HARPER WOODS PUBLIC LIBI
19601 HARPER AVE.
HARPER WOODS, MI 48225
343-2575

MW01713151

DISCARD

STOP LOOKING

DATE DUE

OCT 12 2007	
NOV 06 2007	
NOV 20 2007	
DEC 07 2007	
JAN 29 2008	
MAR 15 2008	
APR 16 2008	
MAY 21 2008	

DEMCO, INC. 38-2931

Brou

Fic G
9/07

HARPER WOODS PUBLIC LIBRARY
19601 HARPER AVE.
HARPER WOODS, MI 48225
343-2575

DISCARD

TH PUB

Truth Hurts Publications
c/o Jazoli Publishing
P.O. Box 1316
Brookhaven PA 19015

This book is a work of fiction. Names, characters, places and incidents either are products of the author's imagination or are used fictitiously. Any resemblance to actual events, locales or persons, living or dead, is entirely coincidental.

A note about this work of reality fiction: Some words and phrases in this novel are purposely spelled differently or used in a different context than what is generally accepted by English language standards. This is because it is mandatory that a genuine work of reality fiction be written to read in the same way that it would actually be expressed by a human being in these situations.

Copyright © 2007 by J.Gail

All rights reserved. No part of this book may be reproduced in whole or in part in any form.

Stop Looking at Me!
Second edition August 2007
Truth Hurts Publications
an imprint of Jazoli Publishing

Manufactured in the United States of America

ISBN10 (paperback): 0-9726978-4-5
ISBN13 (paperback): 978-0-9726978-4-2
LCCN: 2007900538

3 1519 00096 5949

This is written for all people who are sometimes misunderstood.

TRUTH HURTS
PUBLICATIONS

an imprint of

Jazoli publishing

This is Real Life.
It Ain't No Fairytale.

Chapter 1

"God I thought you were my homie! But you are cold sometimes, so cold," Tracy joked silently with her maker, but she wasn't smiling about it. She took one look at Reggie's cold, hard-lined face as she walked out of the revolving doors at her job and wanted to throw up. She was already having the worst day of her life, plus she was PMSing, and now this.

"Hey baby!" Reggie said with a fake smile. "What's going on?"

"What the hell do you want?" Tracy said with an attitude as she hustled by him towards the train station. She was going to leave it at that, but she began blurting instead. "Talking about 'what's going on.' You a damn fool. Ain't shit going on when it's about you!"

"Where'd you get that attitude from? Man," Reggie said as he followed close behind her. Reggie worked two buildings over in the mailroom of an advertising agency. He swore up and down he was executive status just because he worked in midtown Manhattan and felt the need to wear fresh new Polo dress shirts and Dockers pants to work with the mail. He had dark skin and a bad complexion with pimples all over his forehead. Tracy didn't know why he wouldn't just go out and get some Proactiv or something. It was always a surprise to see how stark white his teeth were, even though they had several gaps and imperfections in the front.

Tracy just ignored him and kept moving. Reggie had disappointed her on so many levels during their two year relationship. He not only cheated on her, but also ran up $2,000 on her credit for traffic tickets, court fees, and new clothes which of course he never paid back.

"I was wondering if I could take you out to dinner, the happy hour at Applebee's?" Reggie asked.

"Ha. In your dreams," Tracy said with a wicked laugh.

"Come on Trace, I wanna talk to you about some things. I'm really sorry for how things went down, you know?"

Tracy stopped and turned to look Reggie in his face. She spoke to him as if she were a man because she had absolutely no respect for him. "No, I don't know. If you were really sorry you would have paid me my money back a long time ago."

"See that's what I wanted to talk to you about," Reggie said. He pulled his wallet out of his back pocket and withdrew five $100 bills. "Here's $500. That's a start, right?"

Tracy was pretty stunned at this gesture. Reggie had never pulled more than a few dollars out of his pocket to give her when they were together. Now he was paying her back some of her money in hundreds? She hurried up and took the $500 from his hands before he had a chance to say "sike."

"I hit the lotto, five grand baby! I wanted to give you something, I would give you more but I need the rest to put down on my new house. I'm trying to buy this duplex in Queens." He lied about the amount—he had actually won $15,000.

"Hey, that's the shit Reggie, thanks," Tracy said, melting as she folded the money and put it in her purse.

"Come on, let me treat you to a meal and some drinks, all on me," Reggie asked again. Tracy could never turn down a free drink.

After her fifth $4 margarita, Tracy was feeling nice, and Reggie was looking like gold. She hadn't had sex in over three months now, and anything with an Adam's apple was looking good to her right now.

As Tracy studied Reggie's strong, muscular physique under the collared shirt he wore, sex with him was looking like the only way to go that night. The margaritas had almost completely removed those memories of the way Reggie used to emotionally abuse her, calling her fat and comparing her complexion to the color of piss after a forty of St. Ides. Today, she thought of Reggie as strictly after hours jump-off status—he would never be something to introduce to her friends or family ever again, not that Tracy would ever introduce a man to her family and friends anyway.

"You look like you about to take off your clothes right at the bar Strippy," Reggie said as he eyed the way Tracy was slowly rubbing her nipples up against the bar. When she realized what she had been doing involuntarily, she stopped abruptly.

"I'm just feeling good," she said to cover herself. "The bartender made those margaritas just right."

"Well, I wish I was that bar right now," Reggie commented as he took another sip from his Courvoisier on ice. Tracy laughed to herself about how he was really trying to ball. He could barely pronounce the drink when he ordered it.

"Shut up." But secretly Tracy had been wishing the same thing.

"Yo, why is that girl looking at you like that? Yo, I think you need to go handle that," Reggie said with a serious look on his face as he looked over at a white girl sitting on the other end of the bar.

"Stop fucking with me Reggie, why do you do that?" Tracy complained. She was not amused. "You know I ain't one to play."

"Do what?" Reggie smiled mischevously. He found amusement in playing on Tracy's weaknesses. He decided to back off at the moment though, he didn't want to screw up his chances of getting some later. Out of all the women he probably could have snagged up after winning that money, Tracy was the one that kept returning to his visions. She had been the best woman he'd ever bedded, with perfectly shaped double D breasts, and legs that could open all the way into a split—she knew how to keep him longing for more. And she was gangsta in bed; calling him all kinds of names that would make a soldier cringe and choking him out with one hand at times—she was strong—he loved that kinky stuff.

Tracy couldn't help but look over at the white girl herself after a few minutes. The girl was over there minding her own business. Reggie chuckled under his breath and then started daydreaming about what would happen later.

Reggie pushed into Tracy's soft backside and jerked at the doorknob as Tracy struggled with the keys. She finally fit it in the lock correctly and the door flew open as Tracy turned to throw her arms up to meet Reggie's embrace. Reggie kicked the door closed and immediately started pulling up Tracy's button-down blouse along with her pink laced bra until he had both of his hands on her thick, fleshy breasts. He knew exactly what she liked. He watched his own work as he squeezed the area around her areolas, and flicked at her nipples with his pointer fingers. Tracy had a fetish with her breasts—they were extremely sensitive and she loved having them handled. After teasing her some more, he lowered his head to lick and suck on each dark brown nipple. Tracy moaned in delight as he lifted her up off of the ground with his strong muscular arms and carried her over to the far side of the room where her bed was.

Reggie turned her around and unbuttoned her loose fitting pants, letting them fall down to the floor. Tracy was brimming with anticipation, and lifted her hips up higher to entice Reggie.

"Put it in already motherfucker! Damn you slow," she almost begged him to hurry up and put a condom on so that he could enter her from behind.

They had intense, powerful, high-speed sex three times in two hours. Reggie wasn't known for lasting long, but he was able to recover after sex quickly and go again. Tracy marveled the whole time at how cut up Reggie's body was; it was his best asset. His face left much to be desired, but his body was worth the trouble. Hard bodies were another of Tracy's weaknesses. She would run her hands up and down his dark muscles making him feel safe and secure at first but then grab him by the neck and throw him down on the bed so that she could ride him out. She kept him excited the entire time because he never knew what was going to happen next.

"Damn Tracy," Reggie said as he rolled over onto his stomach and fell asleep.

When Tracy woke at six in the morning, she wasn't surprised to see that Reggie wasn't there. She had a splitting headache and wanted to go back to sleep so badly, but she needed to be out the door by seven. She reached over and searched her nightstand drawer for her Excedrins.

She didn't feel the need to check for her pocketbook, because she had gone to her car the previous night while Reggie waited in her building's foyer and left the small purse under the passenger seat. Drunk or not, she didn't trust leaving Reggie around her credit cards and cash, especially after he had stolen one of her credit cards one time and charged a $250 Avirex sweater on it.

Tracy left her apartment a little later than usual at 7:15. She hurried down the stairs, skipping two steps at a time. Reggie may have been a loser, but he sure had her light on her feet that morning.

She made her way down to her car to retrieve her purse and was shocked at how nice a day it was outside. The birds were chirping, and the sun was shining and glimmering across the hood of her car. As she opened the passenger door and reached in, she glanced out her car window across the street and was surprised to see someone examining her closely.

He was with one other guy, but the other dude might as well have faded into the background of the lowered metal gate they were leaning against compared to his drop dead gorgeous companion. Tracy couldn't help but stare as she watched the tall, light-skinned brother's pensive glare in her direction slowly transform into a sly, sexy smirk. He had bedroom eyes that were a strange dark tint of green and hazel, and a smooth complexion that shone in the sunlight. Tracy wasn't usually attracted to light-skinned brothers, especially thug types, but this one was on point. Damn! His mustache and goatee were low cut and well trimmed, and his clothes were clean and stylish. Tracy smiled crooked as she grabbed her purse from beneath the seat. She stood up too quickly and hit the back of her head on the roof of the car.

"Oww," she complained as she rubbed the back of her head and came back out. She was too embarrassed to look back across the street so she just slammed the door and turned in the direction of the subway. She sensed someone coming towards her and jumped back.

"Why you jumpin', you aiight?" Mr. Eyes said as he approached her with his hands in his pockets. He opted not to wear a jacket that day and instead had on a white tee embroidered with black letters, dark blue jeans, a white baseball cap, and fresh new Air Force ones. He was at least 6'2. He was solid, right in the middle of a football and basketball player in stature, and had an intimidating presence. His lips were thick and juicy red like he had just drunk some bangin' ass Kool Aid. She scanned the area right beneath the sleeve on his T-shirt and her knees almost became weak seeing the bluish veins popping out of his cut up arms. He had a tat on his forearm that said 'Bad Ass'. Even as he held his arms resting at his sides his biceps looked as strong and cut as most guys did when they were flexing.

"Well, you scared me," Tracy said, trying to stay calm as she backed up a few steps. Never before in her life had she been more nervous around a guy than at that moment.

"I ain't mean to. So what's up wit it?" he asked casually as he watched her face with a serious expression on his own. He looked even sexier when he didn't smile. His tone was commanding and loud. He had a grit to his voice that sounded like he had swallowed hot soup and never healed from the burn. Tracy loved a masculine man.

"Umm. Not much," Tracy said, trying to play off how anxious she was, now that she felt sweat beginning to bead on her forehead. She wiped at it, trying not to look obvious. She hoped she hadn't smeared any of her foundation off.

"You live around here don't you? I think I seen you a couple times," he said with a nod in that strong, gritty voice again.

Tracy cringed a little at his extreme ebonics. "Yea, I moved out here for school."

"I don't be coming up to chicks like this," he started, and even sounded uneasy at first, but he quickly figured out what he wanted to say and continued. "You heading to the subway right? Let me walk wit you for a minute."

Tracy wondered why and how he would know she was going to the subway. *Has he been watching me? And why is he out hanging around outside at seven in the morning?*

"You aiight?" he asked when Tracy just looked at him like he was crazy. He softened a little and realized why she was tripping. "Look I'm Mike. But they call me Moony. I live at Prince's Towers."

Tracy reluctantly started walking down the street. "Why do they call you 'Moony'?"

"Long story," he said as he turned back towards his partner and nodded his head up in the air as if to say "holla at you later."

They walked and made small talk during the short walk to the '4' train station. Tracy was still feeling on edge and trying to figure this guy out. During a moment of silence in their conversation, she looked at him and caught his eye. She became fixated on his face for a while as they continued walking. He just looked back at her and winked, never so much as moving his lips. He was so serious.

What was this overwhelming tingly feeling she had going on between her thighs? To her surprise he kept walking her down the stairs descending to the subway, but instead of comforting her, it made her guards go up until they were finally downstairs near other people again. She still didn't know this guy.

"Yo Tracy," he finally said and stopped when they were a few steps from the subway turnstyles.

"Yes?" Tracy asked expectantly. She liked the way her name rolled off his tongue, ever since she first told it to him.

"Imma check you out later," he said as he frowned up his forehead to convey a deeper meaning behind his words.

Tracy was speechless as she again became entranced by his steady gaze. "Okay."

She turned and hurriedly swiped her Metrocard to go through. Her body was hot and she was sure that she had sweat circles forming on her blouse in the armpit area. She felt like a complete idiot and didn't know what to do or say. She didn't turn back again to look at Mike, but could feel his gaze on her sweaty neck.

On the entire train ride, Tracy couldn't get the image of Mike out of her mind's eye. His face was the kind that made women sell all their shit just to get a nice new outfit to show off in front of him. His body was that of a brother that *stayed* in the gym. And those eyes; so intense and… severe. And genuine. That was what really had turned her on. Boy what was it about him? There were plenty of attractive hood types in the South Bronx, but none of them had ever caught her eye like that. This brother from the neighborhood was making her giddy!

She had never in her life dated anyone that didn't have a corporate or professional job like herself. She preferred preppies, smart guys, and nerds. She looked down on men that stayed in the streets, putting them all inside one neat category—dangerous and ignorant. She never gave any of the guys in her neighborhood the time of day for more reasons than one. The biggest reason was that she didn't like people around where she lived being in her business and knowing where she lived. She lived by the credo "don't shit where you eat" and believed it was a bad idea on any day to take on a jump-off or boyfriend who lived nearby.

But Mike. *He might be the exception.*

As soon at that thought crossed her mind, she felt her period about to come down.

* * *

At her job Tracy was usually a wreck on the inside, and a picture of composure on the outside. She had a nagging feeling that three people in her department were out to get her fired.

There was Sheryl Cromby, the head admin on her floor. She had a mean streak like no other, and it was only towards the admins who she believed to be 'beneath' her. She and Tracy had bumped heads on more than one occasion.

Jerry Miller was an arrogant bastard who worked as a consultant in the creative department, which really meant he did nothing but drink coffee, attend meetings, and send emails. Tracy always believed that she should have his job—she was way more qualified and twice as brilliant. He had tried to hit on Tracy one time in the break room. Or at least it seemed as if he were making a pass, in Tracy's opinion. They were talking about a difficult project that Tracy had basically orchestrated which turned into a positive sales trend for the store. He had said "That compilation was a doozy. But you're probably like me, you like it when things are hard." Tracy became so infuriated at his comment that she reported him to HR. They came to a compromise, making it impossible for Tracy to ever be placed on his team again for future projects. Ever since that episode she felt as if Jerry had it out for her for dragging his name through the mud, and that others in her office thought she had exaggerated the whole situation. She kept her guard up.

Finally, there was good old Mary Higgans. She was, but wasn't really, one of Tracy's bosses. It was never written in stone or communicated directly to Tracy that this woman was someone she would have to report to, but she always, *always*, had work that needed to be done. So whenever Mary requested that Tracy perform work for her, Tracy would do a half-assed job, hoping it would make her go to some other administrative secretary in the future. But that never worked, and instead Mary eventually reported her shoddy work to the department head, James Clark, who had a 'talk' with Tracy in his office. Despite her argument to James that she didn't even report to Mary, James told her that whenever Mary had a work overflow she was clear to ask Tracy for help and that it needed to be of the utmost quality. Tracy was fuming after that one.

So needless to say, Tracy was walking on eggshells at work and watching her enemies closely.

Whenever one of those three people entered the breakroom while she was there, Tracy would leave it promptly. When they came in the bathroom she would stop doing her makeup or hurry to finish washing up and *leave.* She wanted to have as little an opportunity to interact with these people as possible. But sometimes she felt like they were fucking with her, and purposely trying to corner her in awkward situations to confront them. In her mind they hated her, and they knew that just one more office scandal involving Tracy might lead to her eventual firing.

"Hey Tracy," Stacey said as she passed Tracy in the hall.

"Hey Stacey, how are you," Tracy responded. Her thoughts of Mike from that morning had clouded her vision, and she hadn't even realized that her co-worker was coming. She couldn't stand Stacey's happy ass, but tolerated her because she usually had the best office gossip. When they first met and spoke at a diversity training session, Stacey went on and on about how cool it was that their names rhymed. Tracy was immediately irritated by her presence. Stacey was so light-skinned that Tracy thought she was white at first. And she had natural, bright red hair. That's why she had looked at Stacey in amazement when she made a comment about how black people in the office shouldn't be so sensitive to the race thing. But after examining her features more on the sly she realized that Stacey was black herself.

"Oh Trace," Stacey said suddenly and headed back in Tracy's direction. Tracy hated when she called her by that nickname—she didn't really consider her a friend, only an associate. Stacey lowered her voice as Tracy came to meet her halfway. "Guess what I heard."

Tracy looked at Stacey with a blank stare, praying that she

would just come out with it. Tracy had a very low tolerance for Stacey.

"I heard that Mary Higgans was getting transferred," she finally said in her hush-hush voice. She sounded like she was in pain for having to let the cat out of the bag so soon.

"No fucking way," Tracy whispered, a smile growing on her lips.

"Yes way, she's going up to Operations. I thought you'd like that news, being that everybody knows you can't even stay in the same room with her ass," Stacey said freely with a chuckle, not even considering the fact that Tracy and Mary's strained relationship was a part of secret office gossip. Big mistake. It was something everyone knew, but Tracy didn't know that everyone knew.

Tracy looked at Stacey like she had evaporated and reappeared before her eyes brand new. "What do you mean, everybody knows?"

Stacey looked into Tracy's newly troubled eyes, then down at Tracy's neck where a vein had popped out, trying to think of what to say. "You know, how you leave the room whenever she's around."

Tracy stared Stacey down for a moment as if she were counting the rings around her eyes.

"Let me tell you something bitch," Tracy said, stepping forward until she had her right foot held tightly on top of Stacey's left pump. Stacey tried to back up but couldn't move her foot from under Tracy's hoof. When Tracy spoke her voice was hushed.

"What I do ain't none of your damn concern, you hear me? If I *ever* find out you been talking about me behind my back Stacey… oooo. I swear to God Imma ram your ass *good* one time and I don't give a fuck who sees it." Tracy pounded one fist into her other hand. "They can fire my black ass little girl, I just don't give a fuck!"

Stacey couldn't stop herself from gulping hard and even if she had something to say her throat wouldn't have allowed it to leave her mouth. She parted her lips as if she were going to speak.

"Don't say shit!" Tracy stopped her before she could even open her mouth, her voice a husky whisper. "You ain't allowed to say shit to, nor about me, ever again."

Right about now, Stacey was feeling like a big retard for saying anything about Mary in the first place. Despite wanting to scream, shout, apologize, and cry at the same time, she just stood there patiently, like a child being punished, and waited for Tracy to let her go.

"That's what I mean," Tracy said, a little louder than she would have liked. They were standing not too far from someone's cubicle. She released her high-heeled foot from Stacey's. "Now, you are dismissed!"

Stacey high-tailed it out of there like the devil was chasing her. Tracy watched her leave with her face frowned up in anger. *How could she do this to me?* She finally started taking slow even steps back to her cubicle, and when she got there she was so mad that she felt dizzy. She sat down and felt the sweat starting on her forehead, then on her lip. She bobbed back and forward in her chair, clasping her hands together every few seconds. She was pissed. But she knew this was an office atmosphere, and she couldn't go off like she really wanted to. *Calm down Tracy*, she told herself. It was getting hot, and she searched around her to find out where the source of the heat was, but didn't see anything. Roger, one of the writers walked by her desk, smiled, and gave a little wave.

What the fuck is he smiling at? she thought as she eyed him as if he had done something wrong instead of saying hello back. *He's probably talking about me too. What else do they know about me?*

The heat from her cubicle became too much, and before anyone could come up to her and ask her to do something, Tracy went to the office bathroom to cool off.

She locked herself in the handicapped stall and leaned up against the wall. Putting her head in her hands, she went over situation after situation in her head. Did people know that she sometimes ate her lunch in the empty conference rooms on other floors so that people wouldn't see her eating? Did they talk about how she tried to take the routes around the office where she knew there were no video cameras from the lobby watching? God, did they know how she kept three or four nips of Vodka locked in her drawer which she guzzled anytime the coast was clear? And now Stacey's ass—would she tell on her? *Nah*, Tracy thought, *because she knows that I will kick her ass employed here or not. She had better watch her step, for real.*

Tracy was a wreck. She suddenly had the overwhelming urge to shit. She didn't like going #2 at the office, especially when she had her period, but this one wasn't going to wait. Hesitating for a moment, she wrapped her hand in toilet paper and rubbed down the toilet seat. She put about five toilet covers on the seat and sat down, praying that no one would come in until she had finished.

Then, as if her prayers meant absolutely nothing, someone came into the bathroom brusquely, pushing the door open with a vengeance. The person boldly walked up to the handicapped stall and shook at the door, despite the fact that it was obviously locked. Tracy jumped and was about to curse the person out, but she just moved onto the next stall.

What are you handicapped bitch? And there are eight stalls in here. This bitch just has to sit next to me, Tracy complained to herself. She struggled to hold it in until the woman next door finished peeing, but it was coming fast. Tracy felt as if she were about to faint right there in the stall, the sweat was running down her face at that point. Her cramps were returning. She started to think that she should just hurry up and get it out now so that the sound of the woman's tinkling might drown out her own undesirable sounds.

After hearing the last few drops, Tracy waited impatiently for the mystery woman to wrap it up and leave the bathroom. She stood and seemed to hang out in the stall for a minute before finally flushing and opening the door. She washed her hands for a long time. Tracy felt as if she were going to die when she realized that the woman was just standing quietly in front of the mirror. The urge was too much to bear any longer, so Tracy let loose and flushed the toilet at the same time. She cringed when she felt the sprinkling of water on her backside from the flushing toilet as she nervously grabbed for more toilet seat covers. Wrinkling the toilet seat covers up in her hand, she listened for what was going on outside the stall door.

The bathroom door opened again, and Tracy heard two more ladies come in, talking to each other.

"Hey Mary," one of them said. *Mary!* Tracy thought. *Ooooo. I should swipe that bitch!*

"Oh, hey Barb," Mary almost sounded shocked and dismayed that they had said her name outloud. She now seemed anxious to get out of the bathroom. "Bye, bye."

This was exactly the type of thing about Mary that Tracy couldn't stand. She always seemed to know exactly what to do to irk her. She probably already knew that Tracy was in the bathroom and took that moment to go in and disturb her, for no particular reason.

Tracy was going on 10 minutes in the bathroom now, and had no plans to exit until everyone had left. Plus the bathroom was starting to stink.

Another five minutes later the two ladies left and Tracy was alone again. Thankfully, they didn't take forever like Mary had.

Tracy hurriedly left the stall. She felt comfortable now that she wasn't the 'woman behind door number one' anymore. The last thing she needed was for everybody to be talking about how "Tracy stank up the women's bathroom" too.

She splashed her face with cold water several times, not caring that she was messing up her foundation. *I bet Mary knew it was me in here and came in to fuck with me. She's lucky she's leaving cause I'll put her right on the ass whooping to-do list right under Stacey's if she keeps playing with me.* She thought mean thoughts about Mary for a while longer and finally headed out of the bathroom with a frown etched across her face. She dared anyone to mess with her the rest of that day.

The fact that Tracy was able to make it the rest of the day, even though it was already 4pm when she left the bathroom, was an amazing feat. She looked at everyone in the office that afternoon with a new eye. Could they really be talking about her behind her back?

The train was overly crowded on the ride home, and as usual Tracy had guzzled down a drink at the bar down the street before getting on. She sometimes kept a blade under her tongue 'hood style,' just in case something jumped off. Riding the subway at rush hour was the worst part of her day, yet a necessary evil. All the people pushing and prodding, and the weirdos who had nothing better to do but stare at her dressed in her business attire. She hated that she couldn't afford to park her car in the city anymore. She still sometimes drove to work and paid the $25-30 to park when she was having a bad day, but money was tight.

She perched herself near the sliding subway door and tried to concentrate on something positive. All she could think about was all her colleagues talking about her behind her back. She wanted to do something about it, confront someone, but she didn't know who. What was she going to do, yell at everybody? That would be sure to get her ass fired on the spot. She needed that job.

Tracy frowned her nose up at an older Indian guy who was looking at her as if he had never seen a woman before. *Why do these nuts think they have the right to oogle down black women like that? I bet they never do that to white women.* Tracy's stop was coming up soon, and there was room on the farther end of the car, so she eased her way over to that area, out of the view of the perverted man, and settled in a corner chair near the door. After a while, she calmed down and tried to think positive thoughts again. The heat in the train was beginning to become unbearable.

Tracy looked off into space and for the first time since she had told off Stacey, her mind drifted to Mike. She could see his face clearly. He was smirking at her in that sexy way again. She wondered what it would be like to kiss those red, juicy lips. She smiled and looked down a little in shame for her thoughts. But her mood was murdered when she saw the same dirty looking man standing up nearby, now in clear view, again looking at her like a piece of meat. A seat became available across from Tracy, and he sat down in it. He had actually gotten up from his original seat and moved to continue staring at Tracy's body. Tracy began feeling nauseous and a rage was building up in her loins. *Who the hell does this motherfucker think he's looking at?* After a few more moments of riding, Tracy could no longer bear the audacity of this man who was still boldly staring at her, looking down at her privacy and licking his bottom lip with no shame in his game. She saw that her stop was coming up after the next, so she made her way to the door. She saw that the man's eyes were following her every step. She couldn't take it any longer.

"What the fuck are you looking at?" Tracy said all of sudden on the now semi-crowded train as she pointed her finger right at the Indian man. She came up real close to him, ignoring the swaying of the train, and stood with her feet apart, solid to the ground, looking down at his face. "I know you don't think you got a chance with me, look at you you dirty, rock-headed motherfucker!"

The Indian man looked at her with wide eyes and an open mouth, while everyone else on the train pretended not to see what was going on. Some teenagers nearby broke out in laughter and pointed at the man to taunt him. "She called him rock-head!"

"What do you want from me? I am a man," was all the guy said, with a smug look on his face now as if he were entitled to look.

"So what, you wanna see my breasts," Tracy cupped her breasts momentarily and looked down on the man as if he were an ant. "Why don't I just whip my pussy out right now for you to see, since you're already staring at it as if it's on display! I'm tired of you sick, perverted assholes looking at me like a piece of meat all the time!"

When the man had the nerve to look down at Tracy's crack again, he quickly found out it was a bad choice. Tracy cold cocked him with her clenched fist right in the forehead. The man's head went back and Tracy made a mad dash for the just-opened subway door. It closed right behind her. She could still hear the teenagers dying of laughter inside of the train as it pulled off.

Tracy ran up the stairs, two at a time, not even feeling the pain in her hand yet. She checked back once to make sure the pervert didn't manage to get off the same stop. He didn't. When she got to the top of the stairs, she finally saw what stop she had gotten off; 149th Street. *Damn.* She had 18 blocks to walk.

Her adrenaline was jumping as she powerwalked down the busy sidewalk. She felt a rush having given justice to that perv. She was sure every woman on that train was clapping in her mind. No one was going to mess with her and get away with it. Living in New York, she had to be two steps ahead of everything—what if she were to let that guy stare, and then he started studying her movements. What if then he started stalking her every day on the train until he found the right moment to grab her in a deserted subway hall and rape her. Hell no, she had to address that issue right away. Now, he would know not to ever mess with her again.

Tracy had changed into her sneakers before leaving the office, so the walk was comfortable. But by the 10th block, she was starting to become weary, and her hair was feeling as if it were being sweated out. She remembered the $500 Reggie had given her and considered catching a cab the rest of the way. She saw a cab parked across the street and put up her finger to get his attention.

"Ay mama, let me take you for a ride," a Spanish man commented when he saw Tracy trying to get the cabbie's attention.

"Fuck off," Tracy said and crossed the street. She finally felt the pain in her knuckles and shook her hand to get some relief.

"Hey, can you take me for a few blocks," Tracy asked into the open cab window.

The cabbie just shook his head and pointed to the 'off duty' sign on the top of his car.

"Shit," Tracy cursed, sucked her teeth, and walked on. She glanced back over at the Spanish guy across the street who was looking right back at her, and was starting to worry that it was getting dark outside. She really didn't like being in this area of the

Bronx after dark. As her walk grew slower, she started to get nauseous again.

There was a group of guys hanging out at a bodega that she would have to pass by. By the time she reached the intersection her feet were already turned to cross the street. *Who cares what they think it looks like*, she thought. When she reached the other side she picked up her speed. She glanced to the left to see if anyone at the store was looking or coming her way. Instead, she saw a sleek, black, late model Honda with tinted windows creeping beside her. Tracy looked horrified.

She walked quicker, and had to restrain everything in her being to stop from breaking into a full run. She glanced back again, terror in her eyes. All she could think of was the drive-by scenes she'd seen in gangster movies. She thought about the razor under her tongue but what good was that going to do if they had guns?

"Tracy, Tracy," she could hear a voice saying strongly as the tinted passenger side window came down. The first thing she recognized was the lips moving. "Ay yo Queen, slow down."

"Mike?" she said in amazement and stopped in her tracks.

"Yea, what you doin' down here?" he asked as he lifted his head to see from beneath his hat. "I'll take you back to the spot. Come on."

"To the spot?" Tracy asked, still cautious, as she looked at him in disbelief.

"Yea, to your crib. You ain't about to walk 10 blocks down *here* is you? It's getting dark as shit out here."

"I know, but…" Tracy hesitated. She didn't really know this dude. And who was the guy driving? She shook her hand a few times again, still trying to relieve the pain from punching the man on the train in the forehead. *I was right, rock-headed motherfucker.*

"This my man Coupe, he cool," Mike assured. "Don't worry,

I got your back."

It was as if Mike were reading into her inner insecurities. He winked at her and smiled the way Jay-Z did in his videos. Tracy's knees got weak again.

"Okay," she said, relaxing as she came over. Mike got out of the car and opened the back seat door for her. *What a gentleman*, Tracy thought.

"Didn't you take the train home?" he asked.

"Yea," Tracy answered with a quick head nod.

"Why ain't you get off at 167th Street then?" he inquired. Tracy just smirked at him. If he only knew, but he never would. She wasn't about to tell the guy she could potentially marry about any of that mess. When she got in the car, she leaned her head forward and quickly retrieved the blade from under her tongue.

They rode home, with Mike cracking jokes the whole way in that loud, deep voice. When he spoke, people listened with perked ears. He had Tracy almost falling to the side in the back of the car laughing. He told the story of how his boy Coupe had some crazy white chick he had slept with just once stalking him. He also teased Tracy for speed-walking down the block as if Jason were after her. And he was so cool. He never even laughed when he told a joke, he just let it slide and slip off his tongue. Tracy's cheeks hurt as she looked down at her now-swollen hand, but kept it hidden from Mike and Coupe's view. She had gone from mad to happy in a matter of a few minutes.

Tracy felt so comfortable around Mike and Coupe that she actually let them drive her up to the front door of her building. She almost didn't want to get out of the car.

"Thank you so much," Tracy said as she grabbed up her purse and opened the car door.

"No problem sweetheart," Mike said, never really looking her way. She got out shyly and headed up the front walk. A smile was plastered across her face. He was so cool.

Then she heard the whirring sound of the car window coming down again.

"Imma see you tomorrow," Mike told her. He wasn't really asking.

"Maybe," Tracy said with a smirk and opened the glass door to go inside.

When Tracy got inside, she was so full of heat between her thighs that she had to get in the tub immediately. On the way to the bathroom she grabbed her 'toy,' Mr. Wiggles, out of the drawer by her bed, and a plastic baggie full of ice for her hand. She stripped bare in the bathroom in what seemed like one furious motion.

As she soaked in the tub with her legs open, the sound of Mr. Wiggles soothing all the stress of the day away, Tracy thought about Mike, and how different it would be to have a relationship with a neighborhood thug. She had never felt this hot for a man, sexually, before. As she moved Mr. Wiggles around slowly, she imagined it was Mike's thick lips exploring her womanhood with that same determination and confidence he oozed with every step he took, and every word he spoke.

* * *

Mike became an obsession for Tracy. Every day he would meet her outside her building and walk her to the train station, and every evening he would grab her from the train station and either walk or drive her home. Mike kept Tracy laughing and giggling all the time like a young schoolgirl, and knew just what to say to make her smile. It was bliss—Tracy looked forward to waking earlier in the morning than she used to and taking her time on hair and makeup. She wanted to look her best for Mike.

She knew he had to be feeling her, because what guy, especially as fine as Mike, was going to get up at seven every morning for a short walk down the street with a girl he just met? Tracy didn't know if he was a night person who was just finished working that early in the morning, or what. Tracy was longing for him, and it was mostly because he never pressured her—he never tried to get invited into her apartment, never asked any prying questions, and never even asked Tracy for her phone number. He just spent quality time with her.

Then finally, after a few of days of this courting, Mike took it to the next level.

"I eat at this place downtown a lot. They got the bangin'est Chinese food in the city," he said out of the blue when he was driving Tracy home from the train one night.

"I love Chinese food," Tracy said matter-of-factly.

Mike's cellphone rang, interrupting the inevitable. He looked at the caller ID as the sounds of Lil' John singing "Snap Your Fingers" blasted from the phone. To Tracy's delight, he shut it off. *Thank God,* she thought. Sometimes his phone conversations could go on and on for 15 minutes or more.

"So, we going?" he said as he put the phone back in his jacket pocket.

"Huh?"

"Going to eat. You forgot already?" Mike said with a smirk. "My Chinese spot."

"Oh. Yea," Tracy smiled back. "Let's do that."

When Tracy smelled the hot Chow Mein dish wafting up her nose it was as if she had already taken a bite. When she used her chopsticks to take that first taste, she was in heaven. She didn't even feel self-conscious eating in front of Mike.

"Wow," is all she could say as she ate.

"I don't play when it comes to my grub," Mike said as he stabbed a piece of Sesame Chicken from his plate. It was surrounded by fragrant broccoli, drizzled with a delicious sauce. When Mike said they were going to a Chinese place, he neglected to tell Tracy that it was a *restaurant* restaurant, a small place with white cloth napkins and tablecloths. It was a good thing she had on her work clothes, otherwise she would have felt out of place in the nice scenery. Mike was dressed down in a pair of blue jeans and a black jacket, but was so good-looking that he looked like he belonged *any*where.

"I'm coming down here all the time," Tracy said as she looked out the window. She still couldn't help being aware of her surroundings. She was trying to see the people who were walking by, and making sure no one was watching them. "They do takeout, right?"

"Oh now you're just gonna jack my spot and leave me behind," Mike said lightly. "I don't tell everybody about this place you know. I don't even bring my team down here."

Tracy chuckled. "I won't come without you, okay?"

Mike just smiled. His phone rang in his pocket again, and this time he picked it up.

"Excuse me," he said as he stood up from his chair to leave and swung his leg over it in one motion. Tracy watched the Akademiks logo on the back of his jacket as he walked towards the back where the bathroom was. He said "hello" into the phone a few steps from the bathroom. Tracy sighed and continued eating.

Ten minutes later she was still sitting at the table, almost done eating. She suddenly began to get an uneasy feeling. Who was he talking to in there during their date for all that time. Why couldn't he at least pop his head out and tell her "one minute."

Why couldn't he just not answer his phone on their date. This was the exact type of thing that caused her to never date men like Mike, the thugs and 'desperately trying to be' ballers that crawled through the streets of New York. What made Mike any different?

Then Tracy began to feel as if maybe she had been blind, naïve with Mike. He was better looking than most men in New York, which was a feat all in itself, *and* he was cool, *and* he was funny, *and* he was powerful around other men. So what in the world would he want with Tracy. There was no way she was the only woman in his world. He probably had a whole stable of chicks on call, and he was probably talking to one right now. How disrespectful!

"My bad," Mike said, breaking her thoughts as he sat back down at the table. "Had to take that call. That was my man Jones. That nigga's breath was stinking so bad I could smell it over the phone. Damn!"

Tracy chuckled. "Maybe it was the bathroom you were hiding in."

"Naw, it was fat ass Jones. His breath stink like he stores chitlins in his cheeks. He went to see a doctor about it, but he just gave him prescription strength altoids, and those ain't work neither!" Mike said jokingly, and Tracy giggled. Mike paused to wolf down what seemed like half of what was left on his plate. "Yo, you ever been to a Yankees game? I got some tickets."

"Uh, no," Tracy said, trying to hide a smile and relaxing again in Mike's presence. He was already planning their next date.

"We should go," he said. Tracy just watched his gorgeous face and smiled.

Tracy was happy, but still needed a cigarette to shake off the last of her anxiety from his private phone call. Though she had quit almost a year before, she had begun smoking occasionally again. "I'm gonna go outside for a minute and get a smoke," she said as she grabbed her purse.

"Hold up, I'm almost done," Mike said, putting his hand up to stop Tracy from getting up and then motioning for the Chinese waitress, who came right over with the check. *She was probably staring at him the whole time*, Tracy thought. *Eyes off bitch, that's mine.* She imagined dumping the waitress' face into a hot vat of chicken grease and frying it until it was extra crispy.

Mike took a few more bites, pulled out his wallet and put money on the table to cover the check and a small tip. He grabbed Tracy's hand and as they walked out together she stole a glance at their reflection in the window. Tracy thought she looked way out of her league. She usually didn't catch the super fine ones for more than a booty call.

"You shouldn't smoke, it messes up your looks," Mike said when they were outside.

"You trying to say I look bad or something?" Tracy looked back at Mike with eyes wider than saucers.

"No, I'm talkin' about in the long run. Cigarettes make you look older, quicker," Mike explained as he stood right next to Tracy in the cool night air. He shoved his hands in his pockets. "That's why most of those celebrities you see, who look old as shit at 30? It's because they smoke. Don't you know somebody who smokes?"

Tracy thought of her crazy Aunt Yamina, who smoked like a chimney. She went through three cartons of Pall Malls in a day. At only 50, she looked like she could be mistaken for 80. What was even scarier was that people always said Tracy favored Yamina in her youth. Then she thought about her friend Rachel, who probably smoked half a pack a day. She didn't have hard lines or signs of aging on her face, but that was probably because of all that good living on the beach.

"I do, but I don't smoke that much," Tracy reasoned. "Only

once in a while."

"That's what they all say," Mike said loudly with a smile as he looked at his ringing phone again. "Look I ain't trynna get down on you or nothin', but I tell everybody I know who smokes they should stop. Those things kill people. And it's so stupid because they don't even know why they do it. Everybody that smokes started because of peer pressure, cause they think it'll make them look cool or cause they saw somebody else doing it. Then they get hooked. How stupid is it to do something that can kill you, that ain't nothin' but a force of habit, all because you followed behind somebody else who was following behind somebody else who did it?"

Tracy looked down at the ground and took another guilty puff off of her cigarette. Then she looked at the cigarette as if *it* was the reason for all of her problems. But it was just a little cigarette, why was he making such a big deal? Mike sensed her discomfort.

"I apologize. Don't feel bad Ma. Do you," Mike shuffled from side to side as he kept watch over everything around him. "It's just that my moms died from throat cancer. She smoked her whole life away."

"Oh. I'm so sorry to hear that," Tracy sympathized but strangely felt a little better now knowing why Mike was so passionate about the cigarette thing. She was starting to learn more about Mike's character. He didn't talk much, but when he was passionate about something he went on and on about it with so much fervor that it could be intimidating.

"You ready to go?" he turned to look at Tracy and grabbed her free hand. His deep, greenish-hazel eyes gazed into her brown ones, and all of Tracy's daydreams were coming true.

Tracy smiled at him, and threw the cigarette down on the ground. Mike stamped it out and grabbed her by the small of her back to lead her down the street. That was all Tracy needed to ease her newfound apprehension about Mike. The small-of-the-back hold was clear relationship language for Tracy. It meant that she was now his girl, he was her man, and thug or not, there was no place she would rather be. *Now he had just better not fuck up,* Tracy thought.

Chapter 2

Tracy's mother sat on her perch in the dining room watching a tape that her niece had made for her of old Dynasty episodes. She cringed when she heard that familiar sound of the Hyundai grinding up the driveway. She didn't know what was worse—hearing that grating sound of Tracy's front bumper dragging along the concrete, the bumper that had gotten bashed in by a drunk driver while parked, or hearing the grating sound of her daughter's problems and obsessions. Tracy was always afraid of her mother being sick.

"Why can't this girl just go home after her hair appointment?" Tracy's mother groaned and then got up reluctantly to open the door. She at least had hoped not to see her until after 2pm; that's when she usually finished getting her hair done.

Don't get it twisted. Mrs. Terri Samuels loved her daughter with all her being and soul, but loving and liking were two totally different things. Mrs. Samuels hadn't liked her daughter in over 10 years. It was a sad fact, but it was true. Tracy was a constant drain on her mother, with all of her fits, obsessions and delusions. It was unbearable for even a mother to persevere through. Mrs. Samuels had been joyous when Tracy moved out of her house and all the way out to the Bronx to attend college, but now it seemed as if Tracy still spent too much of her time in her mother's presence.

"Mother!" Mrs. Samuels heard her daughter shriek out, as usual.

"Daughter," Mrs. Samuels replied weakly.

Hmmm… I wonder why she sounds like that… She sounds a little sick.

"Mom, when was the last time you saw a doctor?" Tracy asked, revealing her thoughts as she finally stepped inside the door and closed it behind her.

"Child, I don't know. What are you doing here so early?" her mother wanted to know.

Mom wouldn't hide something like a health problem from me, would she?

"Well in any case Mom, I heard on the news that there is a stronger strain of the flu that could begin soon. You can't be playing around with your health like that."

"Like what? Tracy, am I supposed to go to the doctor everyday or something? Just to be sure I didn't get the flu yet? Girl, give me a break," Mrs. Samuels replied with attitude.

"Well dang, I'm just saying. I just want you to be healthy," Tracy rolled her eyes at her mom's attitude and then walked on into the house to get comfortable.

"Ma, can you do my hair?" Tracy said as she pulled at her greasy auburn strands and headed toward her mother's spacious master bedroom. It was almost the same size as her whole apartment. "I need it braided."

"Why didn't you go get your hair done today?" Mrs. Samuels asked as she came behind Tracy and went to sit at her vanity. She pulled out a powder brush and started blotting her face with it. Despite approaching 50, Tracy's mother still looked like she could pass for mid-thirties.

"Some guy at the salon, he just didn't feel right to me. I just had to leave," Tracy said as she grabbed a couch pillow from her mother's white cloth loveseat, which was perfectly seated adjacent to the large bay window. She hovered near her mother with the pillow in hand until Mrs. Samuels realized that Tracy was right there behind her.

"Oh!" Mrs. Samuels gasped when she turned around and saw Tracy standing there with a pillow clasped between both hands. She looked like she was about to take her mother's breath away with that pillow. "Damn girl, you scared me."

"Ooo, sorry Mom!" Tracy chuckled, unaware that she had put her mother on a higher level of alertness. "You're gonna braid my hair right? Cornrows?"

"Oh yes, of course," Mrs. Samuels nodded as she waved Tracy on to sit between her legs on the pillow.

As she wove lock after lock of her daughter's hair into tight, neat cornrows, Mrs. Samuels endured a long story about how suspicious the guy at the salon seemed, and how the other women were completely oblivious to the fact that the strange man was just sitting in the salon; he wasn't there with anyone. She then almost lectured her own mom about how dangerous it was "out there," and how women had to be careful "these days." Tracy decided not to say anything to her mother about Mike, at least not just yet. She had only known him for a few weeks. After a while the monotonous pulling and wringing of her head from the braiding motions her Mom was performing on her head, combined with the comfort of her mother's presence finally caused Tracy to nod off.

Tracy couldn't believe how empty the streets were as she walked down Main Street in the small shopping district in Babylon. There were usually plenty of people strolling down the quaint blocks lined with old-style stores, potted flowers, and banners touting the many years the Town of Babylon had been incorporated.

Tracy passed by the nail salon with the racist nail ladies inside. She had gone in there once before to get her nails done, and they took not one, not two, but three white ladies before her, all who arrived after her. When she complained about it, they snubbed her and told her to wait. However justifiable, she felt like she was making a scene, and the white women were looking at her like "Oh Lord, this is why we don't want black people around here." The last thing she needed was the Babylon police after her. She looked inside the salon as she passed and frowned up her face at the Korean lady who looked back up at her as she buffed someone's nails.

Then Tracy got the odd feeling that someone was following her. She turned around and saw a faceless man walking about 50 yards behind her. She stopped and looked back again. Now the guy was 25 yards behind her. She continued on and started picking up her speed. Now she was tripping, this guy was no more than three car lengths from her and getting faster… and he had no face! She scanned the sidewalk and couldn't see anyone else in sight, not on the sidewalk, and not even driving by. What was going on? She was speed walking now and took about two more steps before breaking into a full run. The faceless guy began running after her!

Tracy finally just threw down her oversized purse, thinking that that was what he wanted, and sprinted until she saw a large parking lot coming up on the right. She crossed the street and was making her way across the lot when she felt the man's presence close behind. She peeked over her shoulder and he was literally ten steps behind her. He got closer and closer. No matter how fast she ran, he just got closer. She suddenly felt the tip of his hard-bottomed shoe hit the back of her flip-flopped heel…

"Tracy sweetheart, Tracy," Tracy heard her mother's voice calling her from beyond. She was starting to get concerned about the movements and mumblings Tracy was making in her sleep.

"Ah!!" Tracy shrieked and took a wild swing at her mother.

"Tracy!" her mother screamed as she ducked back from her

daughter.

Tracy reoriented herself and realized that she was still on her mother's floor, leaned back on the chair. She had fallen asleep that quickly.

"My bad mom," she said regretfully. "I thought you were someone else."

"Tracy you better get going, it's going to get dark outside soon," Mrs. Samuels became cold. "You know how it gets dark quicker this time of year."

Tracy looked at the clock on her mother's wall. It was barely 1:30 in the afternoon. She was starting to get the feeling that her mom was trying to get rid of her more and more, each time she came to visit.

"Ma, I might stay over tonight anyway," Tracy said groggily with a yawn as she felt the back of her head to see how her mother's work had come out.

"Why?" Mrs. Samuels asked with a shock and dismay in her voice that she could not hide to save her life.

"Uhhh, because? I want to make sure you're alright. And I'm too tired to drive all the way back to the Bronx right now. I don't know why I'm so tired these days," Tracy pulled herself up off the floor and looked into her mother's vanity mirror.

"Girl I'm fine, I'm fine! You go ahead home and hang out with some of your friends today," Mrs. Samuels almost pleaded.

"No, I think I want to stay over," Tracy said, being stubborn. But her mother wasn't having it.

"You ain't staying over here tonight Tracy, I got things to do," her mother said sternly in that tone of voice that told her daughter she wasn't playing.

Tracy looked at her mother with a familiar rage in her eyes that she could never duplicate with anyone else. *I knew she hated me. My own mother hates me.* "Fine then, I'm out."

Without another word Tracy turned on her heel and brushed by her mother on her way out of the room. She made her way to the front door and stormed out. She put so much force on the screen door as it flew open that it almost fell off the hinges. She stomped down her mother's steps, but on the last step she put her foot down wrong and twisted her ankle. She fell forward to balance herself on her sister's car in the driveway. It happened because she had been thinking too hard about how much she hated her mother back. *She hates me!* she thought as she reached down to grab her ankle in pain.

"So Ma, Jenny can live here, but I can't even stay over a night!?" Tracy screamed so loud that someone mowing their lawn two doors down looked up to see what was going on. She hadn't even realized until that moment that her sister was probably home, being that her car was in the driveway.

"What?" Mrs. Samuels asked as she opened the screen door and came outside almost as angrily as her daughter had just done.

"I said, how come Jenny can stay at the house, but you don't want me here!?" Tracy screamed as she threw her hands up wildly and shook her head furiously. Droplets of sweat began forming on her forehead and she was breathing hard from frustration. Mrs. Samuels could tell she was about to go through one of her attacks.

"Tracy, your sister ain't here, she's out of town remember?" Mrs. Samuels fibbed. Jenny was in fact living there, for the time being anyway. "Why don't you stop acting so damn crazy all the time? Go home Tracy! I don't want to deal with your bullshit right now!"

Mrs. Samuels wanted so badly to go over to her daughter and smack her upside the head repeatedly until she got some sense. But Tracy was much larger than her mother now, and could get pretty violent when she wanted to.

"Oh I know what it is, you got that Shaft-wannabe Robert coming over here tonight don't you," Tracy said with a smirk, her words dripping with venomous pleasure, as she shook her ankle a few times and headed back to her car with a slight limp.

"Go ahead Ma, get your freak on," Tracy again yelled loud enough for the neighbors to hear. She started being obnoxious and did her own song and dance version of the Missy song before getting into her car. Her mother opened her mouth to say something, but was more shocked than anything at her daughter's remark. She prided herself in her Christian behavior, and didn't want anyone assuming those things about her. But instead of responding and causing even more of a scene, she just turned around and headed back into the house.

Evil bitch! She didn't even ask if I was alright. What kind of mother is that. How is she going to kick her tired child out on the street?

Tracy sat in her mother's driveway for five minutes before realizing that her mother wasn't moving away from the screen door until her troubled daughter left the premises. That's when Tracy finally put the car in reverse and pulled away from the house.

I wish Dad were here. He would never kick me out of his house!

Tracy turned the corner heading towards the main street, and then made a sharp left turn towards the highway. As soon as she hit the Southern State, she began crying her eyes out. This wasn't the first time this type of scene had played out at Mrs. Samuel's house, but each time it hurt Tracy more and more.

Chapter 3

"I think this is the first time I've ever really, *really* wanted to keep a dude around. You know how I am," Tracy said into her cellphone as she pulled into a nearby Sunoco station. "So you know I'm not giving you any details."

"Oh come on Tra," Kamira begged. "Just tell us what he looks like, or his name at least!"

"I'm saying, you've been MIA for the past two weeks, you don't call nobody bitch," Joy, Tracy's other friend, said with disappointment in her voice. "I usually hear from you at least twice a week."

"I know, I know," Tracy admitted. She was loving the attention she was getting from her friends. It was kind of like the way things were when they were all in high school. Tracy was the leader of their group back then, but now that they were separate they were all doing their own thing.

"So then tell us who this dude is that is taking up all your time," Kamira reiterated.

"Uh uh." Tracy had a rule about telling her friends about guys she liked. She was afraid that as soon as she told them how great he was, he would turn from a prince back into a frog, making her look bad. There was no way she was going to mess up this thing with Mike, the first man who had ever given her goosebumps on sight. "Listen y'all, I gotta go. I'm at the gas station and you know I don't talk on the cellphone around all the gas fumes."

Kamira sighed. "Lord, go ahead. But call me when you get done. I wanted to tell you about some things."

"Alright girl. Joy, I'll be seeing you soon. Next Saturday at my hair appointment," Tracy confirmed.

"Why wasn't I invited?" Kamira butted in, half serious.

"When was the last time you came with me to get my hair done Kami? Besides you know you'll be with that dude Karif laid up until 4 in the afternoon on Saturday," Tracy reasoned.

"Yeaaa, you're right," Kamira daydreamed.

"Talk to y'all later," Tracy hung up the phone before either one of her friends could keep her again. She hated to sit in an idling car for too long.

Tracy finally shut off the car and went to retrieve her credit card. She quickly got out and looked around, keeping a close eye on the bum who was sitting on a stoop at the side of the small service booth in the middle of the gas station. She swiped her card through and waited while her car was being filled to $20.

Tracy was born and raised in Queens, NY. Her family moved out to Long Island when her Dad started making real money with his carpentry business. Most people would think she was lucky to be raised on the Island, but she hated it. Which was why she and her friends would spend any extra time they had in the city as teens.

Tracy usually lied about her age to other people. She was really 24, but she constantly told people she had just turned 21. She did it because she liked that age, it was a good year for her, and she wished she could just stay that age all her life. Nobody believed her though, people actually thought she looked *older* than she was. Her face had a few hard lines that were the remnants of a stressful life. Tracy couldn't ever really relax, and it showed in her physical features.

She was tall for a female at 5'9, and thick bodied at 170 pounds. She was athletic, but had some flab around her mid section, and she also had big legs. Her most prized assets were her double D breasts, which sat perfectly atop her chest. They didn't sag or fall because she always wore bras, even to bed, no matter how uncomfortable. She had toffee-colored skin and usually wore her amber-tinted hair in a curly loose style that fell to her shoulders. But her hair mostly looked wild and untamed inbetween hair appointments because she was a really bad sweater—sometimes she could sweat out her hair in less than an hour after getting it done. It was embarrassing. All it took was someone, something, or someplace that she didn't like to send her into one of her little 'attacks.' But through all the rough details of her features, Tracy was still a very pretty young lady.

When Tracy was just 12 years old she was the most popular girl in school. Everyone wanted to be like her or associated *with* her. She had all the boys buying her Candy Grams on Valentine's day, even the rich white boys, and the girls wanting to fight her for any reason they could conjure. Tracy always mopped the floor with them, never getting so much as a scratch on her face. She did exceedingly well in all of her classes, and even was admitted to a special class for smart students. But then one day her world changed.

It was an unusually warm day in November when Tracy found out that her father died. She was sitting in her special history class when a teacher's aide came to the classroom door and knocked lightly to come in.

"Tracy Samuels, please go to the Principal's office."

Tracy reluctantly gathered her things and made her way down to the Principal's office with the aide by her side. The aide was quiet, she didn't say anything, and Tracy didn't ask. She had the eery feeling that something was wrong. When she reached the Principal's office, Tracy's uncle was there waiting for her. His eyes were red and swollen. And his expression read like a book. There was definitely something wrong.

After discovering that her father had died of a sudden heart attack, Tracy's whole attitude changed towards life. She began to do worse and worse in school. Her friends were starting to alienate her because she barely even spoke to them, and when she did she would wild out on them over the littlest things. She was mad at most of them because they still had fathers in their lives. She hated the suburbs and would actually tell people that it killed her father. Tracy and her father were crazy tight, so losing him was a little too much for her to deal with at that young age. She had never been very close with her mother and her sister Jennifer, and felt as if her father dying left her in a very compromising position alone in the house with them.

That's around the time that the attacks began. They were angry, outrageous episodes that happened once in a while where Tracy usually revealed her innermost feelings and fears. Tracy had always been a little 'on edge' about people, places, and things around her, even as a young child, but after her father died she started becoming more suspicious of things that happened around her. On the schoolyard, she would pick fights with girls who looked at her sideways, because she was afraid that they were plotting to jump her afterschool. So she would just fight them immediately to thwart the impending attack. She loved to be two steps ahead of other people.

Her mother would come all the way up to the school to confront her teachers because Tracy thought they had it out for her. But no one really did; it was all in her mind. Everyone started walking on eggshells around her when they realized that she was a little throwed off.

Despite all of this, Tracy managed to maintain three close friends throughout school and in life—Kamira, a tough but sweet girl who most people thought of as the school slut, Rachel, a rich, eccentric white girl who drove everyone around in her pearl white

Benz throughout high school and didn't take shit from anybody, and Joy, a rough around the edges, model-like, athletic type that Tracy had played on the field hockey team with for two years. All of Tracy's friends had three things in common—they all had lost their real fathers to divorce, abandonment, or death, they all were fearless, and they all were secretly afraid of Tracy. Deep down, they all knew that they hung out with Tracy because her craziness made them feel more sane.

When the car was done being filled, Tracy snapped out of her thoughts and waited for her receipt to come out, but it never did.

"What?" she said to herself as she read the small screen that said 'See Attendant'.

She locked up her car and stormed up to the window of the booth, where the Indian attendant sat reading a paper. She hated being inconvenienced. He opened the drawer and just looked at her as if to say "What?"

"The machine. It didn't give me a receipt."

"Yea, we're out of receipt paper right now, it's okay," the Indian man said shortly with his deep accent and tried to wave her off.

"It's not okay, I always get my receipt, I used my damn credit card."

"I'm sorry I can't give you a receipt right now—"

"Look," Tracy banged her fist down on the open silver drawer, creating a small dent in the tray. "I don't go for this type of shit. How in the hell can I prove you charged my card right, if I have no receipt. I ain't leaving without one," Tracy argued.

"I don't know what to tell you," the man said and shrugged his shoulders.

"This is some kind of scam isn't it? I leave here without a receipt, and you charge up my card for more than what it really was, then I have no way to prove what I really charged! Y'all think you're slick!"

"Miss I—"

"Aaah, aah. I'm not trying to hear all that bullshit," Tracy interrupted him again. "I'm not leaving here without a receipt!"

"What do you want me to do?" the attendant asked with his shoulders in a suspended shrug, thinking that he was dealing with a crazy person.

"Hold up, I'm calling my bank," Tracy said, resting her arm on the tray so that the attendant couldn't close it, and pulled out her cellphone. She wanted to make it clear to this joker that his day was being interrupted until she got what she wanted. They told her that the only transaction they saw for that day was a $1 hold. After cursing the people out for not telling her more information, she slapped the flip phone closed and turned her mean mug back to the attendant. Before she could even speak, he held something out for her.

"Here, it's a handwritten receipt for pump number three," he said as he waited for her to let go of the metal drawer so that he could pass the ripped piece of looseleaf paper to her.

Tracy examined it like she worked for CSI Miami. "What is this gonna do?"

"Miss, it's got my signature, the amount purchased at pump three, and the name of the station…"

"What is your name," Tracy asked.

"My name is Chandrashekhar."

"Write that on the back please," Tracy commanded. The attendant went ahead and did as she asked. All he wanted was for her to leave.

"Okay, Chan-dras-hekhar," Tracy badly mispronounced his name and stared him down. "If something goes wrong on my credit card statement *you're* responsible, and I mean that."

Tracy went back to her car and drove off annoyed. She had a very bad feeling that they were either going to charge her wrong, or steal her credit card information. She had heard of that gas station scheme where the attendants record credit card numbers and then sell them in bulk.

But Tracy was most annoyed because now she was really late getting home to get ready for her date with Mike. He was taking her to her first Yankees game. Even though she lived less than 15 minutes from the stadium, she had never attended a baseball game there. She was late now coming from work, having driven in to work that day so that she could get home quicker—but that plan had backfired due to the extra heavy rush hour traffic on the FDR. She needed at least 45 minutes to get ready, and it was already going on 6:30. The game started at 8pm. Just as she was leaning out the car window screaming at the car in front of her for taking three seconds extra at the green light, Mike was calling. She sped up in the lane with oncoming traffic and passed the Volkswagen bug rudely. He honked back at her.

"What's the deal? It's 6:30 and I don't see you," Mike said, sounding a lot more laid back than his words would suggest.

"My bad, I had an issue at the gas station, I'll be there in three minutes. But I need like a half hour to change," Tracy said into her speaker phone. She watched for cops because she wasn't supposed to be on the phone while she was driving.

"Aiight, I'm just messin' wit you anyway, it don't matter to me if we a little late," Mike assured, and Tracy breathed a sigh of relief.

"Great, so give me until like 7:15 then," she said as she made a one-handed turn down her street.

"See you then, I gotta handle a little business real quick anyway," Mike said and hung up the phone.

Tracy decided not to rush anymore. *Ain't got to tell me twice,* she thought. She pulled up in a spot a few blocks down from her building and took her sweet time strolling down the sidewalk.

"I see you ain't in no rush," she heard a voice say from behind her. She whipped around so quickly that her hair got caught in her eye. She brushed it away to get a clear view of her Mike, standing there in what looked like a brand new jacket. He was looking very good, clean, calm, and relaxed as usual. *He sure didn't buy my ass anything when he went shopping,* Tracy thought selfishly.

"Oh, hey. Well you said you were doing something," she answered with a wide smile growing across her face, noticing that his boy's car was double-parked, idling nearby.

"I'm just fuckin' wit you. I'll see you around 7:30," Mike said with no smile ever appearing on his face.

"What time does the game start?" Tracy asked.

"It starts at 7, but don't worry about all that. Just look good, aiight?" Mike said and leaned over to give Tracy a kiss on the forehead.

When they got to the stadium it was eerily quiet in the halls as they looked for their entrance. As soon as they sat down in their seats, a big, fat man with a greasy sweatshirt on came back with his nachos and beer to sit right next to Tracy's seat. Mike immediately grabbed Tracy's hand and switched seats with her. He must have read her mind. Mike had seen Tracy flip out before, and now wasn't the time.

"Thank you," she whispered.

Tracy knew about baseball, but had to ask a few questions during the game. Halfway through, and a few Coors Lights in, she had to go to the bathroom badly.

"I'll be back," she said, maneuvering her way past Mike and

the fat man.

"Aiight, be careful," Mike said mindlessly.

"Why?" Tracy turned back and asked him in shock.

He looked back up at her at first with confusion, but then with understanding. "It's nothing. Just go ahead Ma."

But it was something. When Tracy got to the women's bathroom she almost had a heart attack at the number of women on line. As the line inched up, she felt more and more trapped. She didn't like feeling trapped.

There were all kinds of women on that line. Suburban housewives, working women, older ladies, but the ones Tracy kept a close peripheral eye on were the couple of hood chicks that were lurking nearby, watching everybody else. They looked like the only reason why they were there was to try to rip somebody off. They looked poised to snatch somebody's bag at any moment.

Tracy clutched her bag closer to her hip and wished she never even had to go to the bathroom in the first place. *No more beers for me after this.*

She finally had only two women in front of her on line. That's when some ghetto-looking Puerto Rican chick walked right up past the line and stood next to her, as if she were waiting next. A bathroom opened up and the next lady waiting went inside. The Puerto Rican girl had the nerve to take a step again, right in front of Tracy. Tracy's heart was pounding, but she had to say something to this rude girl.

"Ay Mami, the line starts back there," Tracy tried to say calmly as she pointed at the end of the line.

The girl just rolled her eyes and ignored Tracy. Tracy noticed a long scar running from the girl's nose down below her ear. The next lady on line went into the stall, the Puerto Rican girl inched up again, and now Tracy was mad. Her blood was boiling. Tracy would have been next. She sized the Puerto Rican chick up; she was about an inch taller than Tracy but they were probably about the same weight. But she was probably one to fight dirty. Tracy wished she would have brought her razor with her. *I don't care, there is no way this bitch is gonna take my spot in this line!*

Several tension building minutes later, a bathroom stall opened and Tracy made a beeline for it. The woman who was coming out barely had an opportunity to get out of the stall before she saw Tracy, and the Puerto Rican girl close behind, trying to get in.

"That's my stall, where you going!" the girl said wildly as she held the door open from Tracy closing it.

"Bitch you know it was my turn on line!" Tracy said and grabbed the door. They struggled with the door—the Puerto Rican girl to hold it open, and Tracy to close it shut. The other women on line were mostly watching in amusement. No one even opened their mouth.

"Get the fuck off!" Tracy screamed and finally managed to shut the door. The Puerto Rican girl reached her hand inside the door one more time and it shut closed on her arm.

"Owww!" she screamed. "Puta! Esperate! When you come out there you better be ready for me bitch!"

Tracy locked the stall and almost fainted from her heart beating so fast. *Why me!* she thought. *Why couldn't she cut somebody else in line. Now I might have to fuck this girl up!*

Tracy figured the girl was probably peeing in another stall, so she decided it would be better to get out sooner than later. She didn't mind a fight, but would prefer not to at this time being that she was on a date with Mike and didn't want him seeing her looking all fucked up. Plus the girl was a match—she would probably give her a run for her money. After quickly peeing and neglecting to wipe, she snatched open the door with one of the meanest looks she could muster. She washed her hands with a quickness and hustled out of the bathroom, lightly pushing past some ladies who were blocking her way. Surprisingly, the line was much lighter than before.

As soon as she got back out in the hall she felt a foot reach out beneath her and she fell face forward onto the ground, her hands slapping on the cold floor.

"That's for stealing my stall bitch!" the same Puerto Rican girl from before said in a loud whisper. Tracy turned around and saw three other little hoodish girls that couldn't have been over 16 hovering nearby. Their leader moved quickly to snatch Tracy's bag up from the floor.

"Now beat it!" the Puerto Rican girl demanded, but started walking away herself. She was hyped up. "You be glad I didn't get my Mami's to stomp on your stupid ass."

"Celia, I think I hear a security guard," one of the other girls she was with warned.

"You stupid trick, why you gonna say my name?" Celia turned and scolded the young girl.

Tracy finally got up and grabbed her exposed knees, which were scraped up and starting to bleed. She regretted wearing a skirt to a baseball game on so many levels at this point. Their leader, the hood princess Celia came back over to Tracy and mushed her in the back of her head. Then Tracy snapped. She turned around and reacted without even thinking.

Tracy punched Celia so hard that she almost did a 180 degree swivel. Celia was stunned and stumbled a few steps before dropping to the ground in a daze. The other girls stood around motionless, debating on whether they wanted to fuck with Tracy after seeing that. Tracy came up and started to stomp on Celia's head, but when Celia tried to shield her head, Tracy got her in the chest instead. The blood from Tracy's knees started dripping onto Celia's white wife beater tee. When she saw Celia start to wheeze for air she stopped.

Celia's crew looked at their leader on the floor, who was shaking her head to reorient herself, and then back at Tracy, then at each other.

Tracy lunged forward, causing two of the girls to jump back and put up their fists in defense. She reached down and snatched back her purse from the floor. One of the girls got enough nerve to take a swing at Tracy, but she was so small that Tracy could have taken a big bite out of her. Tracy violently smacked the girl down so hard that all the girl could do was hold her face in shock. Tracy felt a rush of exhiliration go through her body after that. A couple more women came out of the bathroom and were taken aback by the sight of Tracy screaming, and the two girls looking like they had just been hit by a bus.

"Who else? I got something for all y'all dumb asses if you want it! Y'all just don't even know," Tracy threatened with a shaky, scary chuckle and shook her head. She pointed to her knees and her disheveled clothing. She was so mad that she was almost growling her words.

"I should fuck all y'all up for real! And you bitch, I hope I busted that ugly scar on your neck open!" she yelled, pointing at Celia who was desperately trying to breathe properly again so that she could get up from the floor and retaliate.

They all heard a walkie talkie radio coming in the distance, and the other two girls took off running in the opposite direction. The third girl ran behind them with her hand still over the side of her face. Celia was just now getting up off the floor.

"Eh. What's goin' on ova here?" the pasty white Italian security guard said as he took his time getting to the bathroom.

Celia tried to take off but the security guard grabbed her arm and held her back.

"Get off me! Usted no sabe!" she complained as she struggled to lose his grip.

"Ain't shit goin' on," Tracy wiped some of the sweat off her face and started walking away. The security guard held his grip on Celia and started to come after Tracy. Tracy turned back around just in time and gave the security guard the look of death—she dared him with her eyes to put his hands on her. He stopped in his tracks—he saw her eyes flash and decided to just let her go on. Tracy turned and continued back down the hallway.

"Tu perra sucia! I'll kill your ass! You just wait," Celia threatened. Tracy looked back one more time and got another good look at this woman who was throwing threats her way.

"You got a ticket?" the security guard turned and asked Celia.

When she got back to her seat, Mike was so engrossed in the last inning of the game that he didn't even look at Tracy when she came and sat down with her knees scraped. She tried to cross her legs to look feminine, but then realized that the blood was dripping too fast.

"They tied up, and it's the bottom of the 9th inning," he said as he watched a man get walked. He finally looked back over at Tracy and his eyes grew wide.

"What the fuck happened to you?" He looked at her hair, which was all over her head, and then down at her knees.

"Some stupid bitch tried to rob me in the bathroom!" Tracy said, starting to come to terms with what did actually happen. She felt as if she had just had an out of body experience. She hadn't even felt the pain of her scraped knees until that very moment, and didn't even think to go back into the bathroom to clean up. She had just wanted to get out of there.

"What?" Mike stood up immediately and looked at Tracy for more information. When she didn't say anything, he patted his pocket where his keys were and started making his way out of the aisle. "Come on."

"Mike, naw, it's cool baby. I handled that. And I still have my purse, look," Tracy called after him as she held her purse up for him to see.

Mike stopped and turned around with a rage in his hazel eyes that Tracy had never seen before. "Uh uh, ain't no silly hoes gonna try to rob my girl and get away with it. They just don't know who they fucked with this time."

He continued out of the aisle, annoying everyone in it as he passed, and Tracy jumped up to follow him. What did he think he was going to do? They would surely be gone by then.

When they reached the hall a few people were walking by. Mike looked around. "What they look like?"

"I don't know, Spanish, my height, scar on her face, but it doesn't matter because I got my purse," Tracy confirmed. "She tripped me up coming out of the bathroom and I fell, but I got my shit back."

Mike looked at Tracy again and saw that she was still holding her purse. He finally just grabbed her up around her neck in a bear hug. "Didn't I tell you to be careful?"

"I know, I know. But you should have told me what I should be careful *of*," Tracy said, warming up to his embrace. All of the negativity was sliding off her shoulders as she relished in the feeling of having Mike's strong arms holding her close.

"You sure you alright though?" he said, letting her go a little and looking into her eyes.

"Yea, but I think I need a napkin or something," she said and reached down to wipe at the blood that was still dripping down her knee cap. Mike didn't even look squeamish as he leaned down and examined her knee as well. He pulled a napkin out of his pocket and started patting at the blood. Then Tracy looked up and saw her reflection in a glass door. She couldn't believe she was looking like that around Mike. "And let me get your hat too?"

Mike passed her his hat, revealing his bare hustler's cut. Tracy couldn't help staring down at Mike's profile. His smooth, light-brown skin and well-trimmed goatee made him look like he should be in the movies. She wanted to plant kisses all over that handsome face.

"Come on, let's just get outta here," Mike told her as he stood back up and grabbed her hand.

"Don't you want to finish the game?"

"Naw, you're more important than that game; I gotta get you home. I'll check out ESPN later," he assured her.

Tracy beamed on the entire walk back to Mike's car. She couldn't even feel the pain in her leg as she strutted down the hall on Mike's arm, and she let the thoughts of Celia and her minions float out of her consciousness. Right now, it was all about her and Mike. No one was going to rain on her parade.

Chapter 4

"You had to see that shit to believe it Kami," Tracy said into her cellphone as she raked through the circular clothing rack, searching out her size. "I don't even remember hitting her ass, it was like an out of body experience. All I know was afterwards that chick was laid out on the floor where she needed to be. And it felt sooo good."

"I bet. You used to go off on girls like that in high school, remember?" Kami replied. She was over her boyfriend Karif's house chilling.

"I didn't never really go *off* off on those girls."

"Like hell you didn't. On more than one occasion I felt so bad for the other girl that I almost jumped in for her!" Kamira confided.

"What? No."

"Yes! That one girl almost choked on her spit," Kamira recalled as she paused to suck on a red ice pop, trying to entice Karif who was sitting on the other couch engrossed in ESPN. He looked at her, rolled his eyes, and got up to fix himself something to eat. Kamira sighed and then focused back on her conversation. "You could've caught a body at 11. If Joy didn't turn her over and pat her back she would have choked. You were vicious."

"That's crazy, I don't even remember that shit," Tracy tried to remember. "What was her name?"

"Shameka, with the long braids, remember her?"

"Oh yea. The one that was telling people I smelled like fish. But I didn't get her that bad." In all honesty though, Tracy couldn't remember what she did to Shameka. She blanked out that day after hearing that people were talking behind her back, saying that her coochie stank.

"That was bad. But anyway, you have to be more careful going places by yourself around there," Kamira warned.

"But why? You would think it'd be safe going to the bathroom at a major baseball stadium. When are you heading down?"

"To where? Rachel's aunt's house? Probably about four. You?"

"Right after I find a new outfit to wear. I need something nice. You know her mom is going to be there too right?"

"I heard her Mom was dating some new guy. He's supposed to be a big shot lawyer. A millionaire too," Kamira gossipped.

"I heard that too. I wonder if she is going to bring him by."

"I wish I could meet a millionaire. Damn!" Kamira checked behind her to make sure Karif wasn't nearby. Sometimes he could be all up in her personal business. "I've gotta go hang with Mrs. Moretti one day. You know she and Joy still hang out sometimes."

"Well I'm happy with my man," Tracy said proudly. "Millionaire or not. I gotta go Kami."

"Whatever. Alright, what did you get her?" Kamira asked.

"I don't know, nothing? It's not like they need anything right?" Tracy said, half-kidding, but suddenly began to panic about what she was going to bring. For the first time since she entered the store she realized that a skinny, gay-looking guy who worked at the store was around her all the time.

"But it's still her birthday, you've gotta bring something," Kamira said. "I'm bringing cupcakes I made."

"How cute," Tracy cut her eyes at the gay salesperson, who was pretending to fold some clothes nearby. "But I've gotta go okay girl?"

"Alright, I'll see you there." Kamira hung up. Tracy put the shirt down that she was looking at and went over to the other side of the store to look at jeans.

Lo and behold, just as she had figured, Mr. Loose Hips was in her area less than a minute later. He came right over to the jeans and started cleaning up some that were out of place. Tracy turned her head to the side and looked at him.

Tracy didn't play these games anymore. Yes, she and her girlfriends had shoplifted a couple of times for fun when they were young (until Kamira got caught), but she was no thief. She would not tolerate someone following her around a clothing store just because she was black. She confronted the salesman on the spot, whipping her whole body around to face him.

"Those jeans don't look that damn messy," she commented with her hand on her hip.

He just smiled and kept pretending to refold things that looked out of place.

"I don't appreciate you following me around this store like I'm some kind of potential criminal," she blurted out and took a step towards him. "Where's your manager?"

Tracy stood with arms folded as she watched him squirm. He looked like he was debating on whether to ignore her or speak.

"I'm sorry, is there anything I can help you with?" he finally said.

"Now you want to help me? I'm not stupid, you're following me around as if just because I'm black I steal. Who is the manager of this store?"

"I'm the manager on duty," he said with his lips almost pursed into a kiss. He looked so nervous and shaky that Tracy thought he was going to go into a fit.

"I knew you were gonna say that," Tracy shook her head as

she glanced at all the nice shirts draped over her arm. "But that's okay, I'm not gonna punish the owner of this store for your ignorance. You just better stop following me. And I'm not playing with you. You stay off my back."

Tracy went back over to the shirt area and continued looking through her rack. She had 10 solid options, and was about to head to the dressing room when she turned around and saw Loose Hips right behind her, putting a shirt up on a rack.

"Didn't I tell you to stay the fuck out of my face!" Tracy lost it. The lady running the cash register looked up to see what was going on.

"You racist motherfucker! How are you gonna be gay and racist? You need to get your ass kicked!"

"Miss, I'm not following you, I'm just putting some clothes away," the man said pointing at the shirt that he had just put on the rack.

"Like hell you are. Oooo. People like you need to be shot!" Tracy walked up to him and threw the shirts she was holding at his face; they all fell to the floor. Loose Hips looked at her as if she had lost her mind. Tracy's eyes burned as she spat at him. "Keep your motherfucking clothes. Now you really have something to put away. Get to work pussy!"

"Uh uh, I ain't *even* putting this shit away," he began to get an attitude back and rolled his neck at her taunting. Tracy lunged at him and he flinched back.

"That's what I thought. Fuck you," she pushed her way past some racks angrily and kept talking to herself loud enough for him to hear. She knocked over a display rack near the front of the store sending all of its contents flying across the floor. "Teach his ass to follow black people around the store!"

* * *

When Tracy pulled up in front of Rachel's aunt's apartment building she reeled at the sight of the expensive property. Despite being right in the middle of a concrete jungle, there were nicely trimmed trees and bushes lining the walk and going up and down the median that separated both sides of the street. Rachel had told everyone to come right up to the front and beep the horn. Her aunt was nice enough to let Rachel use her sprawling apartment for her birthday party while she was away vacationing in South America.

When Tracy beeped, the doorman came out and smiled. "Here for Ms. Rachel Moretti's party?"

"Yes," Tracy answered with a smile. She felt right in place in her light pink chiffon dress that she had paid over $200 for on sale at a boutique in lower Manhattan. The skirt part flared at the bottom, giving Tracy an airy, flirty feel. After leaving the clothing store in Harlem where they followed her around, she decided to go to a classier part of town in Manhattan to shop. She could afford it, because she had money left over from her yearly bonus - about $350 to do whatever with. She could have paid off some of her $15,000 credit card debt with it, but the urge to shop was too strong.

The doorman blew a whistle and a valet came up. He tossed the valet Tracy's keys and led her inside.

The inside of Rachel's aunt's apartment on the 30th floor of the building looked like a scene out of Scarface. The ceilings were high and vaulted in some areas, the living room was expansive and well decorated, and the kitchen looked like it was transplanted from Emeril's cooking show.

Rachel greeted Tracy at the door and asked her what took so long.

Rachel was a pretty, stylish, Laguna Beachesque, blond girl

that they all had grown up with. Nobody who didn't know them from school really understood why and how she fit into the click. From the outside they looked strange—three suburban-raised but hoodish black girls and a bleach-blond, white, valley girl type—but when you got to know them you figured out that there couldn't have been a more perfect match in a group of friends. They all understood each other in a way that no one else could. They all had one thing in common—a crazy streak.

Rachel was hard to figure out. She could be the sweetest, most cherub-like white girl you ever met, but she could also be slimy as shit. She had bone-straight, blonde hair that fell to her ass, bright sea green eyes, and a walk that killed. She took people's men left and right and rarely felt bad about it. Still, none of the girls whose men she took ever confronted her about it because they were afraid of her. She had a brown belt in karate and knew how to disable people the same way a marine did with pressure points.

"I had a little issue out shopping," Tracy said, leaving out the details. "Kamira and Joy here?"

"Yea, come on in girl," Rachel welcomed her. "We gonna have some fun tonight, I got a lay out that's gonna lay you out."

When Tracy saw the table full of Moet Champagne being chilled on ice, right next to the table laid out with fried chicken, lasagna, macaroni and cheese, empanadas, and other comfort food, she knew she was going to have a good time.

"Here you go girl," Tracy said with a smile as she handed Rachel a box of her favorite candy, Blow Pops. "I hate shopping for you, but I know how you like candy and shit."

"Ohhhh, Blow Popsss. Oh you know that's my shit. These are good for practicing with," she winked deviously.

One thing about Rachel was that she was genuine. When she said thank you, she meant it. Instead of throwing the candy in a corner she immediately opened the box and went over to the living room table and started dumping them into a bowl on her aunt's coffee table. She took a watermelon one for herself, threw one at Joy who she knew would want one too, sat down, and started unwrapping it.

"So where you been Tra?" Joy asked as she flipped her long black hair over her shoulder. "We were about to eat without you."

"She had to go shopping earlier," Kamira answered for Tracy.

Tracy went over and gave her two friends a hug and a kiss. "That dress is bad Joy."

Out of them all, Joy was probably the prettiest and most stylish of the crew. Her family wasn't rich, but they were pretty well off. Her father was a doctor with a thriving practice in Connecticut. He had left Joy's mother for one of his assistants years before. Joy's mom got the house and a fair alimony payment each month.

Joy had chocolate brown skin and long black hair, which was mostly extensions, but her real hair reached down to her shoulder blades. She was slim like a model, but with an athletic build from her years playing field hockey in middle school and high school. While she was pretty, she had an edge to her look that served as a warning to ignorant men and jealous women. She never really smiled, and could give you a crazy look like you've never seen. She would usually just glare at people while they talked out of the corner of her slitted eyes. It was very intimidating at times. The wrap dress she was wearing was a black floral Diane von Furstenberg. Joy was almost like a black clone of Rachel. When Joy and Rachel were together it was like Paris and Nicole on the town, only they weren't ditzes—they were not to be fucked with and knew exactly what was going on around them.

"Thanks Tra, I got this for my birthday last year and never

wore it," Joy confided.

Rachel looked at Joy with contempt. "And I guess the only reason why you're wearing it now at my party is because I'm the one that got it for your ass!"

Joy laughed. "Nooo. I just thought it would look nice with my new black boots."

Tracy always felt insufficient around Joy. She loved her close friend, but knew that being around her almost always meant she was getting no play, no attention. Knowing that Joy would be at the party was the reason why she had wanted to go shopping in the first place.

"Tracy, I heard you got a new man," Rachel handed her friend a flute of champagne and then sat down herself.

"Ummm. Yea," Tracy answered cautiously. She took note of the fact that Joy didn't compliment her back on her new outfit, and her shoulders began to slump.

"So come on, tell us about him," Joy interjected, hoping Tracy would finally open up now that they were all there.

"I told you before, I'm not saying anything about him. I've got a good thing going and I'm not gonna to mess it up fuckin' wit y'all crazy bitches."

"Ohh, come on," Rachel pleaded. "Tell us what he looks like at least…"

Tracy rolled her head back after taking a long sip of champagne and relented. "He's tall, light-skinned, and has green eyes."

"What?" they all said in unison.

"What?" she asked them back.

"You don't EVER date light-skinned guys," Kamira answered.

"You said they all look gay," Joy agreed.

"I know, I know. But this one is different. He's very

masculine and strong," Tracy daydreamed.

"He has a big dick or something?" Rachel asked.

"Where does he work?" Joy asked.

"Okay now y'all are getting too deep. Isn't it time to eat?" Tracy tried to change the subject.

"Nooo. You don't get any fried chicken until you give up some more info," Kamira demanded, holding her friend down from standing up. It was then that Tracy realized they all were hovering over her, hanging on her words.

"I'm not giving up any more info, so you all just need to back the hell off okay?" Tracy said as her forehead began sweating. She began to feel as if they were pressuring her, and she didn't like it. Just then, Rachel's mother came flying through the door. She had on a gold pants suit and looked like Jackie Collins' blonde sister.

"Ma!" Rachel said, almost embarrassed that her mom was in the room.

"Hi sweetheart, happy birthday! Am I late?"

"I thought you weren't going to make it?" Rachel almost sounded disappointed.

"No, I canceled my spa appointment, all for you," Mrs. Moretti smiled brightly. "You know I couldn't miss a chance to hang with my daughter and her beautiful friends. How are you all doing?

"Hi Mrs. Moretti," they each got up and hugged Rachel's mom as if she were their own. They had been over Mrs. Moretti's house just about every day when they were all kids. Mrs. Moretti would take them all shopping and to tea parties to teach them proper etiquette. She was a second mother to them all.

"I hope I'm not interrupting something," Mrs. Moretti said with a wink as she sat on the couch right next to Tracy.

Joy cleared her throat. "No, not really. We were just grilling

Tracy for info on her new man. She hasn't even told us his name yet."

"She's trying to keep him top secret because she thinks if she tells us we're going to mess it up somehow," Rachel piped in. *Why are they all in my business like this?* Tracy thought.

Tracy opened her mouth to speak, but Mrs. Moretti spoke in her stead and put her hand around Tracy's shoulders. "If that's what Tracy wants, that's what she gets. Now you all leave my baby alone."

Everybody groaned, and Tracy breathed a sigh of relief. She was afraid that she would say something to her friends that would ruin the whole vibe of the party if they kept pushing. She wondered why they hadn't learned yet when to leave her alone. "Thank you Mrs. Moretti."

For the rest of the party they talked about Mrs. Moretti's new man instead, and she was more than happy to release the details about her latest catch. After the party, they all decided to hit a lounge right down the street. On the way to the elevator, Tracy's cell phone rang. It was Mike.

"Go ahead, I'll be right down guys," Tracy said nervously and everyone seemed to look at her with a smirk. They didn't mess with her though, they just went ahead to the elevator, which took only a few seconds to arrive.

"What's up?" Tracy said into the phone once the elevator doors closed.

"I was just about to ask you. You done with what you had to do today? I wanna see you," Mike said, almost pleading with her. Tracy loved it when he acted like he couldn't go another minute without seeing her. His weakness with her was such a big contrast to how he was around his boys. They saw the mean, shit-talking side of Mike, and she only saw the kind, loving side of him. Not only was he one of the most caring brothers she had ever met, he also was killer in bed. Just seeing his gorgeous face and hypnotic eyes complemented by his well-toned body made Tracy come very quickly. She loved to hold onto his well-sculpted chest in bed and then dig her nails deep into his back right before the moment of truth. Afterwards his back would be red and wounded, but he didn't care. He would just casually get up and go to the kitchen to get them some orange juice.

"I don't know, I just told everyone I'd go to a bar with them," Tracy said, smiling from ear to ear. She was leaning with her face against the wall in her own world.

"Which bar? I can come by—"

"NO. No." Tracy's mind swam with images of Kamira's smiling ass all up in her man's face, and Joy sauntering past Mike with her perfectly molded body in her $300 dress. "No, I'll come out there. Where you at?"

"I'm down at June's bar on Webster Ave. You know where that's at?" he asked.

"Um, yeah," Tracy scrunched her nose up when she heard the name 'June's'. That was the one of the ghettoest, shoot-em-up bars in the Bronx. "Okay, I'll be there in about a half hour or so. Are there a lot of people there?"

"Don't worry Trace, I got you," Mike said, referring to her anxieties about being in crime-ridden areas. He knew Tracy like the back of his hand, and could sense when she was freaking out.

"Okay. I'll see you."

When Tracy told her friends that she was ditching them, they were understandably upset, but they let her go without much of a fight. Mrs. Moretti invited her down to the house that following Saturday. Tracy was glad Rachel had given everyone a bottle of Champagne to take home, because she was going to need it going up into June's on a Saturday night.

Sitting parked in the car down the street from June's, Tracy looked around to make sure no one was walking down the street before taking a long swig from her bottle of Moet. When she opened her eyes, she saw a couple had just passed by and were looking back at her. She rolled her eyes and sunk lower in her seat.

June's was a large hole-in-the-wall bar that you couldn't say many good things about. The walls were dirty, the floors were sticky, the bartenders were mean, and most of the customers were known for criminal behavior. Tracy couldn't understand why Mike would even want to step foot in this bar.

"Hey baby," he said as soon as he saw Tracy walk in. He eyed her down and admired the cute dress she was wearing. He was sitting right next to the door at the bar. There were people dancing on the small dance floor to the sound of Remy Ma's *I'm Conceited* playing on the juke box. It wasn't even 9pm, but the bar was already getting too packed for Tracy's taste.

"Hi," Tracy said shortly and slid onto the bar stool that he had been holding for her. She glanced around and saw all kinds of people she didn't want to be around. But the one person she did want to be with was there, so she would suffer through this.

"I'm glad you here," Mike said in his deep voice, low enough so that only Tracy could hear. He was looking like the star of the bar as usual, in a gray Ecko jacket, a pair of dark blue jeans, and a Kangol hat. His chiseled face reminded her of Michael Ealy from the Barbershop movie—but Mike was better looking and much more rugged. "These nut ass broads always trying to get in my shit. You look so good."

"You like this bar?" Tracy couldn't stop herself from asking, ignoring his compliment. She noticed several dice faced women looking their way. They looked mad as if Tracy had ruined their plans for the night. Tracy ordered a shot of Tequila, straight up.

"This bar is my roots. I do a lot of business up here," Mike responded carelessly.

"And what business is that?" Tracy asked for the 1500th time.

"Princess, you shouldn't ask questions you don't really wanna know the answer to," Mike almost scolded her. He looked at her intensely with a look of concern etched in his scrunched eyebrows. He was starting to think Tracy was either extremely naïve, or just very nosey.

"Whatever," Tracy waved him off with her french manicured fingers. He was right, she probably didn't want to know, because she was too happy right now being in his presence. She loved it when he called her by his pet name for her, 'Princess.' It made her really feel like royalty being around him. Mike was doing wonders for her self-esteem. As she downed her second shot, she began to get bolder and less on edge about her surroundings.

"Damnnn Moony, who this pretty young thang you got ova here," a bummy looking old man came stumbling by on his way out of the bar. He looked like he was eternally drunk.

"Take your ass on somewhere Pete, not now," Mike waved him off. Usually he would go off on someone who made a comment about his girl to his face, but Pete was just an old crackhead drunk who meant nobody any harm.

"Yo Moony, let me holla at you about something," a broad-shouldered, older-looking, brown-skinned brother came into the bar and shouted out Mike on sight.

"Nigga, don't be calling me out in front of my girl," Mike turned around and told him off in a tone that said he wasn't playing. "Who the fuck you think you talking to?"

"Yea, who you think you talkin' to?" Pete mimicked Mike and pointed at the man.

"Petey, I ain't gonna tell your ass again," Mike told him and half stood up from his stool. Pete went scampering out of the bar and Mike sat back down, still grilling down the newcomer, who looked annoyed.

"Listen, my bad Moony wit ya girl and all, but this is urgent business. You know we gotta talk," the other man pushed again. He looked slightly embarrassed as several of the other bar patrons watched him closely. Mike had his head cocked to the side, his hands hanging between his legs, eyeing this guy down like Beenie Sigel at the end of the movie *State Property*. If looks could kill. Tracy became uncomfortable.

"It's about that dude, yo, the one we was talkin' about. Come on man, don't try to play me right now," the brother continued.

Mike finally made his decision after a few awkward moments for Tracy. He excused himself from Tracy and went outside to talk to the guy, who Tracy had never seen before. Before he left, Mike glanced around at certain people in the bar, as if to say "leave my girl alone."

Not even 30 seconds later a brother who Tracy *did* know, Mike's friend Bowen, came from the back of the bar and sat down right in Mike's seat. It was as if he came out of hiding or something. He was tall like Mike, but looked like a cockroach in comparison.

"What's goin' on Trace," Bowen said, trying to sound sweet.

"Uh, nothing. What's up Bowen," Tracy said with an obvious look of dismay on her face. She was annoyed that he thought it was okay to call her by a nickname. She turned and looked out the small window in the door for Mike.

"I never seen you in here before," he continued. Tracy was at a loss for why he was talking to her in the first place. So she just ignored him and kept sipping on her beer.

"You look nice in that dress you got on. That new?" he

asked, trying to make small talk.

Tracy was starting to think something was going on. "What is it you really came over here for. You know Mike is here, right?"

"Yea, I know," he said and looked at the door to make sure Mike wasn't coming in yet. "But look, I had wanted to say something to you. I promised myself if I ever caught you by yourself I would holla at you—"

"You have got to be joking." Tracy looked at Bowen in disbelief.

"Naw, naw, naw, nothing like that," Bowen assured and waved his hand from side to side. Then he started speaking as if he didn't know what he really wanted to say. "It's just that...well, you know I got a lot of women in my family... I know you a good girl, you know?"

"Look, I don't know what you're trying to say, but I'm not catching whatever it is you're throwing at me right now," Tracy cut him off shortly and got up from her stool. She turned and went outside before he had a chance to open his mouth to say something slick again. On the outside, she was the perfect vision of coolness and confidence.

But on the inside Tracy was freaking out. Should she tell Mike about Bowen's advances? Should she shut her mouth to prevent a bad scene at the bar? What if somebody he knew told him she had been talking to Bowen in the bar? Just as she was contemplating what to do, she saw Mike walking back from down the street, his face red from the cold and from whatever heated discussion he had just been having.

"I'm sick of these desperate ass niggas! Can't do nothin' nice for muthafuckas these days," Mike rambled and grabbed Tracy by the waist. "Come on, we outta here."

Tracy didn't even ask him what was wrong; she just let him lead her down the street. It was definitely time to go.

Tracy drove her car, and Mike drove his. Tracy's whole night was ruined by Bowen, and by the time she pulled her car into a spot near her building, she had decided to tell Mike what happened. She didn't want anything messing up her relationship with him.

She waited in front of her building for a long time for Mike to show up, and after ten minutes she began to think something was wrong. She picked up her cellphone and shakily pressed 'call' on Mike's number. She could have sworn he was behind her when they were driving. He didn't pick up.

Later that evening, Tracy sat up in bed, in the dark, staring off into space. Mike hadn't called her all night after they left the bar, and she was starting to become concerned.

Why couldn't he just pick up the phone and call, she thought and became angrier by the moment. She decided to switch on the lamp on her nightstand and do a search through 'The Book' to ease her mind.

'The Book' was an important part of Tracy's life. It was a huge black binder full of scraps of paper and college ruled looseleaf sheets with tiny writing on them to maximize space. Each page contained note after note of messages for Tracy to remember:

"Links between the microwave and health issues. Healthy Woman Magazine—3/2/1998"

"Rat found in chicken box at Chicken King restaurant in Queens on Jamaica Avenue—1/5/2005"

"Woman was shot outside club R.A.M. in Manhattan. Random gunfire. August 14, 2000—8/15/2000"

Tracy would refer to the book regularly. It was now overflowing with pages and falling apart at the seams. But Tracy didn't care—she still came home and inserted notes that she had written on the bus, in the bathroom at work, in the coffee shop, and anywhere else she could find a piece of paper, even a napkin. She kept her receipts of purchases for $100 and more in a pocket at the back of the book. They had to be taped down at some point to stay put. She liked to keep all of her information in one place. She didn't trust to put her private thoughts and reminders on her computer hard drive.

Everyone who had seen 'The Book' now officially considered Tracy to be over the top, and even a few had dared to tell her so. The third person who called her crazy in jest, a guy who she was dating, went running out of the door when Tracy threw a plate of food at him right at the dinner table. Ever since then she didn't allow anyone to look at 'The Book.' Now she kept it locked up in the drawer underneath her night table.

She scanned page after page looking for anything referring to June's bar. If Mike didn't show soon, she was going to go back out and look for him. Suddenly a random thought ran through her mind. *Who would tell my mother if I was dead—nobody even knows me over here except Mike. Would mom even care that I was dead? And Mike never called me back—so who is to say he isn't already dead?*

All kinds of wild thoughts entered Tracy's mind and she felt as if she were going to have a fit. There was a knock on her door and she jumped. She quietly placed 'The Book' down on her bed and switched off the lamp. No one was able to come in her building without being buzzed in. *Uh uh, what if it's that crazy ho across the hall who's been giving me dirty looks whenever I see her?*

The knock came again causing Tracy's heart to nearly jump out of her chest. She gently crept up to the door and peeked out of the peep hole. She almost fainted from relief when she saw it was Mike. She couldn't have opened that door faster.

"Mike! I was so scared. What happened to you? Thank God. I thought something bad happened! Why didn't you call me?"

Tracy asked the questions that had been swimming in her head for the past few hours one after the other.

"Calm down, Princess. Everything is alright. My fault for not calling you. I had some drama," Mike explained as he walked inside. "Why all the lights off?"

Tracy quickly ran to switch on the lights. She knew that looked strange. Then she remembered 'The Book' on her bed!

She tried to stay cool as she watched Mike sit down on the couch and pull his hat off his head revealing his clean hustler cut. Her knees began to get weak as she thought of the possibilities for that night. She tried to ease over to the bed, but Mike quickly reached out for her and grabbed her wrist.

"C'mere," he said with a smirk as he looked up into her eyes.

"Sure, just a second though…" Tracy said, cursing herself. But he wouldn't let her go and snatched her towards where he was seated. He cut his eyes up at Tracy devilishly and bit the side of his lip.

"Dance for me," he said, with the excitement growing in his voice. His face revealed the mischief going on in his mind. "No music this time."

"But baby, just give me a second," she said and then put her hands on her hips.

"Dance," he said again, evenly, and firmly. She instantly became moist.

Tracy glanced up at her window to make sure there were no spaces in the blinds. She then slowly started to move her hips from side to side.

Mike sighed and sat back as he watched Tracy gyrate and dance to the music that was playing in her mind. She ran her hands down the length of her bodice from her torso down to her knees and then split her legs apart exposing herself for a few moments before working her way back up. She turned around this time and did a shimmy move before flashing him with a flip of her skirt.

"Owwww," Mike commented as he watched the show.

Tracy was doing her thing, but she still had 'The Book' in the back of her mind. She had to find a way to get that thing off of the bed before they got there. How would she explain that?

As she was scheming and starting to panic again, Mike jumped up and grabbed her from behind, bringing her in close to his pelvis. She could feel that he was fully grown, and about to burst out of his jeans in a minute. He put his arm around the front of her neck as if he were holding her hostage as he carried over to the bed. He threw her forward over the covers and Tracy collapsed over "The Book," desperately trying to cover it with her bosom. Mike was trying to lift her hips off the bed but she was resisting and moving forward to the other side.

"What you doin' baby," Mike said in his sexy voice that said he was gone, lost in horny-ville, as he tried to pull her back towards him. "Where you tryin' to go?"

Suddenly Tracy jerked forward, 'The Book' tucked like a football and rolled off the other side of the bed.

"Tracy!" Mike yelled at her and scrambled across the bed to see if she was alright. Tracy shoved the book under the bed with a quickness.

"I'm okay, I'm okay," she said, holding her hand up as he looked at her as if she had lost her mind.

"What the hell you doing?"

"I just got so excited, I had a spasm," Tracy lied quickly. It sounded stupid to her, so she knew Mike had to be thinking the same thing.

"Would you get your ass back up here?" he asked as he offered her a hand.

Gladly, she thought as she got back up there with him and fell into his arms. He looked at her a few more moments with concern, and then let her head fall to his chest.

"I love you Tracy," Mike said out of nowhere. "I don't never have to worry about you, do I?"

He felt Tracy melt in his arms after he said that. It was the first time she had heard him say those three magical words. "I love you too."

"I said, can I trust you?" Mike repeated firmly with his head resting on the top of hers. Tracy could feel the vibrations from his deep voice.

"You know you can," Tracy assured. "But will you protect me?"

"You know I will Princess." Mike pulled back from their embrace and grabbed Tracy by her chin. His eyes shone even in the dim light, and Tracy closed her eyes as she anticipated the euphoric feeling of Mike's thick, wet lips swallowing hers in a loving kiss. Everytime they kissed it was even more blissful for Tracy than before. She truly was in love with this man.

They kissed and played with each other's tongues for so long that Tracy lost track of time. Truly, she lost track of her whole being as she got lost in Mike's world. By the time he had pinned her roughly against her headboard, she was completely gone, a slave on Mike's plantation. More and more, this was the world she wanted to take residence in, for life.

Chapter 5

Mrs. Moretti's house was set behind a long line of trees. It was the biggest house in the neighborhood by far, and only a hop, skip, and a jump from the marina. Fire Island was a short boat ride away.

"Tracyyyy! Kami!!" Mrs. Moretti opened her arms and welcomed her house guests. They had brought overnight bags and were looking forward to spending the night at the house. Mrs. Moretti had told them she had a surprise for everyone.

Joy and Rachel greeted Tracy and Kami in the foyer. As usual, Joy was looking like she had just stepped out of a fashion house in Milan. She was wearing a long, white blouse belted underneath her perfect size C breasts and skinny, black jeans that hugged her skinny legs.

Tracy had no idea when this envy of Joy had begun, but it was beginning to consume her. She and Joy had been so close in their youth—especially when Tracy was president of the FBLA club in high school, and Joy was her vice president. They traveled together in the club all the time, which was the real reason why they both joined, and hung out with each other more than with Kami and Rachel at one point. They also had started on the same field hockey team in high school. Joy was always athletic in school, and looked more like a stick figure for the most part while Tracy had the sexy curves. But Joy had blossomed after high school, and even seemed to have grown a few inches taller.

"I can't believe we're all getting together again in one place," Joy commented as her slanted brown eyes gave the only impression of delight.

"Twice in two weeks, that's a record," Rachel agreed as she sat back down on the loveseat in the grand room. "So come on Ma, what's the surprise?"

Mrs. Moretti could barely contain her excitement as she stood before them as if she were making a huge presentation. "I'm sending you all to LA!"

"What?" they all said in unison.

"I bought you all a plane ticket to LA, and I booked a ritzy hotel near Hollywood for a week. It's my gift to you all, because I'm feeling guilty. Last week when I saw you all, I realized that I haven't been keeping touch like I used to. Tracy, I haven't even seen you in over two years! Kamira, the last time I saw you your hair was bright red. I never see you guys, and I wish you'd all stay tight and close. It's hard to find good, true friends. You have to stick together. So how about a trip together!"

Joy and Kamira hopped out of their seats and bumrushed Rachel's mom with kisses and hugs. Mrs. Moretti was overwhelmed. Rachel smiled and got up as well to thank her mother. But Tracy sat stone silent.

"Tracy are you okay?" Rachel was the first to realize it.

"We would have to fly?" Tracy asked nervously.

"Yes, how else would you get to Los Angeles, it's across the country," Rachel laughed.

"Tracy's afraid of planes," Kamira reminded everyone, and sat down next to her friend. All of the air in their celebration was zapped out of them in one swift realization.

"You're afraid of planes like that Tra? Why?" Rachel asked.

"Ever since 9-11, she refuses to board a plane," Kamira answered for Tracy again.

"What am I your mime? I can speak for myself. And there is no way in hell I'm getting on a plane, so forget it!" Tracy snapped.

The room was quiet as everyone prepared for what would

happen next.

"Maybe it's time to face that fear," Joy was the first to have the balls to suggest what they all were thinking. "I mean, it's LA. You never know, you might get discovered or something!"

"You mean *you* might get discovered. That's the real reason why you want to go so bad anyway," Tracy said snidely in response.

"What the hell is that supposed to mean?" Joy scrunched up her nose and asked defensively.

"You know exactly what it means."

"Girls!" Mrs. Moretti wanted to stop this before it got worse. She went over and sat on the arm of the chair where Tracy was seated. "Sweetie, 9-11 happened almost five years ago. There's nothing to be afraid of."

"You know, they have those nerve calming pills don't they? They make you lose all your inhibitions right before a flight," Rachel thought outloud.

"I'm not getting on anybody's fucking plane!" Tracy stood up and screamed. "I don't care what any of you say."

When Kamira stood up and tried to grab Tracy's arm to calm her down, Tracy shook off her hand violently. Everyone was quiet again. Rachel's mom looked down at her hands, Rachel looked out of the window, and Joy rubbed her right temple.

Tracy finally just grabbed her bag and left the room. When they all heard the front door shut, they waited a few more moments to make sure she was gone. Mrs. Moretti was the first to speak.

"So she hasn't gotten much better?"

"No, not really," Kamira confirmed.

"Hasn't anyone tried to get her some help?"

"I think her mom convinced her to see a psychotherapist a few months ago. But she stopped going after a couple of visits.

She didn't see the point."

"They say the first step to recovery of anything is to admit you have a problem, but I don't think Tracy would admit she has a problem in a million years," Joy said, shaking her head.

"God, let's stop talking about her. If she knew we were talking about her she'd probably come in here and slice all our asses up," Kamira said seriously, and Rachel chuckled but knew deep down that Kamira wasn't that far from the truth.

"But seriously, it's not funny. It's never been funny. Remember that time in high school she thought her boyfriend was cheating on her, and slept in her car outside his mom's house for two straight days?" Rachel remembered. "She's lucky they didn't call the cops when they finally caught her. She missed school and everything."

"That was nothing. Once, a few months ago, we were at a party, a classy party, and Tracy swore up and down that some girl had said something to her when she passed us. I didn't hear anything. She actually walked up on the girl and cursed her out, for nothing. The girl didn't know what Tracy was talking about. It was so embarrassing, and security kicked us out on our asses, in front of everyone."

"Well, something needs to be done *now* before it gets even worse," Mrs. Moretti commented. "But it's not my call. Maybe I should talk to her mom."

"Okay Mrs. Moretti, but whatever you do, don't let on to Tracy that you were talking behind her back. She will add you to her book," Kamira warned.

"What book?" Mrs. Moretti looked confused.

"*The* book," Kamira answered.

"She still does that?" Joy asked in near horror.

"Yup."

"She's had that book for over a decade now. She hides it

from people now though. She thinks I don't know where it is. You don't wanna know what's in it."

"All of her crazy thoughts and delusions," Rachel confirmed.

Kamira got up and went out of the room to check and make sure Tracy wasn't still in the house listening to everything they were saying. Truth be told, Kamira was still kind of scared of Tracy and what she was capable of. She even checked a few closets. When she was sure Tracy had left, she came back into the room.

"Seriously though y'all, let's stop talking about her. She really hates this," Kamira pleaded.

"Okay. But I still want you all to go on this trip. Can any of you convince her to go? Or is that a dead issue?" Mrs. Moretti asked.

"The only way she is going to LA is by car or train," Joy answered the question in the air.

"So she'll take a train?"

"She might take a train," Kamira nodded.

"But that's like a three day trip!" Rachel said in shock.

"Doesn't matter. If you want us all together in LA, she'll have to take a train. I'll talk to her about it when she calms down. Let me go out there and make sure she didn't try to walk to her mom's house or something," Kamira said, taking control over the situation.

About 15 minutes later, Tracy and Kamira came back in. Tracy seemed apologetic.

"Listen everybody, I'm sorry for earlier. Mrs. Moretti, I'd love to go on the trip, thank you so much. But I have to take a train," Tracy confirmed.

"Okay," Mrs. Moretti clapped her hands. She just wanted to get the positive vibe back in her home. "It's settled then. I'll get you a train ticket and you can meet the rest of the girls in LA.

Anybody else want to ride the train with Tracy?"

Kamira looked at the houseplant, Joy looked at the Rembrandt painting on the wall, and Rachel looked at the empty brown leather recliner.

Tracy laughed. "Yea, thanks guys."

"Sorry girl," Kamira laughed. "But there is no way I'm getting on a train cross country!"

"Me neither," Rachel agreed. She came over and hugged her friend. "But I still love you."

"That's alright, I'll be okay on my own. But I guess I'll have to leave a few days before you guys."

"Yea, we'll probably be there before you," Rachel pondered the time schedules.

"If your plane doesn't crash," Tracy joked.

They all talked about their trip and Mrs. Moretti had the maid bring out food and drinks for their sleep over. They were so excited about Los Angeles that they forgot all about the drama from earlier. But Mrs. Moretti didn't forget about one thing—she was definitely going to talk to Tracy's mom.

Chapter 6

Mike turned the corner in his black Acura knowing that he had to handle this. It was a tricky situation, but who better to do it but him. He puffed on a fat blunt being careful not to let it touch his lips—he didn't want them turning black from the cigar. He let the smoke flow out of his nostrils and permeate throughout his car as he drove down the block. He was looking for someone.

The one he had a problem with was unfortunately his sister's boyfriend Jimmy a.k.a. JM, a dude who people usually didn't like to mess with. He had been to jail twice—once for robbery, and once for attempted murder. He was a Trini brother, about 35 years old and a cold killer. He was living with his brother Marcus and Marcus' girlfriend Shauntea. Jimmy and Marcus ran their own block in Castle Hill. They held it down, never getting any problems from the young kids with street dreams who were on the come up. It was mostly because Jimmy was feared—it was known that he would kill somebody without much of a thought.

Not only did Jimmy owe Mike's crew money, he also had been messing around on Mike's sister Janet. He had always been doing it, but now he was getting obnoxious about it. He was bringing chicks around the spots where he knew Janet and her people rolled. Random chicks were calling Janet's phone cussing Janet out as if she were the one that did something wrong, and Jimmy was rumored to have some other girl on the other side of town pregnant.

Then Mike had been feeling the pressure lately to collect on a few ounces of coke that he had consigned to Jimmy over four months ago. Mike hadn't been stressing the matter much, because it wasn't like he had to come out of pocket for the coke—he and his boy had robbed it off a white kid in Brooklyn who had been trying to get in the game. But one of Mike's running partners, the guy from the bar, was starting to feel some kind of way about how Jimmy was ditching the bill. He didn't like being played, and his pressuring was starting to piss Mike off. Mike knew he had to do something about it since that was his sister's man, and he had vouched for him.

"Yooo JM," Mike said, slapping hands with Jimmy, who was standing on his regular corner, posted up not far from a bodega, talking to some girl with big silver hoop earrings and dimples in her cheeks from smiling so hard.

"What's up cousin? What goin' on deez days," Jimmy said in response. He had a distinctive Trini accent that came out more when he was mad. His forehead was permanently indented; people said it was because he was always thinking about money. He wasn't really that happy to see his future brother-in-law.

"Can I holla at you for a minute playa?" Mike asked with his hands in his pockets. "It's important."

"Yah, I doh know man, I'm kinda busy right now. Maybe later," Jimmy said disrespectfully and turned his back to Mike.

"Nigga, I ain't gonna ask you again," Mike said, getting loud. Mike's second nickname was 'Snaps', because he was known to snap off in a hot second. He had been hoping this would go down peacefully but was prepared if it didn't.

"Well damn, you ent got to be gettin' so loud nah," Jimmy said, beginning to stress his Trini accent as he turned his head back around to look directly into Mike's eyes. It was a way of intimidating his enemies. "Wham now? Why yuh harrassin' me so?"

"I don't know who the fuck you think you talkin' to, but you really pushin' ya luck. I asked to speak to you in private," Mike said, giving Jimmy dagger eyes that said he meant business. He glanced at the girl Jimmy was talking to. "I don't wanna have to embarrass you in front of your lil smut, but I can and I will!"

"Who the fuck you callin' a smut?" the girl started, but Jimmy shushed her.

Jimmy locked stares with Mike for a long time before excusing himself from the girl's presence and walking down the street with him.

Mike got right down to business when they stopped near a street light post. "First, I need that double stack you copped off me and Chewy so we can keep things moving. Today."

"Huh? Wha' dat?" Jimmy played stupid.

"Yo, don't do that duke. All I want is a settle up so that we can go on with business as usual, feel me? You a business man, so you should already know the deal. You takin' money outta both our pockets at this point. You know I gave you a deal on that package, and I can do it again if you cooperate."

Jimmy stopped speaking with his heavy accent, and became serious as he bargained. "Well I 'ent got da settle up. I'll give you a half G when I see you next time, on da re-up."

"A re-up? With 1/4 of the bill and no deposit? Yo, you buggin'! You trynna play me like some dumb little hoe now huh?" Mike asked, his voice wavering with anger as he pointed at Jimmy's head.

"Fool yuh 'bout to get yuh limbs cracked, keep puttin' yuh fingers in my face. Doh make me haf to cut ass," Jimmy said in a threatening tone as he stood toe to toe with Mike.

"Oh you threatening me? All that time jerkin' off upstate done made you catch amnesia. Let me jog ya memory then," Mike said, trying to keep calm as he put up his both of his hands in a challenging stance. He began gesturing wildly and punching one fist into his other open hand as he continued speaking. He was getting madder by the moment, but trying his best to keep his cool. "See you might got all these Castle Hill muthafuckas out here shook, but I ain't them, and you ain't me. JM, listen to me real good, you my sister's man and all, but don't get spun over no couple of stacks aiight? Right now you in my game, and you play by *my* rules. I want my money, two G's by tonight, or it's gonna be a serious problem between us. And you know when we *got* to, we go *at* it ock."

The fire in Mike's eyes was burning brightly. Jimmy knew that if he played his cards wrong he could create problems he didn't really have time for. His little operation on this block was going well, and the last thing he needed was a beef, especially against Mike's crew, which was at least 50 deep.

"Murda!! Two G's in four hours? Moony, you cyah be serious," Jimmy said incredulously, but really his face showed that he was surrendering.

"I coulda gave you til tomorrow if you ain't come out your face wrong. Pay up tonight, I'll get you a re-up, half from before, that's all I can get you this time, but you gotta pay that shit on time," Mike commanded as if he were reading him orders. "And then we got to come to a understanding about my sister. We both know you gonna do your thing, but don't be flaunting them other hoes in front of her no more. I'm tired of hearin' her mouth."

"Aww, doh talk to me 'bout no bitches Moony," Jimmy was getting annoyed again. "That be 'tween me and yuh hoe ass sister. She be doin' her ting too."

"You callin' my sister a hoe now? To my face?" Mike shouted and looked like he was about to explode. He had never been disrespected that blatantly in his lifetime.

"Well shit, 'ent like I'm de only one dat know," Jimmy put his hands up in a 'what do you want me to say' gesture and chuckled coldly. It made him unprepared for the sudden, powerful jab Mike hit him with, right between the eyes. Jimmy's head jerked back and he stumbled backwards. As he was holding the bridge of his nose in pain, Mike came up and punched him again, this time harder. Jimmy fell helplessly to the ground, and Mike could hear someone coming up from behind. He pulled out his brand new .44 and pointed it at Jimmy's young boy, who was coming to his defense.

"Back up, this is ain't none of your concern youngin'," Mike warned him. Jimmy's boy put up his hands and backed off when he saw who it was. He knew Mike had a reputation for being ruthless when it came to his money and his family. Mike looked around him to make sure the coast was clear. The girl Jimmy had been talking to was just standing there, silent, with her hand over her mouth.

While Jimmy sat in a daze, holding his face, Mike searched through his pockets and found his earnings for the day—about $1,800.

"Lyin' ass nigga. Consider this a done deal. And I don't want you coming near Jan no more," Mike said as he walked to his car and put his gun back in his jeans. "If I hear about you comin' at her, I don't care if it's to apologize, I'm gonna dust yo ass so quick they'll put it in the ghetto book of 'hood records."

Mike hopped into his car and looked over at Jimmy on the sidewalk one more time before driving away from the bodega. Calmly, he sparked his blunt back up and blew smoke out the side of his mouth.

"Now why this nigga make me have to do that shit!" he said shaking his head as he turned the corner. He wished that things would have went down smoother, and hoped that Jimmy would just heed the message and move on. Knowing Jimmy for over four years though, he knew this wasn't the last he would hear from this Trini killer.

Chapter 7

"No Karif, seriously. Where were you all night?" Kamira went ahead and began the conversation that always grew into an all out fight.

"None of your fucking business, leave me alone," Karif waved her off as he tore into his newly made cheeseburger. It was one in the afternoon on Saturday, and he had just stepped in the door not even a half hour before.

"How can you say that? We live together, of course it's my business!" Kamira pressed on, but really she was pressing her luck. She knew how Karif could be, but still she continued to do this regular song and dance with him.

Karif was silent as he picked up the universal remote control and switched on the small television in the kitchen.

Karif was everything Kamira had been looking for in a man for a while. He worked as a stock broker making over $70,000 a year in lower Manhattan, had a spacious loft on the upper west side, and drove a brand new red convertible BMW. That was all Kamira could ever ask for at this point in her life. When Karif agreed to let her live with him after a lot of complaining, she was ecstatic. Her friends thought she was the ultimate idiot for giving up her rent controlled apartment in Manhattan that previous month, which had been granted to her by her aunt who died several years before, to move in with this man that she had only known for six months. But she was too far deep to see his true character before making that life changing move.

"Karif! Do you hear me?" Kamira yelled, sounding desperate.

"Get the fuck off my back!" Karif screamed back and gave her the look of death.

Kamira stormed out of the room and Karif thought that it was over. He was on the last bite of his burger when Kamira came back into the kitchen holding his cellphone.

"I just called the last number on your phone and some bitch answered. Who the hell is that!" she screamed hysterically. "You talked to her like five times yesterday!"

Karif threw the last of his food into his mouth and pushed himself back from the table. He got up and grabbed Kamira by the arm violently and led her to the bathroom. When he got there he locked the door.

"Give me that fucking phone," he screamed, snatching the phone out of her hand. Kamira was already crying when he grabbed her hair from the back and made her get on her knees in front of the toilet.

"I don't know who the fuck you think you are Kamira. I told you about fucking with my phone, didn't I?" Karif asked, sounding like a Dad about to dole out punishment. He lifted the toilet seat cover.

"Karif don't," Kamira said, crying even harder as she began to realize what he was doing. She tried to pry his grip from her head but in response he just jerked even harder, causing her to stop for fear of losing a chunk of hair. "Okay, I won't do it again."

"Didn't I!" he yelled into her ear this time. Kamira just responded with more crying.

Her ear was ringing when Karif started pushing her face down into the toilet water.

"Hold your breath!" he told her.

She resisted, straining her neck as she cried for mercy. "Karif, no! I said I'm sorry. I'm sorry!"

But Karif was too strong for her. He kept pushing her head down until her face was submerged in the cloudy toilet water. Kamira was hysterical as she grasped for anything in her reach to help her out of this situation. When holding on the toilet and trying to push herself up didn't work, she hit her hand on the sink and knocked over the plunger as she struggled.

Karif finally let her head up out of the water and turned it so that he could look right at her. Kamira gasped for air with her eyes still shut closed from the water.

"You think it's a good idea to call people on my phone?"

Kamira didn't respond quick enough as she tried to wipe the excess water from her eyes and Karif snatched her head back and then pushed it toward the toilet water.

"No! It wasn't a good idea. I'm sorry Karif!" she begged pitifully. Toilet water was getting into her mouth.

Karif stopped for a moment. "So what if somebody calls me and you're near my phone? You're gonna answer it?"

"No!" Kamira said quickly and obediently. "That's your phone and I have no business touching it."

"What if you see my cell phone bill in the mail again?"

"I won't touch it, I promise!" Kamira screamed and cried, praying to God that he didn't dunk her face again. She could taste the rancid impurities in the water and felt herself getting sick already.

Karif tossed her aside, nearly causing her to hit her head on the tub. As he left the room, Kamira lay to the side, crying and holding onto the back of her head which was throbbing in pain.

After almost a half hour of feeling sorry for herself, Kamira finally pulled herself together. She turned on the shower and started stripping. She felt so embarrassed that she was scared to even leave the bathroom.

This definitely wasn't the first time something like this

happened. As the warm shower water sprinkled down, replacing the germ-filled toilet water that covered her face, she thought about the time that Karif had held her over his balcony and threatened to throw her off after she had called his mother to tell her how he was treating her. His mother had cursed Kamira out and told her to never call her house again. Karif was so mad when he got the call from his mother that Kamira actually thought that he was going to kill her.

Kamira soaped her face over and over as she considered why she was still with Karif. He had been abusive to her even before she moved in with him, yet she had believed that he would somehow get better with time. Of course, he got worse. She was afraid to let him go because it was so hard to find a good-looking black man in New York who made close to six figures in a legitimate job. Karif had the potential to advance to a junior partner at his firm within five years, and that could mean an income of $250,000 or more. They would be set. He would probably buy them a nice house in Long Island or Jersey, and Kamira could live out her dream of the picture perfect suburban life.

Kamira's father had abandoned her mother early on her childhood, causing Kamira and her mom to move from their ranch-style home to a one bedroom apartment. Kamira was ashamed of the way she lived, especially being that all of her friends—Tracy, Joy, and Rachel—had between three and ten bedroom houses. She felt inadequate, like a poser, and never wanted her children to ever have to go through that type of struggle.

When she was finished with her shower, she turned the water off, stood in the stall, and didn't move for several minutes. She was thinking about how she was going to react to Karif when she left the bathroom. Her head was still pounding and she needed an aspirin badly.

She came out of the bathroom wrapped in a large white towel, having rubbed down with a cinnamon apple scented Bath & Body Works lotion and popping a few prescription strength tylenols. She didn't see Karif in the living room or the kitchen, so she went back to the bedroom. He was laying back on the bed with his eyes shut closed and his feet hanging over the side.

Perfect, Kamira thought. She turned down the lights in the room and eased slowly towards him, not sure if he was still pissed about the phone situation. She heard him snoring softly.

She threw her leg over his legs, as if she was mounting a horse, and when she sat down he snorted as he was woken from his light slumber.

"What?" he asked sleepily as Kamira let her towel fall to the bed. She began unzipping his pants quickly before he had a chance to protest. Before Karif knew it, Kamira had his penis in the back of her throat. She closed her eyes and concentrated to keep from gagging because she was still feeling sick from the toilet water.

She knew how much he loved a good head job. The way he was moaning with each movement told her that he was totally over what happened earlier. She pushed the negativity to the back of her mind and did her best to please her man. It would just take a little more time and a lot more pleasuring to mold Karif into true husband material. Just a little more time.

Chapter 8

"Hello? Hello?" the voice on the other end of the line said over and over.

"Oh yea, what's up Kami," Tracy finally answered, immediately recognizing her friend's voice. She didn't recognize the phone number at first, so she was listening in to see who it was.

"Trace!! Yoo, where you been, I've been tryin' to get at you all day!" Kami said, happy that she was finally able to get in touch with her best friend. "We're gonna hit Black tonight, you coming?"

"Black?" Tracy said as she involuntarily got up and walked over to where 'The Book' was stashed. "Wasn't there a shooting there? And what is this number you're calling me from, why didn't you call me on your cell?"

"No, there wasn't a shooting there! And girl you better not be looking in that damn book. We're trying to get out there early, like 12:30 so that we don't have to wait on line long. Rach is coming out."

Tracy took note of how Kamira completely dodged her question about the cellphone, but didn't say anything about it. "Rachel's coming out huh? Yea, I want to see that girl. The last time I saw her was when we were all at Mrs. Moretti's."

"Oh, so you tryin' to say you ain't coming out see me? Shit, being that I'm the one calling you," Kamira complained.

"You know what I mean. I always want to see you, but we don't get to see Rachel that much since we moved out to the city."

"Yea, I know, I'm just fuckin' with you. Be ready at

midnite—we'll take my car."

"What you wearing?"

"I don't know yet, just something cute, maybe my new skirt I got on Canal Street."

Oh Lord, here we go. She knows that skirt is way too short to be wearing in the club. She is just asking *to be singled out and harassed. And I bet she didn't even get 'permission' to go out from that jackass Karif. Maybe I should rethink this, before she gets me caught up in something.*

Kamira took Tracy's silence as something bad. "Let me get off this phone before you change your mind or something. I'll see you at midnight."

Tracy heard the dial tone in her ear before she could say anything else. She flipped through the pages of 'The Book' against Kamira's command, and after 20 minutes of searching, didn't find anything about Black night club in it.

She got up and went to her wine cabinet. The cherry finished cabinet was the most stylish thing Tracy owned in her small apartment, and she was proud of it. She took out a bottle of Cuervo and poured it into a crystal shot glass. She threw the shot back and filled the glass up again quickly. She poured the bitter golden liquid down her throat once more and barely winced. This was her ritual to calm herself down and get ready for a night on the town. Sober, the risks and dangers of being in New York City after midnight terrified her. But she wanted to be around her friends.

Kamira had Mariah blasting out of her maroon Jeep Cherokee SUV, which she could barely afford, when she pulled up in front of Tracy's building. She was right on time at midnight, just like she said she would be. That's what Tracy liked about Kamira; she was a woman of her word.

"What's up girl!!!" Kamira screamed over the loud music. It

was obvious that Kamira had been toasting it up before she left the house too. Tracy looked at her short, bubbly, brown-skinned friend. She was a cutie that almost always made men do a double take because of her shapely figure. She wore her hair in a short style and was really shaped like a glass coke bottle, without the help of a girdle, with a DD chest, 26 inch waist and 38 inch hips. Kamira's dad was half black, half Puerto Rican, and her mom was a dark-skinned Dominican woman. You wouldn't even know she had Spanish roots by looking at her.

"Girl get me to the club, I am ready to shake my ass. I'm gonna make y'all pretend you don't know me tonight," Tracy cackled as she struggled to keep her balance enough to hop up in the passenger side of the Jeep.

"Rach said she was gonna meet us there, and I asked Joy but she couldn't make it. You know what that's about," Kamira said, rolling her eyes.

"Yea, I know. That white boy Mark. She acts like she don't even know our asses when he's around. They goin' out or something?"

"I don't know, probably not. Probably just gonna sit up in the house up under each other."

"And he'll probably just find a reason to pick a fight with her like he always does. Then she'll be calling us talking about 'where we at'," Tracy predicted, her head bobbing with each word in her half drunken state. She had thrown back a couple more shots before leaving the house.

"Anyway. You look good girl," Kamira said with a head nod, and then was quiet.

What the hell does all that mean. The head nod. Either she's jealous or she's lying. I can't tell. I probably look crazy. That's what she's trying to tell me. She's just being nice. I wish she'd just tell me the truth so I can go change.

"Do you mean that, or are you just saying that?" Tracy asked outloud. She was never afraid to express her thoughts to her friends.

"What? Yea, I mean that! Come on Tracy, don't start baby. Let's have a good night," Kamira said, and then pressed her CD changer. A new Kelis song started playing with a bass so strong that Kamira's windows were shaking.

She better not be lying to me. She's supposed to be my friend.

When they drove past the club they saw the line was quickly beginning to grow. Kamira started driving faster as she scanned the streets nearby for an open parking spot. She was trying to avoid having to pay $30 to park the car in a lot. Luckily, she found a sweet spot two blocks down, and two blocks over from the club.

Tracy and Kamira strutted down the block like they usually did when they hit the club. In New York, you never knew who was watching, or who you were going to meet, so you always had to be on point. Kamira had on the white, three-tiered ruffle skirt she had just bought, a sexy white halter top contrasting against her brown skin with a pair of silver rhinestone-studded stilletos ending it off, and Tracy had on a pair of tight-fitting black pants and a caramel Armani Exchange blouse that had the back out with a pair of matching leather pumps. She had put on one of her best wigs for the evening.

They stood in line at the club for a little over 20 minutes before finally getting to the front where they could pay their admission. Tracy was so happy to get in and get another drink. She was starting to sober up, and that was scary for her.

Tracy's phone rang and when she saw that it was Rachel, she picked up quickly and started yelling into the phone so that Rachel could hear what she was saying. When she got off the phone, Kamira looked at her with raised eyebrows as she sipped on her Belvee and Cranberry as if to say, "So what's up?"

"She's outside," Tracy said and they started walking towards the entrance to meet their friend. "How come she didn't call you?"

"Oh I forgot to tell you." Kamira sounded like she was hiding something. "I told her to call you, I don't have my phone on me."

They saw Rachel pulling cash out of her black Gucci purse. She had on a sexy black dress that was sure to have been made by some designer that 90% of the country hadn't even heard of yet. Her family was loaded because of her late father, Harold Miner, who was a tycoon high on the supply chain of the oil business who caused a lot of drama after his death when it was discovered that he had left 50% of his money to his two children, 20% to his mistress, and the rest to his wife, who he really couldn't stand but still decided to leave in his will. Despite her family's wealth, Rachel was down to earth and realer than most poor folks. Most of the white people at their high school would sniff up her ass on a daily basis, trying to be a part of her circle, but Rachel wasn't having it. She knew that if she didn't have money those West Islip kids wouldn't even *tell* her the time of day. She had always preferred hanging out with Kamira, and then soon after Tracy and Joy came along. Rachel and Kamira had been friends since the 3rd grade, and they had gotten tighter and tighter with Tracy and Joy since middle school. Rachel, Kamira, and Joy were the only people who were able to deal with the wrath and idiosyncracies of Tracy after her father died when she was in the 7th grade.

Rachel turned her head and flashed a huge bright smile at her two friends.

"Heyyyy!!!" they all exclaimed at the same time. They did a group hug and immediately started chatting and catching up with all the latest gossip, right there in the lobby of the club.

"Girl, I'm almost through with this club already, but now that you're here I think we can have some real fun," Tracy screamed, starting to really slur her words. Kamira looked up at Tracy with dismay in her eyes. Kamira felt some kind of way about the fact that Tracy was acting as if she was having such a boring time with her before Rachel arrived.

"I see y'all didn't wait for my ass to start throwin' back shots," Rachel said playfully with her mouth twisted to the side.

"Who's throwin' *back shots*?" Tracy joked and looked around to see. Rachel chuckled at her play on words.

"Apparently your new man. I haven't seen you this happy in ages. Either you're drunk or you just got some," Rachel teased.

"Well, you know Tracy ain't never wait for nobody about some liquor in her life," Kamira said snidely. Tracy just gave Kamira a glazed over look and a smile. Nobody was ruining her high.

"Did you hear about John Bustamante and Lisa Conroe? He got caught red-handed cheating," Rachel interjected. She loved to gossip—it was her thing. "He and the ho were sitting right up in *a fucking McDonald's* eating. Cheap bastard."

Tracy laughed. "How old is he? You don't take anyone to McDonald's anymore, unless you're in the 5th grade."

"I know. And then you know what's even more fucked up? Lisa walked right up into Mickie D's and saw them together, and don't you know that silly bitch took him right back two days later. I swear, she believes everything John tells her."

"Well Rachel, everybody can't be as independent as you I guess," Kamira said with a smile and an eye roll. Rachel was a notorious female player in Suffolk County. She had guys waiting on her from Deer Park all the way down to the Hamptons. And all of them usually looked the same—tall, athletic, reddish-blonde hair, and green or blue eyes. Either that or a 'guido' Italian look. Blue eyes, black hair were her favorite. Kamira could stand to take a lesson from Rachel on how to handle men—she was constantly being played by them.

"I'm telling you—fuck these dudes. They're only good for a hook up. All they want is some pussy anyway," Rachel commented as she licked her lips, wanting a cosmo.

"Regardless of what they want, I needed one, and he got it," Tracy said as she turned on her heel and gave the cue for her friends to follow her back to the main club area.

"Girls like Lisa burn me. John came over the other day and was laughing about the whole thing. She doesn't have a clue," Rachel said in her 'valley girl' voice, shaking her head as she followed close behind Tracy, Kamira right behind.

Tracy, Kamira, and Rachel were being virtually stalked by men that night. Out of the three, Tracy was the least interested in the attention—all she thought about was Mike and what she was going to do to him when she got home. The club really started jumping at around 2am, and the quality of men in there was pretty high that night. Everyone was dressed up—one thing that Tracy loved about that club; they didn't tolerate half-assed dressers in there. They always stuck to their rules about attire.

Tracy was beaming with pride as she crept up behind Rachel, who was standing next to the VIP area talking to a tall, light-skinned brother who was wearing a perfectly tailored suit, no tie.

"Boo!" Tracy screamed in Rachel's ear, causing her to jump and turn around in one motion with her fists up, ready to fight.

"Whooaa, chill Rach!" Tracy said, backing up. Rachel had to have gotten her balls from her father, because her mother could be a real pushover. (Things had been exactly the opposite in Tracy's household when her Dad was alive—her mother ran things.) Rachel switched from an air of the whitest white girl to the hoodest chick in the room with ease. She probably would have knocked Tracy out cold if she had had just two more drinks in her.

"Girl don't creep up on me like that," Rachel said with a frown as she playfully smacked Tracy upside the head. She softened up her features when she saw the huge smile on her usually troubled friend's face. "What's up with you?"

"Nothing, I'm just having a real good time and I wanted to talk to my friend is that alright with you?" Tracy asked with a wide smile.

"Oh?" Rachel asked, almost flirting with her friend. She could turn real gay when she was drunk enough. Tracy suspected that Rachel might be selectively bi, but still in the closet. She was now completely ignoring the guy behind her, who was still waiting patiently for her to finish her conversation with Tracy.

"Yes. So what are you doing tomorrow?" Tracy asked as she sipped on her cognac, the third type of liquor she was drinking that night.

Rachel sighed and looked up at the ceiling. After a few seconds she finally spoke. "Well, Joe's family has a house out in Virginia. He wanted me to go see it. I don't know though."

"Ehem…" the guy behind them finally interrupted. Tracy looked over Rachel's shoulder at the attractive young man as he continued to speak. "Uhhh, Rachel right?"

Rachel swung her head around and looked at the guy as if he were a stranger who was bothering her. "Yeah?"

"I was wondering if you'd like to come with me to get that drink now?" he said, trying to hide his impatience with a brilliant smile.

"Uh. Naaa, I'll pass. Maybe some other time," Rachel said, waving him off flippantly as she turned right back around to continue talking to Tracy. The guy's face changed from delight to dejection almost instantly. Tracy almost felt sorry for him as he walked away, but not really. She started laughing at him.

"What was I saying?" Rachel asked Tracy.

Suddenly they heard a loud commotion coming from the other end of the club. They both turned their heads just in time to see Kamira struggling with a guy who was trying to pull her away by the arm. They couldn't see his face at first because his back was towards them, but when he turned and got all up in Kamira's face Tracy refocused her eyes and realized that it was Karif, Kamira's idiot boyfriend. Tracy and Rachel looked at each other as if the devil had arrived in person at the club.

"I said come on, now!" Karif screamed, inches from Kamira's face. There was a guy nearby watching the whole scene; apparently he had been talking to Kamira, and Karif showed up to the club out of nowhere. Tracy was there with Rachel right on her heels.

Karif had taken Kamira's cellphone from her before he went out for the night, assuming that it would discourage her from going out. He was out with one of his jump-offs when he listened to Kamira's recent messages, one of which was from Rachel confirming that she would be at Black in an hour.

"What's going on here?" Tracy asked, pulling off her hoop earrings instinctively.

"Nothing guys, it's okay," Kamira tried to assure behind scared eyes.

"Come on," Karif grabbed her arm again and started to pull her towards the short staircase leading down the platform they were on. Tracy stepped in before they could go and pushed Karif off of her best friend.

"Why you grabbing her like that, who the fuck do you think you are?" she challenged him. Rachel stood side by side with Tracy to back her up.

"Bitch, this ain't none of your concern," Karif said,

annoyed. He couldn't stand any of Kamira's friends. "Don't be putting your damn hands on me."

"Who the fuck are you callin' a bitch?" Rachel jumped in and got in Karif's face, but Tracy pulled her back as if to say, "I got this."

"You little pussy. So you can put your hands on my girl, but I ain't supposed to put my hands on you? Negro please, I will fuck you up!"

"Tracy, it's okay," Kamira held out her hand and pleaded with her friend. Karif turned her around and started pushing her towards the stairs again. Tracy wasn't happy with how Karif was pushing and pulling her friend all over the place. She ran down the steps and grabbed her friend.

"She's coming with us. You, go," Tracy instructed Karif as she kept walking with her friend.

"Kamira!" he shouted as he stomped towards them again. He stood in front of them both, and when Tracy tried to get around, they began to struggle with Kamira in the crowded club. People moved away from them when they realized there was a conflict.

"Get off sicko, what is your problem! She doesn't want to go with you!" Tracy screamed.

"She's my girl! She's going with me," Karif said, sounding like the textbook jealous, possessive boyfriend. "You don't want no problems with me Tracy."

"What is that a threat? You don't scare me. Let go!" Tracy said again. Kamira didn't know what to say at that point, so she just shut her eyes and prayed that this would blow over.

Karif finally won that struggle. He grabbed Kamira around her waist and picked her up to prevent Tracy from getting a hold on her again as he carried Kamira towards the club exit. Tracy became enraged and tried to pull his arm out of the hold.

Without thinking another thought, Karif backhanded Tracy in the eye. She stumbled backwards and held her face, trying to open her eyes but all she saw for a few moments was a flash of light. When she finally regained sight she saw Rachel punching Karif in the back and head with all of her might but was quickly pushed back. A couple of brothers saw what happened and got in Karif's face. It was about to be on.

Tracy charged at Karif with her fist clenched and took the opportunity while he was arguing with the two other men to give him all she had. She punched him hard in the jaw, which was all the motivation the two men needed to start wailing on Karif themselves.

"No! Stop!" Kamira's voice got lost in the crowd as Karif was getting pummeled and kicked by Tracy and the good samaritans. Five burly bouncers came out of nowhere and started pulling people apart. They dragged all three of the attackers plus Karif out of the club. Tracy was still kicking and screaming hysterically.

Rachel and Kamira rushed outside behind the bouncers and as soon as they let Tracy go, Rachel came to her side. But to Tracy's surprised and dismay, Kamira went to Karif! She began nursing his wounds.

"Kamira have you lost your mind!" Rachel was the first to say something.

"Why are you always tripping Tracy! I told you it was fine!" Kamira yelled like a woman possessed in front of the club and stomped her feet like a child, defending her boyfriend.

"Fine! He smacked your best friend you fool, what is wrong with you?" Rachel answered.

"Fuck you Kamira, you are always doing this stupid shit," Tracy finally said. Her eye was throbbing with pain. "Everybody knows you're getting your ass kicked on the daily!"

"That's not true!" Kamira denied and wanted to cry.

"Dumb ass bitch, I should kill your ass dead," Karif threatened Tracy. His face was bloody and he was holding his sides. The bouncers were standing around with their arms folded, making sure that nothing else popped off.

"Go 'head make a move nigga, so I can crush yo ass," one of the strangers threatened Karif.

"Okay then, y'all need to get the fuck outta here before I call the cops," one of the bouncers finally said.

"Where did you park?" Kamira asked Karif. She helped him towards his car, without saying another word to her friends, or even asking Tracy if she were okay. She loved her friends, but she couldn't afford to let them be the cause of her losing her future with Karif. She would never be able to forgive them if that happened.

"Can you believe this girl?" Tracy turned and asked Rachel. She was so mad—half at the pain in the left side of her face, half at her friend's disloyalty. She caught her breath and they thanked the two brothers who had had their back. That was one thing Tracy loved about New York brothers—they would jump into some drama in a hot second, especially when a woman was being disrespected. These brothers looked like they just loved a good, righteous fight too.

"No problem ma, that nigga needed a reality check. I hope ya girl wake up for real," one had responded.

Rachel drove Tracy home and decided at the last minute to stay over the night.

"What are we going to do about that girl Rach?" Tracy asked as she stripped down to her bra and panties. Rachel watched unconsciously, interested, with her head held up by her hand as she lay on the bed.

"I don't know girl, she is so far gone."

"She's lucky he didn't get his ass killed, that one guy looked like he could be holding heat."

"I doubt it—you know they are thorough about that at the clubs these days, ever since that shooting at the R.A.M. club."

Tracy crawled into the bed and pulled back the covers awkwardly. She was still drunk, but her high was gone. "That would be nice though, if that fool got killed. Then I can have my friend back."

"Kamira's always been like that Trace, if it weren't Karif it'd be some other asshole," Rachel slurred.

"Well I'm through with her. Let her fight her own battles. Maybe she likes getting her ass whooped," Tracy said as she rolled over to go to sleep.

"Dame un beso chica," Rachel demanded and Tracy rolled over to oblige. She puckered up and let Rachel give her a kiss on the lips that lingered a little longer than it was supposed to. Tracy pulled away shyly but Rachel grabbed her chin and to Tracy's surprise they started french kissing. Tracy felt a tingling run up her spine, but it just didn't feel quite right—this was her good friend after all. They had kissed before, at sleepovers and parties in the Hamptons, but never like this. Rachel just went with her first instinct and did whatever she felt like at the moment.

Rachel finally let her go and smirked. "You are so hot."

"You are so crazy," Tracy shook her head and quickly turned back around. She tried to play it off, but her heart was pounding and she could barely catch her breath.

"Can I spoon you?" Rachel asked from behind.

"No horn ball, good night," Tracy told her, and Rachel pouted.

Sometimes Tracy just couldn't figure Rachel out—she was like a modern day hippie. Tracy wasn't gay, but she couldn't deny that she was attracted to Rachel in a very strange way. She wondered if that type of thing qualified as cheating on Mike right before she drifted off to sleep.

The top of the Empire State building was the first thing Tracy saw from the street. But not even a few moments later she was *at* the top of the building looking down. The change in view shook her essence and she started to back away from the ledge slowly. Then she could hear someone's heavy footsteps running up behind her. Before she had a chance to turn around fully to see who it was, she felt a strong shove to her back pushing her over the ledge. She was flying in the air. She screamed wildly but no sounds would come out. She saw the street coming at her fast and couldn't catch her breath. She hoped she would just die. *Die! Die! Die!* she pleaded in her thoughts over and over. But it wouldn't happen. She saw the top of a black car right before she closed her eyes. She didn't want to see her death…

Tracy's eyes shot open. She jumped up off of the bed like a mad woman and screamed. "What the *fuck*!"

She jerked her head from side to side as she examined her surroundings. Luckily, what she saw was familiar. The amber-colored but beat up couch. The silver-plated clock hanging over the faux fireplace. The imitation red-based persian rug that sat underneath her glass coffee table. Kamira had given her that coffee table. She realized that Rachel had left and saw a note across the room probably explaining her absence. Tracy felt a pain in the side of her face that reminded her of what had happened the night before.

She relaxed and did some of the breathing exercises she learned during her short stint in therapy. The therapy that had failed so miserably. In Tracy's heart she knew that therapy wasn't for her, and had refused to return, even after several calls from the psychotherapist and her family doctor.

She was just about to fall back into a deep sleep when her cellphone started ringing. It was really loud too, since she had turned it up at the club.

"Dammit!" she said as she reluctantly pulled herself up off of her comfy bed again and went over to retrieve her phone from her purse.

"What?" she asked callously into the phone when she saw that it was Kamira calling.

"What the fuck is wrong with you? You didn't have to go off like that. You might have fucked up my situation with Karif!" Kamira complained.

"Kamira, don't call me with this shit," Tracy said with a snarl. Kamira was just silent for a long time.

"Whatever, I'm not even gonna stoop to your level. I'm just calling to tell *you* not to call *me* anymore. You ain't no friend of mine."

"What? You're breaking up with *me*? Bitch, you ain't never broke up with a dude in your lifetime, but you can break up with *me* after over ten years. And *over* a dude that beats your ass! Girl you are a trip."

All Tracy heard was a dial tone in her ear. She shook her head and got up from the bed needing to relieve herself. She headed for her small bathroom, stumbling as she went.

As nonchalant as she was acting, she could feel a swelling of anxiety building up in her stomach as she sat on the toilet and closed her eyes. When she got up and looked in the mirror she was entranced by what she saw. She had felt the pain in her face, but had no idea that it had left a mark so prominent on the side of her eye. The bruise was definitely noticeable.

"Ooo!! That—" Tracy couldn't even find a word for Karif.

She wished those guys would have sent him to the hospital last night. She debated on whether she was going to tell Mike the truth about what happened the night before. He would definitely want to know.

She finally peeled herself from the mirror and made her way to the kitchen to find something to eat. She was starving as if she hadn't eaten for days, and when she looked at the microwave clock she realized why. It was 8 o'clock at night, and she had been sleeping pretty much all day.

"Oh God. I can't do this again," she mumbled to herself for the three hundred and thirtieth time. She had been here many times before, having wasted entire days to scary dreams and drunken nightmares. She had wanted to work on her budget that day, but of course that didn't happen and wasn't going to happen within those 24 hours. She had work the next day. She still felt tired, but was more hungry. And as she gazed at the box of baking soda and half full gallon bottle of orange juice on the top shelf of her fridge, she realized that the fridge wasn't going to solve either one of those problems.

She called Mike to see if he was nearby and could bring her some grub. She was surprised that he hadn't called her all that day or last night and thought of all the things he could be doing in that long time period. She had told him she was going out, but still he could have called to see how she was doing.

Mike never picked up. She went over to her double-wide window and pulled back the blinds cautiously. Just as she feared, night had fallen hard. She hated to leave her apartment that late at night, but she had to do something. Her stomach was grumbling so loud every few minutes that she kept jerking her head around thinking that there was someone else in the apartment groaning in pain. She took another look at the time and then headed to her bedroom to throw on some clothes.

As Tracy opened the front door she looked both ways down the hallway to be sure that there wasn't anyone there. She didn't ride the elevator with anyone in her building. Never that. If there was someone waiting at the elevator and she was in a rush, she would take the three flights of stairs down to the bottom. Even if the person waiting was a little old lady with knee high stockings and a wig on, she wasn't doing it. She would wonder if the old lady could be sick or something and go the other way. It was just a thing for her—she barely wanted to ride the janky elevator at all after it had broken down two times since she had moved in three years before.

Unfortunately for Tracy, there was someone in the hall just standing around the door of the family that lived three doors down and across from her. It was a middle aged brown-skinned man who looked as if he were waiting for someone. But Tracy was instantly suspicious. Who was he waiting for? The woman that was living in that apartment had a Latino husband who worked the night shift. She was the same chick that was always giving Tracy dirty looks in the hallway as if she were going to steal her husband away. So what was this guy doing here? She was looking at the guy, but he wasn't paying her any mind.

She kept her eye on the man as she did a tip toe hustle over to the elevator. She pressed the button quickly and prayed that it would hurry up and come. But she moaned in her mind as she listened to the old elevator grind its way down from the eighth floor. It sounded as if it were stopping on every floor.

As Tracy heard the elevator making its third stop, the apartment door that the older black man was standing next to opened and the young Latina woman came out with an attitude. She had her pocketbook over her shoulder as if she were on her way out. Tracy's heart started pounding as she heard the elevator approaching her floor. She stared at the elevator doors as if she had no idea there was anyone else in the hallway.

"What you knockin' on my door like that for, you know the baby's sleep!" the woman said with a heavy spanish accent as she started in on the guy Tracy had been wondering about.

"How the fuck I'm suppose to tell you I'm here when you don't answer your mutherfuckin' phone," he answered.

"That's because it's on silent, I don't want the baby wakin' up!"

"Well who's problem is that?" he replied with a wave of his hand as they strolled down the hall, taking their time. "Those little bastards ain't mine."

The elevator had finally made its way down to the fifth floor and as soon as the doors opened Tracy pushed open the guard door and went in. She settled into the back of the elevator and waited for the doors to close.

"Hold up, hold that elevator! Here we come," the woman yelled out to Tracy. But Tracy ignored her.

"You know you hear me!" Tracy could hear the lady saying as the elevator went down to floor number two. "Stupid bitch!"

Tracy's blood pressure was just about to go back to normal levels when the elevator stopped again and the doors opened for the second floor. *Who pressed the button for the damn second floor, walk downstairs you lazy ass!* She quickly pressed the 'close door' button over and over before anyone had a chance to open the guard door.

When the door didn't close after a few moments she started to get nervous. The people from the third floor were probably going to beat or meet her downstairs now. The last thing she needed right now was a confrontation in the lobby of this apartment building, which was one step up from project living. As she considered whether she should get off now and go back upstairs to the safety of her apartment, the elevator door closed in her face.

Now Tracy was really having problems. The familiar bead of sweat started to form on her brow and she gulped hard as the elevator slowly grinded its way down to the first floor. She could hear a muffled female's voice talking loudly on the other side. She knew it was the same Puerto Rican woman. When the door opened she tried to delay getting off, but when the door almost closed again she had to stop it and open the guard door.

There was the Puerto Rican girl and the dude she was jumping off with right there in the door of the entrance walking out with their backs turned to the elevator. When the woman heard the elevator open she glanced around and saw Tracy.

Now Tracy had to get on ghetto mode, because she wasn't about to back down from this grimy, adulterous bitch. She hated confrontation but when it came, she didn't back down from it. Besides, this was where she lived and she had to establish her strength living alone out there in the Bronx. She put on her 'I ain't tryin' to hear that shit' look and stepped out of the elevator with authority. *This little Puerto Rican bitch better not try to get fly with me, cause I'll show her ass something*, she thought, hyping herself up. The Puerto Rican lady touched the arm of the guy she was with, telling him to stop and look. Then they both stood on the stoop and watched Tracy walk by them.

"Yo, why you couldn't hold the elevator," the girl finally said. Tracy instantly was annoyed that this chick was still stressing that matter.

"I ain't see you," Tracy lied as she kept walking.

"How could you not see us, we was talking loud as shit! You heard us. You buggin'," the guy chimed in. They both started to walk again behind Tracy in her direction, and Tracy was starting to get really pissed. She could feel her top about to blow off now.

Tracy didn't play that following shit.

"I don't know why people gotta be so stupid! She know she heard me calling for the elevator!" the Puerto Rican woman said loud enough for Tracy to hear.

"What are y'all following me for!" Tracy yelled.

"Bitch please, we ain't followin' your dumb ass," the guy said snidely as he twisted his face up and rolled his eyes. He looked at the Puerto Rican girl who was looking right back at Tracy. "'Lena, you was following her?"

"Naw, I'm goin' to my car Tre, I don't know what the hell she talkin' about. That's probably why somebody bust her upside the head too," the Puerto Rican girl Elena said, never taking her eyes off of Tracy's face. Her expression said 'trouble' and they were obviously being sarcastic.

"Keep running your mouth bitch, I can make yours look the same if you want," Tracy threatened as she turned and continued on her way.

"Ooooo," Elena mocked her and started laughing with Tre.

Tracy just kept walking, faster this time. When she got close to the corner she realized that they were still following behind her and she could no longer control herself. She snapped.

"Y'all muthafuckas think you're slick, you better think twice before you start some shit with me. I ain't the one to fuck with. I see your husband every damn day, and he don't look like somebody *you* wanna fuck with either," Tracy said out of nowhere, pointing at the black dude with her last comment. Right after she said it, she regretted it. She had started something.

The smug look on Elena's face disappeared and the guy looked like he wanted to sink into the ground. They both stopped dead in their tracks and looked at Tracy with their mouths open. The feeling of shame was quickly followed by anger on both of their parts. But before they had a chance to react or say something smart in return, Tracy had turned on her heels and left the scene.

As Tracy entered the small restaurant that offered everything from empanadas to chicken feet to Steel Reserve beers, she immediately surveyed the room; for familiar faces, for mischevious looks, and for any indication of potential trouble. It was dark outside, and there was rarely a police officer driving by in that area of the South Bronx. She grabbed a menu off the counter roughly and looked up and down the list.

I think I know this dude right here. With the red beret that's always standing in front of the deli. What the fuck does he think this is Paris? He got a lot of nerve tryin' to holla at that girl, she is wayyy out of his league. Anyway, let me stop looking his way before he recognizes me and starts bothering my *ass.*

"What you want?" the balding Dominican clerk said with his usual attitude. It was just something everybody had to deal with, because the food was too damn good. He was like the Soup Nazi from Seinfeld; the 'Arroz Con Pollo Nazi' Tracy called him. Tracy hadn't gone to the other restaurant, the Jamaican spot, on that block in over two years, ever since she heard something about the Board of Health rejecting its permit for a few weeks. People complained that they had rats running across the tables in there. Tracy was not about to catch a rodent-bourne disease over some jerk chicken.

"Hold up, I'm looking," Tracy answered back with the same amount of attitude. She was trying to decide what she could get for under $10, which was all the cash she had on her at the time. "Ooo. Let me get the roast chicken and a side of plaintains."

"Sweet or green. Manny, where the cups at, I need them up here now!" the clerk yelled, diverting his attention to the white-apron wearing, young, mexican guy who was carrying a white pail to the front door. The guy with the apron just nodded his head over and over again until he reached the outside. "Sweet or green girl."

"Sweet. How long will it be?" Tracy asked.

"15 minutes," the clerk said as he ripped the receipt off the pad and went to the back to give it to the cook.

Tracy went to an empty table in the corner to wait for her food, but she had a bad feeling about her surroundings. There were only a few people in the restaurant eating and mostly minding their business, but it was still dark outside, and this was still the South Bronx.

"Why you all by yourself Ma?" a voice said from her left, waking her up from her thoughts. "You need somebody to keep you company?"

"Hell no," Tracy said, annoyed that the cross-eyed, brown-skinned man had the nerve to even speak to her. He was holding a Colt 45 inside a brown bag and smelled like a walking winery. The small table he was sitting at was covered with other brown bags and an empty white carton full of chicken bones.

"Yooo, that's low. What I ever do to you?" the drunken brother asked as he hung over his chair, oogling at Tracy. "Where you get them kicks?"

"Leave me the fuck alone," Tracy said, rolling her eyes. She got up from her seat and went back up to the front without another word. The wino downed his Colt 45 and followed her to the register. Tracy was getting impatient.

"Papi, my food ain't ready yet?" she asked the clerk who was reading a paper folded in fours.

"I told you, 15 minutes. The other cook's on a smoke break—it's gonna be a while," he answered without ever looking up from his paper.

Tracy turned around with her back to the clerk and watched

the guy who was bothering her intensely. She wished Mike were here because he would set him straight in an instant. He stumbled up closer to her, and she backed away slightly. *I knew I should have brought my knife,* Tracy thought. She was smart enough to leave her pocketbook at her apartment, but didn't bring any type of protection. *Dummy.*

The guy eyed her with a peculiar smirk on his face for a few seconds too long.

"You know what, never mind," she told the clerk and turned around to walk out of the restaurant.

"Uh uh, he already started that shit baby, you gotta pay for it now," the clerk finally looked up from his paper and called after Tracy.

"Nope, sorry. I told you to hurry the fuck up," Tracy said as she walked out the door. *That's what he gets for copping an attitude. Asshole.* She was glad to get away from the drunk. But deep down Tracy knew she shouldn't have walked out on that food like that; the 'Arroz Con Pollo Nazi' might refuse to take an order from her ever again. This was the only restaurant on the block that had halfway decent cooked food. The only other option was the bodega on the corner with their day old bread and month old cold cuts.

"Ohhh, come on," the clerk complained, throwing his hand up in the air. "Carlos, stop that chicken order."

Tracy made her way back down the street and considered stopping at the bodega on the other side, but changed her mind when she saw several men standing out front arguing. One of them was really good-looking, and he was the main one yelling and talking shit to the others. Tracy stopped dead in her tracks when she realized it was Mike. He was scary. She watched as he intimidated each and every one of the men he was talking to. He looked mad, as if someone had done him wrong. She was tempted to go over there and say something to him, but didn't want to punk him out in front of his boys. She decided to just pretend as if she hadn't seen him. She was secretly happy that he was with his boys and not with some trick laid up. That was why he hadn't answered her call.

Tracy was going to have to get into her car and risk losing her parking space, right out in front of the building, to drive over to McDonald's. She really didn't want to do that. She made her final decision when she remembered that her ghetto neighbor and her 'friend' might make their way back to the building by the time she returned from McDonald's. Unless Mike answered his phone, it was going to be another food-free day—nothing new to Tracy, she was going more and more without food ever since she lost her good job at the bank.

She had been on her way to being promoted to the head manager position at Nations Bank, and nobody messed with Tracy when it came to her job. She was quick, decisive, authoritative and informative for customers. The other tellers feared Tracy, but unbeknownst to her, talked about Tracy like a dog whenever she left the room. Tracy hated to think that anyone was in cahoots behind her back about anything, even just a little gossip.

One day Tracy was in the vault helping a customer with his safety deposit box. She was getting frustrated because she was having trouble with turning the key. After a few more minutes of trying she had to assume it was the wrong key.

"Hold on a moment Mr. Trist, I'll be right back," she said, leaving the customer in the vault against her best judgment. She ran to the back room and went back to the closet that held all of the customer depository keys. As she was looking in the T's for Mr. Trist's file, she heard someone come into the back room, but they couldn't see that anyone else was there.

"So where's your girl Tracy?"

"My girl, why does she have to be my girl? I hate that shrew," the other female voice said.

"I thought you loved her after you was kissing her ass yesterday 'Sure Tracy, I'll get that right to you Tracy. Do you need anything else Tracy?' You were all up in her shit," the voice that Tracy now recognized as Stella, an older black woman who was another one of the tellers. Stella was the definition of a bitter woman, having gone through three divorces and now dealing with a younger man who was playing her like a fiddle.

"Whatever. You know she's about to be our boss, I'm just trying to get on her good side. You know she has an attitude problem," the other voice said. It was Sydney, the only Indian teller. She had a huge mole on her cheek that no one could ever miss. People usually focused on that mole when talking to her, and it drove her crazy.

"I don't give a fuck about that little girl's attitude, she ain't firing me. Shoot, I been here for over ten years, and she still got breast milk on her lips," Stella said seriously.

Sydney laughed. "Well don't say I didn't tell you when she puts your head through that plate glass window. I heard she was mental."

The last sentence, Syndey calling her mental, set Tracy off. She had heard enough. When she came out of the closet with her lips curled and a bead of sweat forming on her upper lip, Sydney and Stella knew they were in for something. They looked at Tracy with their mouths wide open in horror.

"So I'm mental huh?" Tracy cocked her head and felt herself blanking out.

That day, it took three large bank security guards to rip Tracy's strong grip from Sydney's long dark brown hair. When she finally let go with the security guards securing her hands, she kicked her foot so high up in the air that it collided with Sydney's chin, knocking her down to the floor. Tracy was lucky Sydney was too embarrassed about getting beat up to press charges. It was enough for Sydney that Tracy had gotten fired and banished from the bank forever.

Now Tracy worked in the corporate offices of Elias Department Stores as an admin to the creative team. Luckily for her, they didn't actually check her references before hiring her. Unluckily for her, she made $8,000 less than what she made as an assistant manager at the bank.

Tracy hustled her way back to her apartment building and went through the side entrance. She took the stairs back up to her apartment, two at a time. She made sure to lock up her door securely before calling Mike again. When he didn't answer, she gave up, not wanting to look desperate—he would call when he was ready. She went into the kitchen to search for some food again. She found a half a container of grits in the cupboard and fired up a small pot of water.

It was starting to get cooler, but the landlord still hadn't turned on the heat. She went into her closet to retrieve a winter sweater to wear around the house. When she heard a muffled sound coming from her couch, she hurried to answer her phone. It might have been Mike—or better yet Kamira calling to apologize.

"Tra, what you doin'?" Rachel's voice came over clearly from her side of the phone over the music from her car stereo playing in the background.

"I'm chilling, hungry," Tracy said casually as she began stirring grits into the pot.

"Huh?"

"I said I'm hungry. I'm sitting here with a box of grits and butter."

"You wanna get something to eat?"

"Yea…" Tracy thought about Mike and her hopes of seeing him that night. "But I thought you went back to LI to go see that dude with the house in VA."

"Naw, I'm driving in the city right now, didn't you get my note? I had some business to tend to and had to come back. I'll see you in a minute."

Before Tracy could respond, Rachel had hung up the phone. There wouldn't have been too much of a protest from Tracy anyway. She liked being around Rachel and didn't get many opportunities. But still, she had been looking forward to seeing Mike that night.

After she had buzzed Rachel in, Tracy still went outside her door to make sure her friend got safely inside; especially after the elevator incident with the Elena chick. But then, she thought, that ho probably wasn't going to be back for hours.

"Oh you're dressed?" Rachel said as soon as she stepped off the elevator. "I thought you were already in your pajamas or something. Come on, let's go somewhere and eat."

Tracy was relieved as she went to retrieve her house keys. "Aiight, but I only have 10 bucks to spend. I'm broke as shit."

"I'm treating, I just want to get something to eat and talk about what happened last night before I head back to LI. You know I don't like leaving you two up here fighting."

This definitely hadn't been the first time Kamira and Tracy had been in a fight. They were probably the closest out of the four friends, but they were also the most prone to infighting. Rachel knew their relationship well.

The first time Kamira and Tracy fought was in high school. It was over a guy they both liked, who ended up asking Kamira to the junior prom. Tracy was jealous and started picking at Kamira for no reason. When the conversation got heated they both stood up and got in each other's faces. Tracy jabbed her finger in Kamira's face and was stunned when the shorter, smaller Kamira took hold of it and twisted Tracy's hand behind her back. She held Tracy in a painful hold for a minute before letting her go and kicking her into the lunch table. Tracy quickly recovered, and lunged at Kamira, grabbing hold of her hair right before someone broke up the fight. They made up not too long after, but ever since that fight Tracy had a respect for little Kami—and none of their fights ever got physical again.

Rachel pulled her year-old black Benz around the back of what used to be *Jimmy's* restaurant and they headed down the sidewalk to the front entrance.

"Kamira needs to stop sluttin' herself out, especially with these slick ass New York brothers," Tracy said suddenly as they entered the smoky restaurant. It wasn't as packed as it usually was on a Sunday night. They easily found a table on the side level near the windows.

"You know that's what she likes, the bad boys," Rachel said as she threw her pocketbook on the seat next to her. Tracy slid in her seat and instantly regretted not doing her makeup and hair before they left. There were some Dominican cuties with expensive suits on sitting at the table next to them. Tracy couldn't help eyeing the darker skinned one. *Doesn't hurt to look*, Tracy chuckled to herself. Not long after they sat down, a waiter came over and took their order.

"I can't believe that she would choose that wife beater over me. We've known each other for over a decade Rachel," Tracy complained.

"You know what I'm about to tell you right?" Rachel asked as she played with the tip of her straw.

"What," Tracy sounded disinterested.

"We've talked about this a lot Trace, about your temper. You can't get so drunk and angry where you can't control yourself," Rachel said. "You know how Kamira is—you should have just let her go."

Tracy rolled her eyes. "Yea, yea, I know. But she's supposed to be my look out partner; she's supposed to make sure I get home safe and vice versa."

"Yea, but when it comes to a man, you know the deal with Kami." Rachel paused to take a long drink of her soda. "Look I ain't taking either one of your sides, but we gotta be there for her still. She is going through some shit."

"But it's her own choice," Tracy said, maintaining her cool.

"Whatever, that's all I'm gonna say about it. It's up to you, but please talk to Kami. I hate when you guys fight," Rachel almost pleaded with her friend as she pulled out a cigarette out of habit and wished she could light it. Instead she played with it, flipping it back and forth between her french manicured fingertips. "Y'all gotta look out for each other out here."

Tracy glanced around and noticed another table with two young black women sitting nearby. They were both facing her as she looked, and appeared to be smirking in amusement. Tracy looked at them with her forehead crunched in, and they looked at each other and then back down at their drinks.

"What's wrong Tra?" Rachel asked.

"Nothing, just those ghetto ass girls over there, I think they're talking about me or something," Tracy answered bluntly.

"Oh boy, Tracy please don't start tripping, they're just young girls, don't pay them no mind."

"I just hate when people talk about me behind my back. Do I look crazy or something?" Tracy asked, running her hands over her hair, which was pulled back into a tight but messy bun.

"You look fine girl," Rachel assured her.

When their food came they ate as Rachel started her story of why she had gone to Manhattan again that day. She was thinking about buying her own apartment in downtown Manhattan. She had almost forgotten her appointment with the realtor that day.

"It's really nice Trace, if I decide to get it you've gotta come see it when the deal is done," Rachel gushed. "That means I'll be able to hang out with you guys more, and you know I'll bring Joy whenever I stay here."

Tracy couldn't have been happier. "Rachel do it! You know you have to get that apartment now right?"

"I guess. And that's why I wanna keep us all tight, because it's gonna be just like high school again," Rachel said getting more excited at the idea, and also at the opportunity to finally smoke her cigarette. "You gonna call Kami?"

"Yea," Tracy sighed. "I will if you give me one of those cigarettes."

"I thought you quit?" Rachel asked in confusion as she passed a Virginia Slim to Tracy and got up from the table.

Tracy couldn't help but eye the stylish way Rachel's designer jeans rested on her hips as she walked ahead of her out of *Jimmy's*. The Bottega Veneta heels she was wearing gave her a cocky gait that cried "I'm wealthy" on each step. Tracy wished she had money like that.

"Excuse me miss," they both heard a voice say behind them. It was one of the good-looking Dominican brothers they had seen in the restaurant; the same exact one Tracy had had her eye on. Tracy quickly tried to look at herself in the reflection from a nearby car window to make sure she looked presentable, but the guy was really trying to get Rachel's attention.

"Yes," Rachel said with a devious smirk, as she blew smoke out of the corner of her mouth. She leaned back against the wall and looked at the guy impatiently.

"I'm Ricardo, I was hoping I could get a minute of your

time. I couldn't pass up an opportunity to speak to such a beautiful lady."

"I already have somebody special in my life," Rachel responded casually, knowing what he wanted.

Tracy was already feeling awkward. She hated being the third wheel, especially when it was with a guy she had had her eye on. Still she listened in as Rachel threw her game at Mr. Ricardo as she puffed desperately at her own cigarette—the first she had had since Mike told her off about her smoking.

"I wish I could be that special," Ricardo responded.

"You went to church today or something?" Rachel asked out of nowhere.

Ricardo looked at her in confusion, until he realized why she said it. "No, no, I just got this suit on cause we had a pretty important business meeting today."

"Oh so you don't love the Lord," Rachel asked, teasing him. He opened his mouth to say something and she stopped him before he responded to the remark. "Don't respond to that. What kind of business do you have on a Sunday afternoon?"

"Rach, let me get the keys," Tracy interrupted. "I'll bring the car around."

"Sure." Rachel threw the keys to her friend. "But hurry, I'll be done soon."

Tracy tried to hold in her envy as she fumed down the sidewalk. She wasn't sure if she was jealous that the guy wanted Rachel and had completely ignored her, or because this guy had stolen away Rachel's attention. She quickly snapped out of it when she remembered that she already had a man twice as gorgeous as him at home.

When she pulled the Benz around the corner, Rachel had already wrapped it up with Ricardo and hopped right into the passenger side. Tweet's song *Best Friend* was playing loudly over

Rachel's sound system. Tracy was in love with that song—it made her relax and forget her anger at being ignored by Ricardo for the moment. *He's probably a loser anyway*, she figured.

"That fool is some kind of drug dealer, talking about he had a business meeting today," Rachel sneered.

"You didn't get his number?" Tracy asked, being nosey, as Rachel chuckled in amusement. "He was so cute."

"Oh I got it, but I doubt I'll use it. I don't do drug dealers."

Tracy thought about Mike, and what she believed he was doing for money. It was even more reason for her not to tell her friends about him.

Tracy was used to driving Rachel's car, ever since they were in high school. When she pulled the Benz up in front of her building she felt on top of the world, and almost bad when she had to get out.

"You sure you don't want to come up? You can stay over if you don't feel like driving all the way back to LI," Tracy bluffed, hoping she would say no. She was trying to spend the night with Mike that night.

"Naw, I'm supposed to go see John tonight."

"John who? John Bustamante? Please say it ain't so."

Rachel pulled her jacket collars high up on her face to hide her expression. She bit her lip before saying in a sing songy voice, "Yea, we're kickin' it now."

Tracy threw her head back and laughed with her hand on her chest. "You scandalous bitch."

"What can I say, he's hot, and he's got a big ass dick. You know I love my Italian brothers," Rachel said with a smile. "That's Lisa's loss. But it's nothing serious, we just started hooking up last week. We're just screwing. I couldn't trust him in a relationship, and he's too cheap."

"Uh, I have nothing more to say to you, goodnight," Tracy

said with a chuckle as she exited the car.

"Bye!"

Tracy took the stairs again, though she hated walking in the stairwell at night. It was going on midnight. Mike still hadn't called. Against her better judgment she called him but it went straight to voicemail again. She pouted and threw her phone on the bed, deciding that he was just too busy handling his business to spend time with her that night. That was okay.

After doing her night routine, she finally sunk into the sheets on her queen sized mattress and let her mind drift to good thoughts. Then she picked up her cellphone and said "Kami" in the receiver.

As she listened to the phone ring she thought of all the good times she had had with Kamira, and how good a friend she had been in hard times. She remembered the one time that she and Kamira got caught with a half a blunt in Tracy's car, and Kamira took all the blame since she already had an infraction on her record. The officer appreciated Kamira's honest gesture and went easy on her with a warning. But it was the fact that Kamira had been willing to take a misdemeanor on her record, a fine, and possibly jail time for her friend.

"Trace I was just about to call you," Kamira said weakly on the other line. She sounded as if she were going to cry.

Chapter 9

"Who the fuck did that to you?" Mike wanted to know.

"Mike, calm down alright baby? I handled it," Tracy said as she peeked around the corner to make sure no one was nearby. Mike had shown up to her job unexpectedly to take her out to lunch, but she was already meeting Joy in a few minutes. Tracy had just told him that she had other plans and a lot of work, no specifics. She was doing her best to rush him out of the building before Joy showed up.

"You always saying that! It's about time I handled something, I'm your man dammit!" Mike said too loud. "What kind of man am I if I can't defend my own girl?"

"Mike you are tripping, seriously. I'm fine, please, just go ahead home and I'll see you tonight," Tracy looked out around the corner again to make sure Joy wasn't coming.

"Fuck that Tracy! I ain't leaving 'til you tell me what happened," Mike said with finality as he crossed his arms and leaned back against the wall.

"I ran into the side of my closet door by accident," Tracy lied.

Mike just looked at her with his eyebrows slightly raised and shook his head as if to say "Don't lie to me Tracy."

Tracy looked at her cellphone for the time and saw that it was 12:53pm. Joy was supposed to meet her at one. Her heart started beating faster as she thought of the possibility of them running into Joy by accident. Joy loved cute light skin guys—she would eat Mike up. Tracy knew Joy would never do her like that, but she was still a shameless flirt. Once Mike laid eyes on Joy he would probably be lost for sure.

"Okay! I got into a fight," Tracy admitted.

"With who?" Mike demanded and stood back upright, looking as if he were about to jump out of his skin.

Tracy rolled her eyes and decided it wouldn't make any sense at this point to keep lying to her boyfriend. He knew her like the back of his hand. "This dude my girl Kamira is messing with—he knocked me aside, it was nothing serious. And he got his ass handed to him by a couple of guys."

"What? Where did this happen?"

"At the club. Listen it's no big deal Mike, please don't trip," Tracy pleaded with her eyes. Since the fight, Kamira had apologized and claimed to be making serious attempts to leave Karif. The next night after the club fight, Karif had taken his frustration out on Kamira's face and torso, leaving her with a black eye and a large strawberry bruise on the lower left side of her back. She said that it would take a little time and support, but she would leave him. Tracy had no choice but to believe her friend. She had always kept her word in the past.

"What's this dude's name?"

"Mike, I'm not telling you. Listen, I need you to go alright? My boss is going to give me problems." Tracy grabbed his arm and tried to lead him out of the hall through the back exit, but he took his arm away and went around her.

"My car's out front," Mike said with an attitude as he stormed out of her building, his hands jammed into his pockets. Tracy watched him as he went through the revolving doors and was relieved when he disappeared from her sight.

Outside, Mike could barely contain his anger as he stood in front of his car staring at the *Friday's* across the street. He thought about going to get a drink. What would people say if they found out some other guy had put his hands on his girl, and he let the guy get away with it? He had to do something.

"Excuse me," someone said from behind, startling him. He turned around and laid eyes on a tall, slim, beautiful, dark-skinned woman with legs for days. He looked at her curiously, at a loss for words, wondering what she wanted.

"I just wanted to give you this," she said with a smirk, as she passed him a slip of paper.

She walked away before he had a chance to respond. Mike watched her switch away towards Tracy's building before looking at the paper.

"Joy 631-561-9358," it said.

Mike just shook his head with a smirk of his own and crumpled the paper up in his fist.

Chapter 10

It took Tracy a whole half hour to drag all of her bags from the taxi stand to the baggage checking area. She still had to pick up her tickets, so now she was crunched for time.

All of the people being helped at the ticket counter seemed to be moving in slow motion. *What is taking them so long! If I miss this train it will fuck up the whole trip!* Tracy began to panic. What if she missed the train and they didn't have another one until the next day? Then she would miss an entire day in LA and probably mess up the girls' plans. *I knew this was a bad idea*, she thought.

Tracy glanced up at the clock, which now read 7:23. Her train was leaving at 7:35, and she still had two people in front of her. One of the people being helped was pointing at his ticket and asking questions, while another was flipping through her wallet to find the right credit card to use. She could no longer contain herself.

"Come on!" she shouted outloud. Everyone looked at her, and the ticket agents just rolled their eyes.

Finally, a line opened and the next person was helped. A few minutes later, another line opened up and the last person before Tracy went up. Luckily, at the same exact time another agent became available.

"Thank you. Thank you. Thank you," Tracy said outloud as she made her way to the agent. "I'm picking up a ticket for Tracy Samuels."

"How do you spell that," the ticket agent asked, taking her time. Tracy looked at her, dumbfounded.

"S-A-M-U-E-L-S," she spelled.

"Do you have ID?"

Several minutes later Tracy had her ticket in hand and was doing a full sprint down the halls towards her train. She was sweating profusely, afraid of missing the train. All of the thoughts of the consequences of missing that train were flying through her head as she picked up speed. She wanted to faint.

As she was running down the steps she heard the train conductor making a last call for her train. They were saying to keep clear of the closing doors. Tracy skipped four steps and made a beeline for the doors, which were closing. Her foot got stuck in the door, causing the train to make a strange beeping sound, and the doors opened back up.

"Sssss," Tracy winced in pain at the pressure the door had put on her foot.

She rushed in and looked around, breathing heavily. Everyone was looking at her again.

"What the hell are you looking at?" she said outloud, and then continued down the car.

The first leg of the trip was tough and long, but Tracy's excitement about going to Los Angeles made it more bearable. She fell asleep for a couple of hours with a small switchblade clutched inside her fist by her side. Even though Mrs. Moretti had gotten her a first class upgrade, she was still on edge about being around all those people for so long. She wished Mike could be there. She still was slightly upset that she had to leave him for a week.

The second leg of the trip was the worst. She had an almost eight hour layover in Chicago which was her worst nightmare. The train station was crawling with homeless people talking to themselves, and strange looking passengers waiting along with her. She was afraid that a perverted-looking, 40ish, white businessman was staring at her, and then turning his head never she would look at him. She grabbed her carry on bag and moved to another area of the train station.

She was looking behind her to make sure the guy wasn't following her when she felt a strong hand grab her leg. Tracy almost tripped.

"It was you! Youse the one!" a crazy black homeless woman said, pointing at Tracy with an indescribable fear in her eyes. Tracy jumped back and looked at the woman in horror.

"She tryin' to kill me. Leave me alone! Stop looking at me *demon.* Get thee behind me!" the woman screamed and scampered to her feet. Tracy backed up a few steps. "You want to kill me 'cause I took your shine. You can't never be me!"

Tracy turned and ran away. She had never been more terrified in her life. She ran until she saw the first exit to leave the train station.

Once outside, she looked around and saw that the sun was shining, but it was colder than she had ever felt. The wind whipped around a corner and smacked her across her face. She had to go somewhere. Then she saw a taxi stand.

Getting into the back of that taxi by herself was more calming than any massage on earth to Tracy. She leaned her head back into the seat and took a deep breath. She tried, but couldn't shake the image of that crazy woman from her mind's eye.

"Crazy bitch," she mumbled to herself as she thought of the woman's dirty clothes, wrinkled skin, and graying hair. She looked like she couldn't have been over 40, but life had done her in. Tracy couldn't help but wonder what path had lead that woman to where she was right now—screaming at people in a train station.

All of a sudden, Tracy broke down and started crying. She couldn't stop the tears from flowing, but had no idea where they were coming from. She sobbed and sobbed, until the taxi cab driver finally had to say something.

"Are you okay?" the African driver asked.

"Just drive man!" Tracy screamed. "What do they have a law in Chicago about crying in the back of taxis?"

"Where to?" he asked.

"I don't know, a coffee shop or something!" she said loudly.

The taxi man just did as he was told. He had had a fare go wrong a few weeks ago, and wasn't trying to have that happen again.

He dropped Tracy off in front of a nearby Starbucks, and was happy when she paid him in silence and got out.

Tracy was dragging herself into the coffee house at that point. She felt emotionally drained. Why in the world did she think taking a three day train ride would be any better than taking a plane? Now here she was, in a strange city she knew nothing about, around people she didn't know. She was all alone right now with no one to help her. She was the perfect target and felt as if she were on the verge of a nervous breakdown.

"What can I get for you?" the Starbucks employee said with a smile.

"Uh, a nonfat latte, grande," Tracy ordered. "And do you know if there's a liquor store around here?"

"Yes, right down the street," the nice employee confirmed. Her smile made Tracy uneasy.

"Thanks."

She sat down at a table facing the door, right next to the window and sipped on her coffee. She looked at her watch, and saw that it was only a little after noon. Even though it was lunchtime there were only a few people in Starbucks. She couldn't wait to get on that train. As she watched the people beginning to bustle by on their lunch hour, she saw the homeless woman's face again.

"That lady was crazy," she mumbled and took another sip. Then she saw a homeless looking person walk by and jumped out of her chair, thinking that the woman from the train station may have followed her. She grabbed her chest when she realized that it was some other guy.

"I need a drink bad," Tracy said to herself as she sat back down. She took a deep breath and looked up at the ceiling.

"You okay honey?" an older black lady who was sitting at the table right next to her asked. She resembled the picture of her thin, dark-skinned great-grandmother in the pictures she'd seen in her grandmother's house, and had stark white hair. All of the women on Tracy's dad's side of the family had passed on. The only family left on her dad's side was his father—who no one had seen or heard from since Tracy's father was five—his younger brother Joseph, and Joseph's numerous children by different baby's mothers scattered throughout Queens and Brooklyn.

When Tracy looked at the lady with her kind eyes, she resisted snapping as she usually did when strangers got in her business. "Yes, thank you for asking."

"If anybody's bothering you, you just let me know. I'll take care of 'em," the kind lady said with a smile as she pointed her finger at Tracy. Tracy chuckled along with her.

"Well I might have to take you up on that," Tracy was surprisingly relaxed talking with this lady. She had a positive aura flowing, and Tracy almost wanted to give her a hug.

"I've been told… that a young woman on her own is one of the strongest beings on the planet. Do you believe that?"

"I guess so. But I don't feel so strong sometimes," Tracy admitted.

"It does tend to be hard. But it's a test of who you are as a person," the lady told her.

"What do you mean?" Tracy wanted to know.

"I mean you're either a rock, a pebble, or the sand. If you're the sand, you just blow every which way the wind takes you. If you're the pebble you can sit unbothered for a long time until that stronggg wind comes and takes you up in one sweep. Just carries you anyway it chooses. But if you're the rock, a strong wind might be able to sway you a little to the left, or a little to the right, but you always hold your ground. You've got to know how to hold your weight, young lady."

Tracy looked at the lady with a blank stare. *Which am I?* She just sat for a while and thought about what this lady was trying to tell her.

"But what if you don't have the support around you?" Tracy said after a few moments.

"The support of God is all you need," the lady said with assuredness. "Besides, how many people do you know who have let you down?"

"Just about all. But that's just what I mean. How can you ever trust people if they always fail you?"

"You have to trust God and yourself first, then you will know the difference between people who are meant to bring you down, and people who truly have your best interest at heart."

Tracy thought about how what this lady was saying was easier said than done. She wished she would be more specific.

"I'm saying that sometimes the problem lies in you, and it takes a strong 'rock' to fix that kind of problem. Most people can't even admit their own faults. If you can learn to do that, you'll be set." The lady must have read her mind.

"I don't know. But how do you get more weight if you're too light?" Tracy asked, playing into the woman's analogy.

"You get weight by experience, by learning, by mistakes. Weight is built by trial and error, knowledge, openness to criticism, and love in your heart. Love for yourself, *and* for others.

I believe you will get it one day."

The lady and Tracy talked for a long time in the back of the Starbucks coffee shop. And Tracy didn't look around her, or even care who was watching her that whole time, talking to the lady. She didn't want to leave—she just wanted to enjoy the company of a caring person, someone that actually sat down and talked to her. Tracy had never had the traditional kind of older female role models most girls have growing up. She wasn't very close to her mother, and her only aunt was a mess.

The lady finally finished off her tea and then stood up. "My grandson is probably waiting for me. And I think I've taken up too much of your time. You take care of yourself baby. But remember, you're never alone. Be strong girl."

Tracy stood up with her and gave the woman a hug. The old lady seemed surprised but smiled and held her back tightly. When they let go, Tracy smiled like she hadn't smiled in years. She choked back the urge to cry.

"You take good care of yourself," the woman said again and walked out with an easy, slow gait. Tracy watched her pass by the window as she waved one more time.

Tracy looked down at her watch and saw that it was 1:53pm.

"Oh snap!" she shrieked. Her train was leaving at three! She grabbed up her things immediately and bustled out of the door. As she was heading to the spot where the taxi had dropped her off, she turned around and looked for the lady down the road to make sure she was okay. The woman was nowhere to be seen.

But she just left, Tracy thought.

Chapter 11

Mike sat in his car, his trademark blunt hanging out of his mouth. He inhaled and then let the smoke out of his nose, never removing the blunt from his teeth. After over an hour and a half of waiting, he was blitted.

"How long we gonna wait out here?" Mike's friend Bowen finally asked. "I got shit to do."

"Shut the fuck up," Mike told him disrespectfully. "Always complaining."

Bowen looked over at him as if he wanted to say something back, but held his tongue. He took a long puff from his cigarette, and after a few more moments he spoke again.

"I'm just sayin' Moon, it's been almost two hours man, that's money out my pocket."

"You ain't got them boys in check yet? They should be self-sufficient by now," Mike took a sip of his beer and then started looking for his gun. "You know that don't even make no damn sense."

"Yea, but I'm sayin' though."

"You ever heard of residual income? That's cash that flows into your pocket without you even being there," Mike schooled his friend. "You plant the seed and watch it grow on its own. You shouldn't even be gettin' ya hands dirty at this point. Besides, it's fucking five-thirty in the morning. When do you stop?"

Mike jerked his head to the side when he heard the front door of the building they were waiting at fly open again. He examined the brother that was coming out and assumed that this was the one.

"That's that nigga right there, it gotta be," he said as he sucked on the blunt once more and then put it out in his ashtray. "Come on."

They hopped out of the car and watched as their target made his way down the street. Mike was counting on this information he had gotten, and was hoping he hadn't spent his night in vain. He had been told that this guy left well before the crack of dawn every morning for work. He had on business attire and was carrying a briefcase, brown-skinned, and short, so it had to be him. They trailed him until they were well within shouting distance.

"Ay yo!" Mike yelled out as he swaggered down the street, his Tims nearly dragging along the sidewalk. "Yo!"

The man turned around to look, but didn't stop.

"You Karif Sanborn?" Mike asked.

The man finally did stop, and turned around with a confused look on his face. "How did you know my name?"

"I know a lot about you," Mike said with a deadly smile. "I know you like to put your hands on women."

"What?" Karif started to back up as Mike and Bowen got closer. He had no protection on him and was suddenly sorry he had stopped. When he glanced over at the car they had emerged from, one of only three cars parked on the block, Mike got in his face.

"What you backin' up for? I had thought you wasn't nobody to fuck with from what I heard? You such a big fuckin' dude, smacking on women. Why don't you smack me fool?" Mike challenged as Bowen suddenly lunged forward and grabbed Karif with one hand as he puffed his Newport with the other. He pushed Karif towards a nearby alley with Mike close behind.

"Go 'head, smack 'em," Bowen repeated, nodding in Mike's direction once they were in the privacy of the alley.

"Listen, I don't know what you all's problem is, but I got somewhere to be," Karif said with his hands up as if they were the cops. He wondered if this was the end.

Mike pulled out his trusty old .380, pointed it directly at Karif's head and continued to speak calmly. "I said smack me."

Karif looked into the barrel of the gun and nearly pissed his pants. He caught himself and gulped down hard. He thought about what and who this stranger could be referring to. "Uhh…I don't want to."

Mike lowered the gun and chuckled. He scratched and shook his head. "So you mean to tell me that you got no problem hitting women, but you can't hit me? I ain't that much bigger than you dude."

Karif shook his head and tried to be cool, but Mike's demeanor was scaring him. He figured this was a robbery, but was stumped about why he kept saying something about hitting women. *Could he be talking about Kamira?* "My man, I don't know what you are talking about. But look, I got money. $200 is yours if you just let this go."

Mike looked at Karif and burst out laughing, along with Bowen who fell back into the wall in amusement. They laughed for about three minutes and Mike waited for Karif to let down his guard before putting the gun back in his face.

"Let me make this clearer. Smack me, or I will shoot you," he said seriously.

Karif was in a predicament. He turned around and saw Bowen had completely recovered and was holding his hand over his own gun, which was tucked in his waist. He had a snarl on his face that dared Karif to make a move to run. Karif turned back around and tried to look Mike in the eye, but couldn't. He knew that either way he was screwed.

"I'll do you a solid and put the gun down," Mike offered as

he lowered the gun again and let it dangle by his side. He leaned forward to within a few inches of Karif's face and looked at Karif intensely from the corner of his eye.

Karif's right hand shook as he lifted it up slightly. For a split second he thought that if he could smack Mike hard enough, maybe he could get an upper hand with the gun down. Maybe wrestle it away. As soon as Mike saw the white side of Karif's hand in the dim light from the street lamp, he stepped back quickly, lifted the gun, and shot him once in the palm. *Pap.*

"Aaaaauuuughhhhhhh," Karif screamed for an eternity as he fell to the ground holding his wrist. Mike hadn't expected him to scream that loud. It must have been because it was at such a close range, but still he didn't feel bad for this woman-beater. Mike watched for a moment as blood dripped down from Karif's hand to the concrete, then peeked his head out of the alley to glance around the nearly empty street and saw a couple of people coming on the other side of the block. He finally just hit Karif on the same side of his head where Tracy had her bruise so that he would shut up. Right before Karif lost consciousness, an image of Kamira's face flashed across his mind.

"An eye for an eye," Mike said. Bowen grabbed Karif's briefcase and they quickly went back to the car. They screeched off down the street, stopping only once five blocks away to take the phony license plate Mike had off of the '87 Chevy he was driving.

Chapter 12

"All aboard," Tracy heard the train conductor call as she finally found her room and threw her oversized shoulder bag down. She had waited a few minutes until a suspicious looking white man had left the area where she had boarded before going to her cabin, because she had no intention of letting him know where she was going to be staying for that long ride.

"Good old Mrs. Moretti," Tracy commented when she saw the spacious room, containing her own personal toilet, sink and shower. "I love that woman."

Tracy immediately pulled out the bunk bed and got ready to go to bed. She couldn't wait to lay her head down. Before she got in, she did a bed bug check. She had read an article about how bed bugs could be found in some hotel and motel beds—it was now also in 'The Book.' She scanned the top of the bed head, underneath the mattress, and on the sheets for remnants or signs of bed bugs. When she was assured that everything was clear, Tracy pulled the shade down over the window and hopped in bed. She grabbed her cellphone to call Mike to update him on her progress.

"Hey Princess. I was just about to call you," Mike said, sounding relieved.

"I just wanted to let you know I'm alright, I'm on the second train," Tracy let him know.

"Damn, I miss you already." Mike laid his head back on his couch and closed his eyes.

"I know, I wish you could have come," Tracy said.

"You're not gonna get all famous and move out there on me

are you?" Mike asked.

Tracy laughed. "Yea right."

"Because I don't think I could handle that," Mike sounded really serious. There was silence for a long while as they both were caught up in their thoughts. "Can you please hurry back? I need you. Especially with this shit going on right now."

"I will," Tracy promised. She knew he was talking about the drama that was popping off within his family. From what he had told her his younger sister Janet had run away from home, causing their grandmother to be hospitalized for stress and depression. They all were afraid that she had run off with her no good boyfriend, who had been known to beat her up on occasion. No one had heard from her in weeks.

"And you'll call me everyday you're there," Mike requested.

"I will put a reminder on my phone to call you everyday at 4 o'clock. How about that?" Tracy said sweetly.

"Sounds good. Well, Imma holla at you later baby," Mike said before hanging up the phone.

Tracy sighed and gazed up at the ceiling. He made her heart pump faster and her soul feel at rest. She almost didn't come on the trip when she thought of being away from him for over a week. Even though they had only been together for a couple of months, she felt as if this could possibly be her future husband. He treated her like a queen, always said the right things, and gave her the security she needed.

But could she ever marry a man that played in the streets? Her mother would have a fit, and her father would have been so disappointed in her choice. What did he have to offer Tracy as her husband? She didn't even really know exactly what it was he did, and felt ashamed about being so naïve. But she was in love with him, and rested on the belief that their love would see them through any hard times.

She fell asleep daydreaming about what it would be like to be Mrs. Mike Jenkins. She wondered about the ups and downs to being a thug's wife…

Tap. Tap. Tap. There was a knocking at Tracy's cabin door and she woke up in a daze.

Rap. Rap. Rap. She was now wide awake and her heart started beating faster. She debated on whether she should even answer. Who the hell could need to knock on her cabin door, and why? She had already given her boarding ticket to the agent.

Tap. Tap. Tap. She heard the knock again, and looked around frantically in the dark. What should she do? What should she do?

Bang. Bang. The knocking became louder, but the person wasn't identifying themselves. Tracy decided there was no way in Amtrak Superliner hell that she was going to answer that door.

The knocking became so loud that she started to wonder why one of the conductors hadn't come to find out what was going on. It was obvious that whoever it was was using his or her fist to beat on the flimpsy wooden door. Tracy wanted to check the peephole, but was afraid that the person would sense her presence. Instead she pulled the covers up over her head and prayed that the person would just go away.

Then she started to hear taps on the window, which the shades were covering.

"What in the world?" she started to say, and snatched the covers back down.

Tap. Tap. Tap. Boom…. Boom…. BOOM!

Tracy jumped up out of the bed when she heard the door crack. The person had busted a crack in the door. Tracy cautiously crept to the other side of the room, and sat in the corner as she watched the door with her eyes wide open in fear. It was dark in the room and she was all alone.

Tracy wanted to scream when she saw a big fist crash through the crack causing more damage to the door but she was too paralyzed by fear. On the third blow, the hand had enough room to reach inside and try to unlock the door.

"Who are you! Go away!" Tracy finally screamed. She jumped up and tried to switch on the mini lamp, but it wouldn't come on. The only thing she could think to do was find something to protect herself but she could barely see in the darkness. She was weezing and sweating profusely and thought she was going to pass out as she searched for something sharp or blunt in her bag. She remembered her knife in the front pocket, and as she was reaching for it she looked back at the door and saw that the hand had unlatched the door.

"Leave me alone!!!" Tracy screamed at the top of her lungs and clutched the knife in her sweaty hand, ready to strike…

Tracy's eyes shot open and searched the room frantically. She was laying face up in her bed on the tough, thin cabin mattress. Her hands shook as she wiped at the moisture dripping down her face. *It was just a dream. Oh, thank God! Thank God.*

Clutching her chest tightly, Tracy sat up and grabbed her cellphone to check the time. She took a huge gulp and let her eyes adjust to the bright light emanating from the phone. It was going on 10pm. She had only been sleeping for about seven hours.

"10 o'clock? I can't believe I still have 30 hours to go!" Tracy complained. She switched on the lamp light and put her hands over her face in frustration. It was about that time that she was wishing she had listened to Rachel's suggestion and had someone knock her out with meds and carry her on the plane to LA. She wanted to bawl her eyes out, but instead just let a few tears fall. The last thing Tracy wanted to do was go back to sleep. She tried to call Mike for comfort several times, but he wasn't answering his phone. His voicemail just kept picking up.

Tracy was pissed because she had forgotten to visit the liquor store before getting on the train. *A bottle of tequila would be so nice*, she thought. "I wonder if the bar is still open," she wondered aloud.

Without thinking, Tracy was dressed and putting her switchblade in her pocket. She grabbed her wallet and sighed. "Please be open."

When she opened the cabin door and looked around, she was happy to confirm that no one was there. *What a dream.* There was nothing worse for Tracy than being in a strange place, by herself and having a bad dream.

"Hello ma'am. How are you?" one of the train crew said as he passed by her. She just nodded without smiling. On her way to the lounge area she could smell the distinct smell of fish—she hated fish. They must have had it for dinner, which she missed.

To her great pleasure, the lounge was open and pretty empty. There was hardly anyone in the way of her enjoying a whole lot of liquor in peace. She sat on the opposite side of the bar far away from the other people who were there. A couple was sitting at the bar talking, a middle aged black gentleman was a few seats down from them drinking a Scotch on the rocks, and there were three white women sitting at a small table talking and laughing loudly. They were obviously drunk.

"Can I please have…" Tracy thought carefully when the balding bartender asked her what she'd like. Whatever she got she was going to be drinking all night. "Let me get two shots of tequila please. Oh wait, can you make a margarita?"

"I sure can," the smiling man answered. "Just not frozen."

"Okay, I'll get a shot of tequila and a margarita on the rocks. Thanks," she said as she pulled two twenties out of her wallet and laid everything out on the bar.

About three drinks later, Tracy was in tequila heaven. All her worries and insecurities melted away and she even allowed herself to smile. She looked over at the other people in the bar and actually had an urge to talk to someone. The black gentleman smiled back at her. He was actually kind of good-looking in a Mayor Royce from *The Wire* kind of way.

Nah, she thought. *I don't know what's up with this guy*. But before she could finish her thought, he had picked up his drink and was heading her way.

"Oh God," she mumbled under her breath, but couldn't hide a smirk. She looked up at him as he approached. He looked like he could be an attorney, or a corporate vice president, no older than 50. His suit definitely wasn't cheap, and his cologne was mesmerizing.

"Mind if I sit?" he asked, clutching his refilled Scotch.

Tracy shrugged her shoulders. "Why not?"

"Those margaritas you've been drinking actually look pretty good, I was about to order one myself."

"Yea, they are good actually," Tracy nodded and swallowed another sip.

"Traveling on your own?" he asked, and Tracy's body tensed.

"Uh, no. I'm here with my sister. I think she's back at the room," she answered cautiously, a lie to keep him out of her business. "What about you?"

"Traveling on business. I hate to fly. But I think I hate riding the train even more," he admitted.

"Hey, me too!" Tracy smiled and was surprised at how comfortable she was talking to strangers on this trip. "I don't fly ever since 9-11."

"I feel ya on that one. My name is Travis," he said, offering his hand. "What's yours?"

"I'm Michelle," Tracy lied again and was surprised by how

strong his shake was. He looked old enough to be her father, but was very youthful in presence.

"Pleased to make your acquaintance Michelle," Travis smiled. He revealed a perfect set of white teeth, and Tracy wondered if they were dentures.

"I'm thinking about taking some classes to better deal with my fear," Travis continued about the flying. "I always have to leave an extra day or two earlier for my business meetings, and I think it's causing a strain at my job."

"In what way?" Tracy asked.

"Well, my boss. He doesn't like the fact that I have to take an extra day for travel. He says I'm being 'difficult'."

"Oh, I see." Tracy wondered what her friends were thinking about her at that very moment. They were probably already laying on the beach, or partying at some exclusive club in LA.

"But I guess it's about time. I'm getting too old for this," he said and took a sip of his drink. "I didn't even have a chance to change after leaving work today, I had to catch this train at three."

They talked for so long that Tracy lost track of the time. As Tracy had guessed, Travis was a corporate lawyer, who worked in the legal department at a major firm in Chicago. He had three sons, but he never mentioned having a wife, and Tracy didn't see a ring. She was quickly becoming drunk after her fourth margarita, and had to go to the bathroom.

"Excuse me, I'll be right back," she said grabbing her wallet and standing up. She swayed a bit, realizing that she was more drunk than she first thought.

When she got to the bathroom she had the urge to throw up. She debated for a while as she sat on the pot as to whether she should get it out or not. The last thing she wanted was to go back out there with throw up breath in front of Travis. He was so attractive and debonair. That would be so low class. But then she remembered that there was a huge pot of peppermints on the bar.

After throwing up mostly liquids, Tracy felt better and came out of the bathroom feeling refreshed, yet still tipsy… and strangely horny. She kept thinking about the way Travis kept looking at her breasts. She was wearing a white cotton shirt that slightly exposed her cleavage. She envisioned him stripping her shirt down and taking advantage of her in the privacy of her cabin room. No one would ever know… Besides, she was ragging, so there wouldn't be any chance of them actually having intercourse anyway.

"I was starting to get a little worried about you there," Travis said with a mixture of concern and levity. Tracy quickly grabbed a peppermint and put it in her mouth.

"Oh no, I'm fine," she played it off. She was praying that he didn't smell anything. She ordered another shot of tequila and Travis again told the barkeep to put it on his corporate tab. Tracy drank half and let the drink penetrate her. "But you know, I did miss dinner, and I'm starving right now."

"You mean you haven't eaten dinner sweetie?" Travis looked as if he were about to scold her for drinking on an empty stomach. "Well look, how about this. I know this is a little forward, but I have a special cabin with a TV built in. It sure isn't like the movies, but it is a good way to pass the time. We can order some food and drinks to the room, and watch some TV, since you said you were trying not to go to sleep… What do you think? Will you keep me company?"

His confidence was infectious. Tracy caught him stealing a glance at her cleavage again, and became even more turned on by his presence. She didn't want to be alone. She felt comfortable around Travis, and their conversation flowed with ease. But still she wasn't really sure. "I don't know…"

"Here," Travis pulled his wallet out and showed Tracy his license, his corporate ID, and a picture of himself with two of his sons, who were both grown. "Just so you know I haven't been lying to you. Honestly, I just don't want to be alone. And I promise I'll keep my hands to myself."

Tracy felt his sincerity, and was soothed by his words. She took another sip of her tequila and let the warm liquid glide down her throat. She finally just gave in. "Alright Travis, I guess it's no big deal. And I really want to watch some TV."

Travis' cabin room was twice as large as Tracy's and the TV was small, but it was a TV. When they came to the door with Tracy's food, she devoured it as if it were her last meal.

"Whoa, slow down lady," Travis laughed at her.

It was two in the morning and Tracy was giggling happily at an old episode of *Martin* on television. It was the episode when Martin went in the ring with Tommy 'The Hit Man' Hearns. She cackled wildly at the end when she saw Martin's swollen head, and Travis chuckled as well. He had taken his jacket off and was sitting with his arm behind Tracy's head.

"I knew a guy that looked *just* like that," Travis said, nodding his head in amusement.

Tracy laughed so hard that she couldn't stop—she couldn't breathe. She fell forward on the floor in laughter. She was hopelessly drunk after a few more margaritas on Travis' account. She wasn't tipsy—she was 'tripsy' now.

"Well damn, I'm glad you never met him. He might have went and hanged himself afterwards," Travis chuckled.

Tracy kept laughing, trying to recover and catch her breath. She placed her hand over her chest and looked up at Travis, smiling. Her cheeks were on fire. Travis could tell she was a little too intoxicated.

"You okay?" Travis said, helping her back up off of the floor with ease in his still-sitting position. Tracy marveled at how strong he was.

"Yea, I'm fine," she responded, her head bobbing from side to side as she stood up in front of him. She bit her lip as she looked at Travis looking at her. His eyes traveled down to her breasts as they had been doing all night, and Tracy could no longer hold it in. She put all thoughts of Mike completely to the back of her mind—the effects of the alcohol made it easier. She tried to be sexy as she traced her curves with her hands and brought them all the way up to her two girls, who were just screaming to get out. She rubbed them with her palms through her shirt, and pinched her nipples before moving closer and straddling Travis' lap. Travis laid his head back on the couch that doubled as a bed and watched. He had held true to his promise—he still hadn't touched Tracy. But now she wanted him to. She tried to fight the devil, but the alcohol made her weak.

"Look Trav," she said with a slur, taking the liberty of abbreviating his name at this point. "I don't want to have sex with you. I just want you to touch me. Right here. Can you do that for me?"

Travis nodded his head as if he had been waiting for that moment all night, and his voice became low as he said, "I'd be more than happy to help you with that little lady."

He grabbed them with both hands hungrily and squeezed them with his fingers. Tracy threw her head back and enjoyed the feeling. Travis became more and more bold with each groan he heard from Tracy. He finally pulled her shirt up and bra down. He groaned himself when he saw that they were just as he had imagined.

"They're perfect," he said, pleased. He felt her bare flesh between his fingers and was overwhelmed. He couldn't wait any longer to put one in his mouth.

Tracy let Travis do what he pleased with her breasts until she couldn't take it anymore. She had to let loose or she was going to burst. But then all of a sudden, thoughts of Mike began to creep back into her consciousness.

"I gotta go," she said, beginning to feel ashamed. She pulled her shirt back on and got up.

"Did I do something?" Travis was flustered. Tracy noticed that he had a huge hard on.

"No, I just gotta go, I'm sorry," she said and when she turned to leave, she tripped on a snag in the carpet and fell head forward into a nearby wall.

"Damn baby, you okay?" Travis stood and tried to help Tracy orient herself. Tracy tried to rub the pain away from her forehead.

"Yes, I'm fine, I'm fine," she said quickly and hustled out of the room. When she got back to her own cabin room in the next car, she was so embarrassed that she wanted to crawl underneath the bunk bed. She was sloppy drunk and had pretty much cheated on the man she loved!

All she could do was flop back into her bed face down. The positive side of being drunk was that she wanted to do nothing more at that moment than sleep the rest of this trip away.

Tracy woke up the next day still in a drunken stupor. She knew it was probably late afternoon, because after being drunk like that she rarely was able to wake before 4pm the next day.

Getting up was a chore. She switched on the light and dragged herself over to the in-room toilet.

"Oh my God. What happened," she said to herself as she sat trying to recall the previous night's events.

Visions flashed back to her from being at the bar and meeting Travis. Then she remembered what she had done and put her head in her hands.

"I don't believe I did that shit. I've got to stop drinking," she said, shaking her head. When she got up to wash her hands, she looked in the mirror and jumped back. "Damn!"

Her head looked like someone had hooked firecrackers up to several locks of her hair and set them off one after the other. Her lipstick was smeared across her face, and there was a dark red strawberry-sized mark on her forehead.

"Where the hell did this come from?" she said in shock. She looked in the mirror with wide eyes and scanned her face. The room was starting to spin and Tracy backed up into the bed to sit down and think. She faintly remembered falling that previous night and calmed down a little.

Tracy grabbed her phone off the floor and read the time. It was after 6pm—she had slept for over 14 hours. She saw several missed calls from Mike, Rachel, and her mother.

She thought harder about what happened the previous night but couldn't think straight. Being that she had missed breakfast, lunch, and dinner at that point, a meal was in order. *That's probably why I feel like such crap right now*, she thought.

Tracy went to retrieve her wallet from her purse, but couldn't find it. She looked in the sheets, but it wasn't there either. She began to panic. When she had torn the entire room up she was finally letting it sink in that she had lost her wallet.

"Where did I leave it!" she screamed and balled her fists up in anger. "The bar! Oh no."

Tracy didn't care what she looked like. She unlocked her door and snatched it open ferociously, heading in the direction of the bar lounge she had been drinking at. When she got there, there was a different bartender from before, and the bar was packed.

"Did someone find a wallet in here? It's a red leather ladies wallet??" she asked the bartender frantically as he looked at her hair in confusion.

He fell out of his trance and called back to the barback. "Did anyone bring up a wallet Chris?"

"Naw, sorry, not that I know about," the barback said and then went about his business.

"I need my wallet. The last place I had it was here! I can't do anything without my ID. My credit cards and my money were in there!" she said to partially deaf ears. The bartender shook his head to let her know that he didn't know what to tell her. That's when she thought that maybe the bar wasn't the last place she had her wallet.

"Travis," she said. Her blood was boiling as she thought about the possibility that Travis had taken her wallet.

She had dangerous thoughts running through her mind. Her mind was so occupied in thought that it was as if she was transported in front of Travis' cabin room. She was there in an instant.

Bam. Bam. Bam. Tracy knocked obnoxiously on his door. By then she was fuming.

"Who is it?" the male voice asked from inside.

"Travis, please open up," Tracy asked impatiently.

She heard some rustling noises and then the door being opened. Travis peeked his head out. He was wearing a wife beater tee. "Oh hey, how are you?"

"Where's my wallet," she asked bluntly with her hands crossed across her chest. She had a look on her twisted face that said she was not in the mood for games and niceties.

"What?"

"I said where's my mother-fucking wallet? What are you some kind of con man? Conning women out of their money on the trains?" she accused.

Travis looked at her as if she were fool. "I don't have any

idea of what you are talking about."

"Like hell you don't! You stole my wallet! The last time I had it was with you!" Catching Travis by surprise, she pushed open his door and busted her way inside. She was taken aback when she saw that there was a woman in there with him. She was sitting on his bed with her legs crossed and only her bra and a pair of jeans on. The woman tried to cover herself up.

"Oh my God, who are you?" Tracy asked with disgust. She looked the young, short-haired brunette up and down as if she were a piece of slime.

"Michelle, get out of here!" Travis raised his voice for the first time since she'd met him. At first Tracy thought he was talking to the other woman, but then remembered that she had given Travis a fake name.

"You have no right to be in here!" he continued.

Tracy turned her attention to his room again, and quickly scanned the room for signs of her wallet. Travis followed her around and gave her a few seconds to look before again demanding that she leave.

"I told you I don't have your wallet! Now would you please leave?" Travis said, trying to refrain from physically grabbing her up out of his room.

"Is this what you do? Tricking women into coming into your cabin room? You dirty bastard," Tracy looked at him with righteous indignation, and then started moving stuff around and opening drawers.

"That's it, you can't be in here. Get out!" Travis screamed.

"Is everything alright in here?" Everyone turned to look at the crew member who was standing at the door, trying to figure out what was going on, but then Tracy just went back to searching through Travis' stuff even more furiously.

"No, this woman won't leave my cabin," Travis complained.

"This man stole my purse!" Tracy fired back.

"I don't know what she is talking about. I don't have her purse. You can search my room yourself," Travis challenged.

"Okay, ma'am, is this your room?" the crew member asked.

"No, but—"

"I'm going to need you to follow me please ma'am," he said and put his hand out for Tracy.

"No! I'm not leaving until I get my purse back!"

The crew member pulled out his walkie talkie and called for security. When he finished talking he turned back to Tracy. "Ma'am, I would advise you to leave on your own will, otherwise this could become a police matter. We may have to stop the train and let you off."

"But I need my money and my ID!" she cried out in frustration. She felt helpless.

"If you come out with me, I will make a report and if you'd like I will search this cabin as the gentleman suggested, with his consent," he reasoned.

"Gentleman. Yea right," Tracy said as she moved towards the door. "Yes, please search his things."

By the time the security guards arrived the crew member had searched the room and was telling Tracy that her wallet was not there.

"This is crazy," Tracy said, holding her head. "I can't believe this."

She looked up at the crew member, the security guards, and then back at Travis. They were all looking at her the same way—like she was loony toons. You could almost hear the cuckoo bird singing over Tracy's head in the thick of that silence.

"You all are probably in on this scam, I bet. He probably rides this same train all the time," Tracy said pointing at Travis. "And you all play damage control for him. So what's *your* cut?"

She began walking away. "That's alright, because I'm going to put in a police report on ALL of you. They're going to put you in *Federal* prison because you're scamming people while we're crossing state lines. You all should be ashamed!"

Tracy passed by a group of people seated in the regular train area and they all were looking at her curiously.

"Watch out for that guy, Travis Johnson. He is scamming women out of money on the train!" Tracy shouted so that everyone could hear.

Chapter 13

It was like the heavens opened when Tracy's train pulled into the station at Los Angeles. She had locked herself in her cabin room the rest of the trip, only coming out to eat. She was crying most of the time, and thinking of how she was going to function in LA with no money, no credit cards, and no identification. She wanted to go to Travis' room again and cut the bastard. She had called Rachel, who was already in the city, and told her everything. She didn't dare tell Mike about what happened, because he was going to wonder why this guy was even around his girl.

She stepped off the train and almost wanted to kiss the ground. Rachel and the girls were probably waiting on her, and she couldn't wait to see her friends. But first, she had some business to handle.

After waiting for her bags for over 20 minutes, Tracy started looking around for an Amtrak information booth. When she found it on the other side of the station she dragged her bags over and looked at the woman with intensity.

"I need to file a report against someone who was riding the train, and some crew members. How would I go about doing that?"

"What was the problem miss?" the lady asked curiously.

"They stole my wallet, and I have reason to believe that it is a part of some kind of ongoing scam."

"Hmm," the lady said and looked down at a sheet of paper. "What is your name and what train were you on?

"Tracy Samuels, and I just got off the train from Chicago." She put her bags down and searched for her boarding pass stub so that she could give the lady her exact train number.

"Ms. Samuels, your wallet was found. They sent a message to us about this situation as soon as your train arrived. It should be at the Lost and Found Kiosk in the baggage area by now."

Tracy looked at the woman dumbfounded. "Did they say where they found it?"

"Uhhh," the lady looked at her sheet again. "It looks like a passenger found it. I'm not sure where."

Tracy's face turned red and she looked down at her ticket stub. The lady looked at her with a polite smile, trying to hide her amusement at the situation.

"Thank you," Tracy said and grabbed her bags quickly. By the time she made her way back over to the other side of the station, her arms were hurting so badly that they were burning from carrying all those bags. She had to rest as she looked around for the lost and found area.

When she reached the kiosk, the man was smiling at her as she approached.

"Tracy Samuels?" he said before Tracy even had an opportunity to open her mouth.

"Yes, how did you know?"

"They called down to let me know you were on your way," the man said as he pulled Tracy's leather wallet out of a small plastic bag. "This is yours?"

"Yes," Tracy said grabbing at it. But the man held onto it for a moment.

"I just have to check the picture on your ID." It seemed to Tracy that he was fucking with her. "Looks like you. Here you go."

Tracy nearly snatched the wallet from him as she eyed him skeptically. She opened it up herself and started looking through it.

"Our policy is that we are not responsible for lost items miss. If there is anything missing from the wallet we can not be held accountable. A nice older lady brought it to us as soon as your train arrived. She found it in the bathroom."

To Tracy's surprise and delight, everything was there. Her money, her license, and her five credit cards. Tracy couldn't help but wonder if the people at the station heard about her outburst on the train, but she wasn't about to ask.

"Thank you."

The sight of Rachel in her green halter top leaning against the blue convertible Mercedes that her mother had rented for their trip was almost too much for Tracy.

"Oh my God! Is this our ride?" Tracy said in amazement as she stared at the car.

"Most def!" Joy said from the back seat as she pointed her finger up in the air. She looked like she had already gotten darker in the LA sun and Tracy was instantly jealous. Kamira was in the back as well smiling from ear to ear. Everyone looked so happy.

"You have got to be kidding me!" Tracy screamed as Rachel helped her put her bags in the trunk.

"What the hell happened to your head Trace?" Kamira was the first to ask when she got in the front passenger seat.

"Oh. I fell into a wall. Don't ask." Tracy said.

"So, I know you don't have your wallet, but my mom told me to give you this," Rachel said, handing over a blank check with Tracy's name on it. "They have a branch out here."

"Oh, I found it," Tracy said casually.

"What?" Rachel asked. "I thought you said you thought someone had stolen it?"

Tracy looked down at her hands and played with her fingernails. "I really don't want to talk about that."

Everyone was quiet and Rachel looked back at the other two.

"Geez, can we just go and have some fun! You all have a headstart, I'm ready to go see some celebrities or something!" Tracy exclaimed.

"Oh my goodness, Tracy you wouldn't believe who I saw!" Kamira became excited and jumped up and down in her seat.

"Who? WHO?" Tracy said excitedly.

"Ashton Kutcher! I know it was him, he was walking to his car. And, oh, Gwyneth Paltrow!"

They all caught Tracy up on their sightings and told her about what they had been doing while waiting for Tracy to arrive. Tracy felt slightly jealous for having missed out on the action, but was determined to make her own history while in LA. She glanced back at Joy again, who was wearing a figure flattering sundress and almost immediately felt a pain in her side. Her extreme excitement was instantly brought down a notch.

Chapter 14

Karif put the last large box on his bed and started throwing the last of his belongings inside. Nobody had even lifted a finger to help him move, none of his family, none of his co-workers, nobody. Kamira wasn't even there because she was off traipsing around in Los Angeles. She still didn't even call him back after he left five messages on her cellphone telling her what happened. Because of this, he had to assume that she had set him up.

"Whenever somebody needs me, I'm there," he complained as he looked at all of his belongings crowding the floor in his room.

He winced in pain each time he had to use his right hand for anything. The doctors had told him he would never be able to properly use that hand again, which was devastating being that his job required a lot of typing, research and use of the phone. He knew that he was in for trouble at work when he returned.

"That dirty ass bitch," he mumbled to himself, referring to Kamira. He blamed her for all of this. If she wouldn't have been at the club slutting herself out he wouldn't have had to come get her and they never would have had that public confrontation. He still didn't know who the guy was that shot him, but he was surely going to report him and Kamira for what happened; as soon as he moved out of this apartment building for good first. He decided that he wasn't going to call Kamira anymore. She would get what she deserved. The guy who shot him knew way too much about him, including where he lived. It had to have been Kamira that told him, who else would have known? Who else could be the woman he was accused of hitting? He was moving to a basement apartment in Connecticut until it was safe to come back to New York.

* * *

"Tracy would you just come on," Rachel begged, as they all waited by the door for her.

"Just one second," she said with a little bit of annoyance in her tone. "I'm looking for my nail tools. Here they go."

"Why are you bringing your nail tools to a nail salon?" Joy asked the obvious question. "They got their own stuff you know."

"I don't trust their equipment. Sometimes they don't sanitize those things. You can get nail fungus and infections like that. Don't you know how hard it is to get rid of a nail fungus?"

Everyone left what they really wanted to say to Tracy to their thoughts. She had been spazzing out ever since she arrived in LA, over the smallest things. Dirty knives and forks at the restaurant they visited on the first night—Tracy accused the waiter of discriminating against their table because they were black. When a man was walking behind them on the strip for a few blocks, Tracy whipped around and called him out for stalking them. When it was her turn to drive, she became frantic when she thought a guy in a white truck was following them. She drove them around so much trying to shake the guy that they got lost on another side of town. Tracy's friends—other than Kamira—couldn't remember her being so obnoxious and outright ridiculous before in her day to day life. Tracy had always had a little 'thing' about her, where she blew things out of proportion, but she had never been that bad. She had gotten much worse since they left high school.

When they arrived at the nail salon, Tracy looked around the shop, seeing how clean it was and was relieved.

"Miss, you're next," the Asian woman called out to Tracy. She led her to the seat for pedicures and made sure Tracy was comfortable before turning on the water basin and putting a special soap inside.

"Was that cleaned?" Tracy asked, looking at the basin as water began to fill it up.

"Yes," the middle aged lady said with a smile. She tested the water and placed Tracy's feet inside. She was very gentle with Tracy and took care to make sure Tracy was comfortable and happy. Everything was great until she pulled out a razor to smooth out the rough spots on Tracy's feet.

"No!" Tracy screamed at the lady, causing her to jump back in fear. She had already taken a few swipes at Tracy's feet with the tool and Tracy was pissed. "I brought my own. Did you even clean that after the lady before me?"

"Is clean," the nice Asian lady said with a nod and a polite smile.

"No, it *is* not. How could you have cleaned that razor that quickly? The woman before me just left the chair," Tracy protested.

The Asian lady just looked at Tracy in confusion. Then she turned around and said something in Korean to another lady, presumably the owner.

"Can I help you?" the owner walked over and asked Tracy.

Joy and Kamira, who were both sitting at a booth getting their nails done, sighed and rolled their eyes at each other.

"She didn't even clean her tools, and she's using them on me. That's gross," Tracy complained and started getting up.

"It's okay miss, her tools are clean," the owner assured her.

"No, never my mind. I didn't really want to get my nails done anyway," Tracy said as she wiped her feet on a towel draped across the basin and put her shoes on.

"Tracy, give me a break," Rachel said to her friend as Tracy sat down next to her in the waiting area. "Go ahead and get your nails done girl."

"Naw, I just don't feel right about it, she broke the skin and I don't think she cleaned that razor."

"You just wiped your feet on a random towel and are worried about her with the nail tool," Rachel said as she flipped her bag open and pulled out a small tube of Advil. She had always loved Tracy, but Tracy was really starting to get on her nerves. Tracy was putting a damper on the whole trip.

Tracy looked back at the towel and scrunched up her nose in disgust. "I've gotta go. I'll be back."

"Where are you going Tra?" Kamira asked when she saw Tracy headed for the door.

"I'll be back," Tracy said, never turning around.

It was all in her mind, but Tracy was feeling as if her feet were on fire as she searched for a single occupant public bathroom. She needed to wash her feet as soon as possible.

"Excuse me, is there a single person bathroom around here?" she asked a young woman who was passing by. The woman took a few moments to process what Tracy had asked.

"Ummm. Yea, there is, at the Mexican restaurant down the block," the woman said, pointing. "I think."

Tracy thanked the woman and rushed down the street.

"Tracy!" Kamira came outside and yelled after her. But Tracy ignored her and kept walking.

She entered the small Mexican restaurant and went right to the back as if she owned the place. When she saw the small bathroom door ajar she was relieved.

If someone were to have walked in on Tracy in that bathroom for some reason, they would have been startled and disgusted. Tracy was washing her feet, one foot at a time, in the small white sink. She scrubbed them with the hand soap from the dispenser and dried them off with toilet paper, the only paper in the bathroom. When she was finished, she slid her feet back into her high heeled sandals and headed back to the salon.

"Where did you go?" Kamira asked immediately when she saw Tracy come back into the shop. Since Kamira was the one who spent the most time with Tracy those days, she felt a responsibility to be the one to calm her down.

"I just went to the bathroom, calm down," Tracy said with a sneer at her friend. Kamira was getting on her nerves, constantly asking her if she was alright.

"Are you going to get your nails done or not?"

"Not. I'll just paint them when I get back to the room," Tracy responded. "You guys go ahead and do your thing."

When they all left the nail salon, the plan was to get something to eat and then go out to the nightclub Joy had been invited to in Hollywood. But Tracy had a different plan.

"Guys I'm going to go to the room and relax for a while. I'll call you later. I'll still go to the club though," she said as she placed her new Coach sunglasses over her eyes.

"Yea right Tracy, you just want to go call that dude," Joy said and sucked her teeth.

"No, really. I'm tired. Plus I have to paint my nails."

"You wouldn't have to do that if you would have just gotten your nails done in there," Kamira reminded her.

"Well I didn't. So that's what I'm going to do alright Kami. Is that alright with you?" Tracy said with an attitude and then spun around and headed back towards their hotel, which was a few blocks down the street. When she turned the corner, the other girls walked to the car.

"God Kamira. Why is she being like this? This isn't the Tracy

I remember," Rachel said seriously. "I don't even want to be around her ass anymore."

"Word. I didn't know she was becoming like this. She needs help. Bad," Joy agreed.

"It's progressive I guess. You know she used to trip a lot when we were kids. I guess living in the Bronx really put her on edge."

"Well, why the hell would she move up to the Bronx of all places then? She should have stayed out on Long Island," Joy wanted to know.

"I don't know, but what I do know is that I'm not letting her or anybody else mess up my vacation. We only have two days left. I feel like I can't enjoy myself. I'm about to lock her ass in the bathroom so I can have fun tonight," Rachel half-joked.

"I was thinking the same thing," Kamira laughed. Joy shook her head and pulled out the remainder of a blunt she had been smoking earlier.

"Girl are you crazy? They will lock your ass up smoking that on the streets!" Kamira said as she watched Joy light the blunt right in the middle of the block.

"They ain't gonna lock me up over a roach Kami, calm down," Joy assured her and took a long puff. "Who are you, Tracy now?"

Kamira paused and thought before breaking out in a nervous laugh. "You're right, what am I sweating about. I guess she's getting to me in more ways than one."

Tracy had been hiding Kamira's phone from her ever since they arrived in Los Angeles. She refused to give it back, because she knew that Kamira wouldn't be able to enjoy the trip with Karif calling her every ten seconds. Kamira had asked Tracy for her phone several times, but was turned down and even completely ignored one time. Tracy was not even kidding, and dared Kamira to try to get her phone back with her eyes. Tracy wasn't about to have her vacation ruined with Kamira's drama. What was ironic was that Kamira wasn't enjoying the trip that much anyway because of Tracy's craziness. She felt like a prisoner. She wasn't even allowed to use the phone at the hotel or be away from Tracy for more than a few seconds. Tracy called Kamira's mom for her several times and let them talk as she stood nearby listening. When Kamira was alone with Rachel and Joy, they were told not to let her touch any phones. For fear of pissing Tracy off, they complied.

"Well at least we can have dinner in peace," Rachel commented as she took the roach from Joy.

"Yea. But what about the club?" Joy asked.

"Don't worry. She's usually cool when she's drunk. She calms down a little," Kamira said, letting her body relax a bit at the thought. "But the only thing is that she .doesn't know when to stop drinking, and can't nobody tell her either. So y'all aren't going to trip about my using the phone this time, are you?"

Rachel and Joy just looked at each other and said nothing.

Chapter 15

The girls looked like a scene out of *America's Top Model* as they strutted to the front of the line at Club Elephante—Joy in her gold metallic blouse that scooped low between her cleavage, Kamira in a red and black bustier that had a flared ruffle at the bottom and black pants, Rachel in a white Vera Wang party dress, and Tracy with her figure flattering white blouse that fell off her shoulders, Capri pants, and a pair of black pumps. From what they heard this was one of the hardest clubs to get into in Hollywood, so their hearts were beating fast as they strolled up to the front door, passing up the line of people waiting behind the velvet rope. Joy had met a guy named Clay who claimed to be a big wig in Hollywood who told her he would get them on the guest list, so here they were, taking a chance on the guy's word.

"Joy Martin, plus three please," Joy said politely, but with a sideways glance at the bouncer, who was trained to reject any and all posers and unworthy partiers. He looked Joy up and down and then scanned his list.

The bouncer never said anything, he just opened the door and let them enter. Joy was relieved, and thankful that her new friend Clay had come through—her rep was on the line. Her first plan upon entering the club was to find him. But when she saw her surroundings, and all of the attractive people in the club, Clay became the last thing on her mind.

"Let's go get a drink," she said as she put on her best model walk and sauntered to the bar farthest from the door with Rachel by her side. Kamira and Tracy just followed close behind. They observed Joy's actions and secretly were trying to mimic them.

"$56," the bartender said simply as he waited for payment on the four drinks they had just ordered.

"Damn, $56, what is this liquor distilled over diamonds. Is this glass platinum lined or something," Tracy said jokingly as she inspected the glass. But really the last thing she needed at that moment was *another* glass of liquor. She had been drinking since 8 o'clock in the evening.

"Tracy, hush," Joy cut her eyes at her scoldingly. She reached into her purse and pulled out her platinum Mastercard and handed it to the bartender. "Can you start a tab please?"

"I'm just saying," Tracy said with an eye roll and then looked back at the dance floor. "Why aren't more people dancing?"

"Because they're too busy profiling, and trying to be seen," Rachel answered. She knew because she had been around people like that all her life, from her mother's holiday parties to her father's business socials.

By the middle of the night, Tracy and Kamira were feeling more and more like the odd women out. Joy and Rachel were clearly the club favorites among the young professional looking men and Hollywood up and comers. They had all been called over to the VIP area by Clay, who was looking more and more to Joy like someone she wanted to get to know. He was a short Jewish white guy, but he had style and a look similar to Scott Storch.

"Heyyy baby, what's going on?" Clay got up to kiss Joy on the cheek. He grabbed her hand and led her to the spot right next to where he was sitting, on a chic black couch set far back in the lounge area, and started pouring her a glass of Dom Perignon, Rose. Rachel was talking to one of his friends, who she found out was his business manager. Tracy and Kamira were forced to sit by themselves on another two seater couch nearby. Tracy was drunk and not really caring, but Kamira was feeling some kind of way about not getting attention.

"I think I want to go back to the regular area," Kamira said, the look of jealousy written all over her button nose.

"Why? This is the VIP. Everyone in this place wishes they were us right now," Tracy said as she did a dance in her seat to the song that was playing—Kelis' *Milkshake* song.

"But no one is talking to me. I came to the club to meet somebody, not to sit and look around like a fool," Kamira complained.

"Then go ahead. You're killing my mood," Tracy said, waving her friend off as she took another sip from her Watermelon Martini.

"Whatever," Kamira grabbed up her bag and walked back over to the velvet rope to look out over the crowd.

The night continued on the same way—Tracy drinking, Kamira hating, and Rachel and Joy getting all of the attention. When it was about time to go, Rachel and Joy were no where to be found. Tracy was way too drunk when she realized that they were missing. She came and sat down next to Kamira at a table in the corner.

"Where the hell did those two go?" Tracy asked as she scanned the VIP area, but Kamira just ignored her. Kamira was pissed.

"Alright, I'll be right back. I gotta find them. They could be in trouble." Tracy stumbled as she got up from the seat and walked towards the back, brushing past a group of people talking, where some velvet curtains hid a section behind the elevated stage.

Kamira smirked as she realized that Tracy had left her bag at the table. She immediately snatched it up and started searching through it for her phone. When she didn't find it there, she took Tracy's phone instead and shakily pressed the keys, dialing into her own personal voice mailbox. The phone rang several times before going to voicemail.

Tracy was reluctant as she found the opening to the velvet curtain and peered inside. She was shocked to see Rachel just finish snorting a long line of cocaine and passing the straw to Joy, who was sitting on a couch next to her. She watched as Joy took the straw and leaned down over the plate just as Rachel had just done. Clay and two of his friends were sitting on the arms of the couch talking.

"Joy!" Tracy screamed and jetted forward to knock the plate away from her friend.

"Tracy! What are you doing in here?" Joy looked at her friend. Her face could have been next to the word 'shame' in the dictionary with a caption.

Rachel got up and dusted herself, trying to play it off. She didn't say anything—she just grabbed her purse and got up to walk back to the VIP section, trying to brush past Tracy but Tracy held up her hand, pressing up against Rachel's chest.

"What are you guys doing? What is this? You're doing *coke*?" Tracy was astonished at her friends.

"Tracy, really, not right now. We'll talk about it later," Joy said with her eyeballs rolled up at Tracy, who was looking like a disappointed mom.

"I don't believe this. Since when have you all been doing drugs?" Tracy wanted to know, but was really focusing on Joy. She had kind of expected something like this out of crazy Rachel, but not Joy. Rachel went around Tracy and left the scene.

"Come on sweetheart, don't come in here ruining the vibe," one of the guys Clay was talking to got up to try to diffuse the situation. He tried to comfort Tracy by rubbing her arm, and that set her off.

"Get the fuck off of me! Who the hell do you think you are,

touching me!?" Tracy screamed as she slapped his hand away.

"Whoa, chill out. I'm just trying to keep the flow going—" he tried to explain, but Tracy cut him off.

"I'm not one of your coke whores you can do whatever you like to," Tracy looked deliberately at Joy. "I should call the cops on all your dumb asses!"

"Okay. Get out," Clay said, getting up. Cops—that was one word he never wanted to hear spoken in his presence. He had priors and couldn't afford another strike on his record. "Joy, I love you babe, but you've got to get your wacked out friend out of here."

"Wacked out? Oh, I'll show you wacked out motherfucker," Tracy said with a tremble in her voice and stepped up to Clay, who was only about two inches taller.

"Tracy no!" Joy jumped up, fearing the worst. She tried to get in between the two, but Tracy knocked her back into the couch.

"And just what are you going to do?" Clay stood with his hands crossed in front of him. He was intimidated by this fiesty black woman, but was trying his damnedest not to show it. If he hit her, and she pressed charges, that would be immediate jail time. His friends, most of whom were high and or drunk, came in the back and looked on in bewilderment as Tracy challenged their friend.

Finally, Clay stepped down. He backed away and held up in his hands in surrender. As he was trying to get away Tracy mushed him in the back of his head. He turned around with a look of shock on his face, but eventually just continued on his way.

"That's what the fuck I thought," she said and then grabbed Joy by the arm.

"Get off of me!" Joy screamed. "Leave me alone you crazy bitch! You are not my mother!"

Joy ran back into the club, leaving Tracy standing there among all of the strangers. Tracy pushed her way past them and went after Joy.

She looked everywhere, but couldn't find even one of her friends. She went back to the table where she left Kamira, but all she saw there was her pocketbook laying open.

"What the?" she said to herself as she rummaged through her things.

Tracy had to take a cab back from the club, by herself at three in the morning, and was highly upset about it. On top of everything else, someone had stolen her phone right out of her purse.

When she arrived at the hotel room everyone was there, moving about, gathering their stuff, and throwing them into bags.

"What the fuck are y'all doing?" Tracy asked as she looked at them curiously. "Why are you packing? And why did you all leave me at the club like that!"

Everybody stopped for a moment and stared, then went back to what they were doing. All except Kamira.

"What did you do Tracy!" she screamed. "You sent somebody to Karif's house? You put a hit out on my fucking boyfriend!? So that's why you didn't want me to answer my phone! You scheming ass bitch!"

Tracy scrunched up her face in confusion. She was stuck, dumbfounded.

"I can't believe you would do that!" Kamira continued, a tear forming in her eye. "You know how much I love Karif! Now he thinks *I* set him up!"

"Kamira, I don't know what the fuck you're talking about, for real," Tracy said, shaking her hands from side to side in front of herself. For a moment, she forgot that she was the one who was angry.

"Yea, whatever," Kamira said flippantly and continued packing. But then she stopped again. "You know Tracy, I knew you were a little crazy, but not that damn crazy. You are just, psycho."

Tracy's eyes bugged out of her head. "What did you call me?"

Kamira was bold at this point, but not bold enough to repeat what she said. She threw a couple more things in her bags, zipped them up and charged for the door with them, but Tracy stopped her.

"No, you ain't goin' nowhere," she said, rolling her neck and blocking the door with her arm.

"Get out of the way Tracy!" Kamira huffed and then tried to push her way past Tracy again. Tracy held her back with her arm on Kamira's neck and they started struggling at the door. Something small quickly grew into something bigger, and when Joy and Rachel saw that Tracy was basically strong arming Kamira they jumped in.

"Let her go!" Joy screamed and she and Rachel tried to pry Tracy's grip off of Kamira's arms. Kamira was punching and scratching at Tracy the best she could.

After an almost silent battle, the three of them finally were able to disable Tracy and hold her down on the ground.

"Go get the bags!" Rachel commanded Joy. Kamira was crying and too furious to think straight by then. Joy obeyed; she grabbed everything she could and threw them outside in the hallway so that they could all get away quickly. She then ran down the hall with a few of the bags and summoned the elevator. When it came she put them in the elevator door and went to retrieve more.

"I hate y'all!" Tracy screamed and tried to get up. Rachel and

Kamira were praying that they could get out of this situation unscathed without having to involve the police.

"Tracy, I love you, but if you put your hands on me or any of us I'm calling the cops. We're going," Rachel tried to state calmly. They let her go and made a beeline for the rest of their stuff.

Tracy finally got up and watched her friends hustle down the hall. She didn't understand what was going on. Why were they betraying her?

"I hate all of you evil bitches! You were never my friends!" was the last thing they heard before the elevator doors closed.

Chapter 16

Tracy looked like a zombie as she passed the stack of papers to her boss, Cathy. Her eyes were sunken into her head, her hair was dry and brittle, and her skin was becoming blotchy.

"Are you alright?" Cathy asked Tracy before she had a chance to leave her office.

Tracy turned around slowly to look at Cathy. "Yea, I'm fine. Why do you say that?"

Cathy's look of concern turned to apprehension at the expression on Tracy's face. "No reason. You have a good day Tracy."

As Tracy was walking back, she heard her desk phone ringing and jetted to her cubicle. Just as she had thought, it was Mike.

"Hey baby!" Tracy said happily. Mike was the only person there for her now, the only person that she could count on.

"What's up," Mike said in an upbeat tone. "I want to take you to Applebee's tonight."

"Applebee's? Sounds good. But why tonight, it's Tuesday?" she asked, beginning to smile as she looked down at the phone.

"Don't you know? It's our four month anniversary," Mike said enthusiastically. The sound of Jadakiss' voice could be heard blasting from his car speakers.

"What, really?" Tracy said, surprised that he would be tracking this information.

"Four months ago today, August 27th, is the day I met you on the street near your car, remember?" Mike reminded her.

Tracy loved this about Mike. He could be so hard and bad-ass on the streets—but when he was with her, he was just like a big kid.

"Wow Mike. I didn't even remember that," Tracy said with a tear in her eye.

"Of course, now come on, ain't you off yet?" he asked, sounding distracted by something. Tracy heard the line stutter and knew he was getting another phone call.

"Not yet, I got about another…five minutes," Tracy said looking at the wall clock. She wouldn't dare leave her job a minute earlier than 5:30 these days—especially after having to take more than a week off of work for her trip to Los Angeles, which had ended in disaster.

"Well I'm outside your building, waiting on you Ma," Mike said, sounding like Tracy's knight in shining armor. Tracy was brimming with excitement now.

"Okay, I'll try to be out as soon as possible," Tracy gushed, and turned back to hang up the phone. She was stunned when she saw Mary, her nemesis, standing at her cubicle. She had been listening to her entire conversation.

"Sorry to have to bother you Tracy, but all of the admins in my department have left for the day," Mary said with a smug look on her face. "I need you to re-type this report with the changes I wrote on this markup by 9pm tonight. Unfortunately, it was sent to me as a fax, so there is no editable file. It will need to be recreated completely."

Was this bitch standing there that whole time, listening to my conversation? Tracy thought. "Uh, sorry, I can't do that Mary. I've got plans."

"Look, Tracy, what is more important, your job or a date? I really would hate to have to bring this up to James again," Mary looked at her with her intense, icy blue eyes attempting to intimidate someone she thought of as 'less' than herself.

Tracy thought her head was about to blow off from steam.

How dare she? "That's really none of your business Mary. It's after work hours right now, and I don't report to you anymore. I think you need to find someone else for your project." Tracy tried to maintain her professionalism, but her voice was already shaking.

"You know Tracy, you have absolutely no sense of professionalism in this work environment. How do you ever expect to advance if you can't excel at your current position? You can go out on dates on the weekends—during the week your work is a priority. If you don't complete this project, I will make it a personal point to be sure that you are written up for this, officially this time."

"Where the hell do you get off?" Tracy had lost her patience. "How dare you violate my privacy like that, why didn't you tell me you were there? Why would you just stand there and listen to my conversation like that? You are way out of line lady."

"No, what is out of line is your attitude Ms. Samuels. This is a place of business, and all calls made on these phones are my and everyone in here's business. I won't tolerate someone at your level talking to me in that way!" Mary became indignant, and hearing the way Mary said 'level' with her nose scrunched up in disgust as if she were talking to a mouse about to be killed made Tracy even more furious. Then the real Tracy, no longer work Tracy, emerged.

"Just who the fuck do you think you are dealing with?" Tracy said, as she came around her desk so that she could stand face to face with Mary. Mary took a few steps back and looked around. Just then a couple of people came out of their offices to see what the commotion was about. Tracy was so livid that she was unaware of their presence.

"Just because I work here don't mean I won't work your ass up and down this floor. You've had it out to get me since I came here, and I know it's cause I'm black! What other reason. There are five other admins on this floor, all white, and you just always gotta come bother my African ass! Advance? I'll never advance in this racist corporation as long as racist ass white folks like you work here. If you *ever* fuck with me again I will make you sorry you ever laid eyes on *this* black face."

Mary looked at Tracy with a scowl, then turned and walked away, her papers still in hand.

"Just like I thought, now who's punking who *bitch*," Tracy spat after her with an unnatural emphasis on *bitch*. She finally looked away from Mary's back and saw the several people who were watching.

Tracy was now extremely annoyed. She had let Mary get the best of her. She was as good as gone from that job. Not only did she curse out a senior in front of other seniors, she had been caught red-handed making a personal call on business time. She stood up and thought about a real showdown with Mary, since she was probably fired anyway, and might not ever get another opportunity. But then she thought about how beating up a white woman in a corporate building would be a definite one way ticket to felony-ville. She decided not to keep Mike waiting any longer.

On the ride down on the crowded elevator, Tracy tried to calm herself but all she kept thinking about was Mary and what had just went down. She couldn't afford to lose her job! This couldn't be happening!

"She set me up!" she screamed outloud suddenly. Everyone in the elevator jumped. She was finished at Eli.

Nowadays, Tracy's only friend in the world to talk to was Mike, who seemed to always know the right thing to say to get her back in a good mood.

"Tracy, I've got some bad news," Mike said sadly as Tracy entered his car. "Something came up—I can't take you out babe."

"Huh?" Tracy looked at him in horror at his words.

"Just kiddinggg," Mike joked. He was trying to keep her spirits up with a little joke, but that had done the exact opposite. The last thing she needed was to hear she had gone and lost her job over a date with him, and now there was no date. "You know I don't put nobody before my baby."

Tracy smiled at his last statement, but she wanted to cry. "Don't do that."

"You are so beautiful," he commented in response.

Mike took Tracy to Applebees to celebrate their anniversary. Tracy devoured her steak and shrimp combo, and Mike had gone with the ribs special. Tracy was quiet most of the meal. She didn't want to tell Mike that she was about to lose her job.

"What is wrong with you Princess?" Mike asked for the fiftieth time.

"I said nothing, damn! Get off my back," Tracy said with much attitude.

"I don't know what the fuck your problem is Tracy, but I ain't having so good a week either. I'm trying to be nice," Mike said, returning the tone.

"When did you say you had to go away again?" Tracy ignored what Mike said and asked with the same attitude in her voice as she sipped on her frozen margarita.

"In a couple weeks. I gotta go visit some relatives," Mike answered.

"Where at?" Tracy asked.

"In Rochester, I told you all of this," Mike said, trying not to sound too impatient. This was the third time she asked about his impending trip.

"And you're sure you'll only be gone for a few days, right?" Tracy wanted him to confirm.

"I'm positive."

"You sure you ain't just gonna be hanging out, making runs with your drug dealer friends?" Tracy said spitefully.

"Nah, but if you want I can go swing by and give your cokehead friends a visit," Mike snapped back.

Tracy stopped chewing and looked at him with contempt, the words splitting her heart like a dagger. Mike looked up and immediately realized he was wrong.

"Baby, my bad, that—"

"I've gotta go to the bathroom, I'll be back," Tracy said sadly, and Mike was at a loss for words.

Tracy splashed cold water over her face several times to bring herself back. She didn't like the image of herself she was seeing in the mirror. Beautiful—what was Mike talking about? She looked more like the before picture in a cosmetics infomercial. She thought about that snide remark from him and wished she had never told him what happened in LA.

After the blowup at the hotel, Tracy had stayed by herself in Los Angeles until her train left. On the entire miserable ride on the train home from LA, Tracy had hardly even left her room for fear that some kind of event would go down. As far as she was concerned, the universe was against her. When she switched trains, she went to the same coffee shop in Chicago she had been to before, hoping to grasp a little of the serenity the old lady she had been chatting with before had given her. But there was no serenity and no old lady—only nervousness and anxiety in the shop when she sensed that two other people drinking coffee were looking at her way too often.

During the trip she spoke to Mike a lot on the phone, and he comforted her about what she had learned about Rachel and Joy.

When she had arrived back in NY, and after making several unsuccessful attempts to resolve the beef with Kamira, Tracy had firmly decided to never call or speak to her 'so-called friends' ever again. When they got back, Kamira wouldn't even accept Tracy's calls because she really believed Tracy had actually sicked someone on Karif. Karif had since left New York and no one knew where he was. Kamira's dreams of marrying a stock broker were dashed. Tracy left Kamira a message, trying to explain that she had no idea what had happened, but it wasn't enough. Now, Kamira spent more time with Rachel and Joy in Long Island, and Tracy had a suspicion of why. They had pushed her out of their little coke clique. Kamira was probably doing it too.

But still, Tracy was surprised when after two weeks, not one, absolutely none of her three friends made an attempt to call her and apologize. Or at least talk. Tracy was beginning to feel hurt, and alone.

If they want it like that, they got it like that, Tracy thought.

Then a thought crossed Tracy's mind that made her whole body quiver as if she were in a snowstorm with no clothes on. What if Mike wasn't genuine; what if he too was against her. She had never thought of Mike that way, but these days with her friends of close to fifteen years betraying her, how could she really trust a man she had only met months ago? She still didn't even know exactly what it was he did for money. As quickly as she let it fall in, she let it fall out of her mind. Mike was the only person who understood her—and he showed it time and time again.

Tracy tripped on her way out of the bathroom and almost fell flat on her face. Some of the waiters saw her and chuckled.

She stopped and eyed them down. "It wouldn't be funny if I fell, sued Applebee's, and caused all of you dumb asses to lose your jobs, now would it?"

They looked at her as if she were joking, but when they saw her expression remain the same they saw that she wasn't *even* playing.

Tracy went back over to her table and saw Mike gazing up at her like a dog that lost it's owner.

"I'm sorry baby," Mike grabbed her hand. "I was dead wrong."

"It's alright. I was trippin'," Tracy admitted.

When they finished their meal, Tracy wanted to go hit a bar, but Mike had different plans.

"I booked us a room at the Marriot in Jersey," he said proudly.

"You did?" Tracy looked surprised.

"Yup, and you know they have nice rooms. I can't wait to get you there."

"Oh wow, that sounds nice!" Tracy was genuinely excited. Her mood was changing.

"You gonna strip for me again?" Mike asked as he leaned forward and bit his lip at the thought. He loved it when they roll played.

"I'll think about it," Tracy smiled shyly. "Can I go home first and change?"

"Sure," Mike answered, breaking his nasty thoughts. "Trace, you know I love you right?"

Tracy bent her head to the side and looked at Mike thoughtfully. "Yes. And I love you too."

"Come on then," Mike said, grabbing her hand, but just before they had a chance to stand, they were interrupted.

"Tracy? I thought that was you. Hey." Tracy looked up and her worst nightmare came true. It was Reggie. He was standing in front of their table casually with his hands in his pockets.

"Umm, yea, hey," she said reluctantly as she glanced at Mike from the corner of her eye. She couldn't believe this was happening.

"I see you're at our place?" Reggie said, disrespectfully.

"Can I help you?" Mike didn't skip a beat. His chest popped out like a peacock.

"I'm Reggie," he offered his hand for Mike to shake, but Mike just looked at it as if his hand were covered in scabies.

Reggie played it off and continued in his mission to get under Tracy's skin. He was boiling at the discovery that Tracy was seeing someone else that good-looking, even though he hadn't been with Tracy for months.

"So why haven't you returned my calls?" Reggie asked Tracy blatantly, right under Mike's piercing glare. Mike looked as if he were going to lose it for real.

"Beat it Reggie," Tracy said, shaking her head. "We haven't been together for close to a year, and I'm completely over your ass. Come on baby."

"A year? Come on now Tra—" Reggie began but was interrupted.

"Yo, what's your name again ock?" Mike asked as he got up from the table, his muscles bulging. It looked like a nature show, with two males flexing and letting off pheromones to show their superiority in front of the female.

"I don't know if that's any of your fucking business at this point, brah," Reggie shot back, trying to look as hard as Mike.

"Ohhhh. But you were so ready to tell me a second ago, when you thought I wouldn't get up and knock your ass out in the middle of this restaurant?"

"Come on Mike!" Tracy mediated as she pulled him towards the exit. Reggie was quiet until she finally seemed to have control over Mike.

"Goodnight Tracy," he said. Mike made a charge back in Reggie's direction, but Reggie had already walked off.

"Reggie you're a loser," Tracy yelled out to confirm what he probably already knew.

"Y'alls place?" Mike repeated what he heard Reggie say earlier.

"It's nothing baby, please. You know how dudes can be sometimes. It's all about you."

The start of their night at the Marriot wasn't as romantic as Tracy had pictured it. Mike had been so mad on the drive there that he totally forgot to take Tracy home to change out of her work clothes.

"How many times that nigga called you?" Mike grilled her.

"I don't fucking know," she said from her spot on the bed. She felt like a little kid being 'talked to.' He had been interviewing her like this for the past hour.

"Why ain't you tell me that some fool was calling you?"

"I didn't think it was that big of a deal, and it isn't," Tracy replied.

"I could have shook him off a long time ago, you know?"

"I know, but like I said, he's a nobody."

"I thought you said I could trust you Tracy," Mike groaned.

"You can Mike, please don't make a bigger deal out of this than it needs to be!" Tracy suddenly broke out in a fit of tears. "It's not my fault!"

Mike was stone silent as he listened to her sob for a long time. He finally melted. "I'm sorry baby, please don't cry."

"Do you realize how much trouble you've gotten me into! My best friend won't even speak to me because she thinks *I* made you go after her boyfriend!"

"I told you baby, that wasn't me."

"Stop lying Mike, I know it was you. It had to be. Who else would have done that?"

"Tracy from what you told me, that dude was a dickhead. He probably has a lot of enemies."

"Whatever." Tracy wiped away her tears and lay back on the bed. She thought about how Mike would have even been able to find out about Karif in the first place.

The tables had turned, and now Mike was feeling bad. He watched Tracy, her eyes closed tightly, and suddenly wished he hadn't taken revenge on weak ass Karif.

"I just want to relax. I don't have any friends right now Mike and I—" Tracy was at a loss of words.

"It's okay, baby, it's okay," Mike shushed her and leaned down over the bed to give her a kiss. "It's gonna be okay."

He started to unzip her tan slacks and caressed her hips as he slid them down over her thighs. When he had her pants off, he pushed her back further on the bed and slowly lifted her legs up until they were at a 90 degree angle. Tracy braced herself. He held them like that as he kissed and licked the back of her thighs.

"Oooo, Mike," Tracy moaned and jumped at each touch of his lips. All of her tears disappeared momentarily.

Mike stopped for a moment to reach over with one hand to switch on the clock radio, while the other hand held Tracy's legs in the air. After he finally had it tuned to 107.5 for some slow jams, he put his hands between Tracy's thighs and separated them until they were at a near split. He loved how flexible Tracy was. He reached in his jeans pocket and pulled a switchblade out, which with a flick of the wrist transformed into a deadly weapon. Tracy opened her eyes just in time to see him lowering the knife to her snatch. She didn't even have time to screech or protest.

Mike used the knife to slice Tracy's thong underwear off. Her panties had turned into a belt that fast. Tracy was mortified, but turned on more than she had ever been in her life. Sometimes Mike was so controlling and unpredictable during sex that it scared Tracy, but that was what really turned her on the most about him. Taking control in the bedroom used to be her M.O., but now she had met her match. Tracy let her head fall back to the bed and sighed as she stared up at the ceiling.

Mike held her legs open and wouldn't let her move as he teased and pecked at her clitoris. He couldn't stand for her to come too fast, so he would agitate it for no more than a minute before letting it go and kissing elsewhere—her thighs, her lips, her lower belly. After about a half an hour he finally decided to let her come. Her entire body burst upward in an explosion of ecstasy when she realized that he wasn't letting her clit go this time. Tears ran down Tracy's face as she felt herself coming. She yelped out as she tried to wiggle away from Mike, but he held her down. When her body relaxed again, she wiped the tears away and trembled as she awaited Mike's next command.

Mike never really like screwing on the bed; he was very unconventional. He decided tonight it would happen on the wall closest to the window, right above the heater. After strapping up with a condom, he picked Tracy up and threw her back up against the wall hard, just like she liked it, and immediately jabbed himself into her soft, wet opening. He was supporting her entire weight with ease. Tracy screamed as if she wanted the cops to come. She opened her eyes and watched his buttocks move in and out in the mirror across the room. He was really doing his thing tonight. She didn't want it to end. They kept going at it like that through about five slow songs on the clock radio.

Suddenly Mike grabbed Tracy by her hair and pulled her head back as far as it could go. He rested his forehead on her neck as he groaned and climaxed for what seemed like an eternity. When he finally finished, he held Tracy with one arm as he slowly let them both sink down to the floor to rest. He lay back on the carpet and let her fall on top of him. Tracy was in heaven. Mike's eyes were closed as he breathed heavily. As Tracy looked up at him from her place on his chest, she figured that he had been threatened by Reggie's presence at the restaurant earlier, and felt the need to throw down even harder than usual to prove his supremacy over one of Tracy's exes. In Tracy's mind, there was no one that was comparing to Mike—he had it all. And he would never have to worry about another man coming between them in life, especially not Reggie's tired ass.

Chapter 17

Mrs. Moretti parked her Jaguar on the street outside of Mrs. Samuel's house. She was dressed down in a pair of jeans and a simple cotton blouse, because she knew how Mrs. Samuels could get sometimes.

There was a time when Mrs. Moretti believed Tracy's mom was jealous of the fact that all of the girls would spend all their time at her house instead of Tracy's when they were kids. Mrs. Samuels assumed it was because Tracy's friends actually believed Tracy when she accused her mom of trying to poison her at dinner, *Flowers in the Attic* style. Of course, that was completely false.

Ding Dong. Tracy's mom heard the bell ring and wondered who could be bothering her that early in the morning on a Sunday while she was watching her favorite pastor, Paul Jones, on television preaching his heart out.

It couldn't be Tracy, because she had stopped going out to Wyandanch on weekends to see her hairstylist Risha after she went in again and Risha called out an hour after her appointment was supposed to start. But in reality, that didn't mean it couldn't be Tracy at the door.

Mrs. Samuels didn't know whether to be upset or relieved when she saw that it was Rachel's mother Mrs. Moretti at the door; not Tracy. She hesitated before opening the door and letting her inside.

"How are you doing Terri," Mrs. Moretti greeted and gave her a small hug. She could hear the sounds of Paul Jones preaching loudly from the television. Mrs. Samuels fake hugged her back, and invited her in.

"I'm doing alright Sandra, how are you?" Mrs. Samuels said politely.

"I'm fine, just coming from church services. I figured I'd stop by," she said as she sat down where Mrs. Samuels directed.

"Coffee?" Mrs. Samuels asked as she turned the volume down on the television.

"Sure."

When they were settled, they had small talk and reminisced on the last time they had seen each other, about three years before at Tracy's graduation.

"I've actually been concerned about Tracy lately, have you spoken to her about the incident that happened in LA?" Mrs. Moretti asked.

Mrs. Samuels looked at her with her eyebrows up, looking confused. "LA? As in Los Angeles?"

"Yes, the trip the girls took a few weeks ago."

"Tracy went on a trip to Los Angeles and didn't tell me?" Mrs. Samuels was visibly hurt and upset. She rolled her eyes. "I can't believe her!"

"Oh Terri. I had no idea you didn't know. The girls took a week long trip to Los Angeles to reconnect with each other, but there was a falling out. The girls told me that Tracy had a fit and attacked Kamira, my daughter, and Joy."

"Oh my God," Mrs. Samuels clutched her shirt together and listened.

"Terri, I don't want to step over my boundaries, but can I ask you, have you tried getting help for Tracy's…problem?"

Something flared in Mrs. Samuels, and she was tempted to curse this woman out for getting in her family's business, but the good sense in her told her to stop lying to herself. "We tried, but she stopped going. She thought the psychotherapist was out to get her, and accused her of being a racist."

Mrs. Moretti let the information sink in, and then reached over to grab Mrs. Samuels hand. "I think she's getting worse Terri, we've got to do something about it. She's beginning to get more and more violent. Kamira told me that she was beating up some girl at a baseball game. She can end up getting into some serious trouble."

"I try to tell her Sandra, time and time again. But she stopped listening to me years ago, ever since her father died," Mrs. Samuels began to get choked up. This conversation was kind of therapeutic for her; it felt good to get all of the problems she had been having with Tracy out on the table with someone.

"I'm willing to help if necessary in finding her the best psychotherapist out there. I have a good friend that works at Good Samaritan who can give me a good reference, and possibly a discounted rate for services."

"Well, money is not the issue," Mrs. Samuels looked at Rachel's mother sideways, feeling slightly insulted. "I want the best for Tracy."

"I think you misunderstood me," Mrs. Moretti tried to clean up. "Anyway, that's not the real issue here. I just wanted to see if I could do anything to help Tracy before things get worse."

"But you're implying that I haven't already done everything I could to help her Sandra, and I have," Mrs. Samuel's tone was changing. She had always been secretly envious of Sandra Moretti's money and lifestyle. When Mrs. Samuels and her husband lived back in the projects in Queens, she was always the most well off wife due to her husband's successful carpentry business, but in Long Island it was a different story. And now for Mrs. Moretti to assume she needed a discount, as if she were some type of welfare story, made her angry. Her eyes glazed over and she stopped caring about the important issue at hand—

Tracy.

"There's got to be someone out there that can talk to her, a professional, and get through—" Mrs. Moretti tried to salvage the conversation.

"You know Sandra, I've heard what you have to say. I'll give you a call if I need you, but I really don't think all of this is necessary," Tracy's mom said as she got up to signify to Mrs. Moretti that it was time for her to go.

Rachel's mom stood up, defeated, and walked in front of Tracy's mom to the door. She turned around once more and gave Tracy's mom a hug. It was the fakest, most insincere hug in history.

"Terri, I really hope you will reconsider and give me a call," she reached in her purse and pulled out a card. "Here's my number."

"Thank you Sandra, but like I said, I really don't think I'll need it," Tracy's mom said abruptly and closed the door on Mrs. Moretti. She flicked the card to the side and it flew behind a stack of boxes near the stairs.

"Rich Long Island bitches," she said under her breath and went back to watching her Christian television show.

"…And what we need most today, is an understanding heart," the pastor on TV bellowed out. "Jesus was understanding of the woman who was to be stoned for her adulterous ways. And she was caught right in the act. I tell you today, that if Jesus can have love for his brothers and sisters, regardless of their sins, we can do the same!"

"Praise Jesus!" Mrs. Samuels shouted from her seat and threw her hands up in the air. She lowered her head and shook it from side to side to show her approval. "Hallelujah!! That's right pastor, preach!"

* * *

"I'm trying to tell you, this was no robbery!" Karif's face had turned beet red from embarrassment and anger at the way the police were treating him.

"Some guys came to your house, stopped you on the street, you lifted your hand to hit one, and they shot you, took your bag and left. Sounds like a robbery to me," the obnoxious detective said smugly.

"No! The guy told me to hit him. He wanted me to hit him!" Karif tried to explain, but they weren't trying to hear him.

"Oh I see. And tell me again why you waited two weeks to report this son?" the detective, who couldn't have been over 40, asked in a patronizing tone.

"I'm not your son," Karif said with his mouth screwed up. "And I told you. He knew where I lived, so I moved to Hartford first—I didn't want to rat on him, and then he comes to my house to kill me completely. I mean, he shot me once, he'd do it again!"

The detective couldn't wipe the smirk off of his face. In his mind, the guilty party was probably sitting right in front of him. He had probably been a part of some kind of drug deal gone wrong, and now that he was out of the food chain, he was over here in the station trying to rat people out for revenge. He had seen Karif's type many times before—they posed as good, honest, working types, but were really cold criminals. He was probably guilty of something.

"*Son*," he exaggerated. "You don't even know what the guy's name is, the license plate of his car, even a good description. How am I supposed to find this *culprit*?"

"I told you, he has something to do with my ex-girlfriend, Kamira Rodriguez. She used to live at 2020 S. 1st Street, Apartment 3A, the Lower East Side. And her mother lives in

Long Island. You can start with her, she knows. She's in on it, I'm telling you. And he was driving a blue Chevy, license plate GTG 346 I think."

"And I told you, that's not a valid plate number in New York. You're missing a digit."

"That's kind of messed up, don't you think?" another police officer asked. "Giving up your girlfriend like that?"

"She ain't my girl no more," Karif confirmed and held up his bandaged palm. "Not after she did what she did. Look at my hand!"

"Sure that ain't from too much jerking off?" the police officer said with a straight face. They were just fucking with him at this point.

"So, I'm going to put this in my report," the detective said as he scribbled something on a piece of paper. *Karif Sanborn, Hartford, CT*, it said. "If anything comes up, we'll let you know."

"That's it?"

"That's it. You have a good day Mr. Sanborn. And stay out of trouble. Officer Smith will show you the way out."

The detective got up and led Karif to the door. He gave one last smirk before shutting the door in his face.

Chapter 18

Mike rubbed his head to ease the pain throbbing against his temples. He hadn't had a headache that bad in months. He was hungry.

He knew the door would be unlocked. He pushed it open and went inside, hoping that there would be no static today.

"Moon, that you?" a girl called out from the back and appeared a few seconds later. The apartment was filled with the sounds of D'Angelo playing from the stereo. "I've been waiting for hours, what took you so long?"

"My fault, I had to make a run," Mike explained and opened his arms wide for her to enter. She came over and gave him a big hug.

"I heard it Janet still ain't come back," she said to him sympathetically. "Trust me, I been hittin' up all my people on the Hill. They got their ear to the pavement. I'll let you know if they hear something."

"Good lookin' C," Mike nodded his head and let her lead him to the kitchen to get something to eat.

"Celia!" her grandmother called out from the back. "Mija, venga y ayudame con la ropa sucia."

"No mommy, I got guests! Leave me alone," she complained.

"Necesito ayuda Celia!" her mother screamed back.

Celia finished microwaving a leftover plate of chicken and rice with plantains and slid it over to Mike on the table. She grabbed a big glass and filled it with red koolaid. "My bad, you know she ain't gonna bother us. So you still need me to do that thing?"

"No, things changed. I got a better idea. That shit will be easier," Mike said, grubbing on the food as if there was a diamond hidden inside. "It should be a done deal on New Year's."

"Yo, imagine if you was doing all of this for nothing," Celia laughed at the thought. "That would be fucked up if she didn't even have nothing."

"Don't even say that shit," Mike shook his head and shoved a piece of plantain in his mouth.

"I'm just sayin' yo, how you know she got dough like that?" Celia asked curiously.

"Her fam live out in LI, in a big ass house, I seen it. And she got a job at one of those huge ass corporations downtown. Plus, I peeped her jewelry box. She got at least $2,000 worth of shit in there," he counted on his fingers.

"Why ain't you snatch the shit then?" Celia's ears perked up at the sound of the word 'jewelry'.

"Cause if it suddenly came up missing from her apartment she'd probably trip—I told you she was throwed off. The only one she be letting in her apartment is me, so she'd put two and two together. Plus, I know I can bag more than that off this chick. She got money, trust me."

"Okay, if you say so. But I seen that beat up Hyundai she be drivin'," she said, letting the thought linger in the air.

Mike and Celia had known each other for over a decade, but had only been dating seriously for a year. They were a con team; they made most of their money gagging stupid, desperate girls out of their money and then disappearing. Mike was irresistible to them, and Celia would usually be the one to take their shit. Usually they would get girls that worked downtown and lived outside of the Bronx, but when Mike first saw Tracy walking home from work one day, he knew that she was a potentially easy target.

"Imma get at least like 10 G's off this broad, watch," Mike said with assurance. "I already got her account numbers, but I still need that ID, and we can drain them credit cards. She be holdin' onto that purse like a second skin."

"But geez, four months you been schemin' on this bitch, and you still couldn't even get her ID. I'm gettin' tired of sharin' you with that ho," Celia grumbled. "Plus I been feenin' to get a chance to stomp on that ass since the Yankees game."

Mike started laughing at the mention of the Yankees game. "Yooo, don't get me started."

"Imma bust you upside your head if you do, that bitch had a lucky shot," Celia became defensive.

"I'll give it to her though, she got a hell of a knock out punch for yo ass!" Mike laughed. "But seriously, I wanna do this right you know? I know this chick will call the cops in a heart beat so she can't know it was me. Besides four months is worth 10 stacks to me. Plus a lil tight pussy on the side don't never hurt."

Celia punched him in his back. "Nigga you buggin'. Don't be talkin' about that shit around me."

Mike turned around and smacked the taste out of Celia's mouth as he stood up from the stool. "Next time I'll knock your ass out like Tracy did, and you won't be gettin' up for *days*."

Celia held her face in shock. Though she had been hit by Mike before, it was never so sudden. "Shit, my bad Moon. I'm just saying…"

Mike glared at her hatefully, and then sat back down on his stool to continue his meal. Celia went to the back and soon after started arguing with her grandmother.

After four months, Mike had to admit, he was starting to actually like Tracy. She was crazy for sure, but he liked how thorough she was. And he also had to admit that Tracy wasn't the only one with paranoid ways—he himself had his moments of watching his back and looking over his shoulder one too many times, especially out there in those streets. And most especially now with this whole feud with his sister's boyfriend Jimmy going on. What was ironic about the whole situation was that Tracy was paranoid about everybody and anything except him, when he was probably her biggest threat. He couldn't help but feel a little guilty about that.

Chapter 19

Joy sat on the phone dialing his number for the hundreth time. But it would just ring and ring until the voicemail picked up.

"Why won't his ass just pick up the phone!" she screamed. She had tried calling him from her house phone, but that didn't work. She had to assume that he was screening all calls from Long Island area codes—516 and 631.

For the first time in over five years, Joy was in love. She had tried, time and time again to forget this dude, but she just couldn't get him out of her mind.

He was tall, strong, nonchalant, and sexy. And light-skinned, just like she liked her men.

She had slept with him on the very first night, something that went totally against all of her rules, but she couldn't resist. The moment he kissed her she knew that she was hooked—those plump red lips explored her face, ears, and neck, and made her feel giddy with excitement. Not to mention the fire weed and coke that he had supplied her and Rachel with the last time she saw him. It was the kind of stuff that fiends lost their minds over. Besides good dick and weed, she didn't know anything else about him except that he was from the Bronx and drove a black Ac.

She dialed his number again and this time it went directly to voicemail.

"Oooo!" she screamed and waited for the annoying white lady to finish telling her to leave a message.

"You have reached the automated voicemail box of *'Moon'*. At the sound of the tone, please leave your message. *Beep*."

"I don't know why you're acting like this. I need to see you," is all Joy said, her tone hopeless and desperate, and then dropped her cordless phone on the bed. She put her head into her hands and started sobbing. This was even worse than how Mark, the white guy she had been dating for the past month, had done her.

Why couldn't she be more like Rachel, the player, who had at least five different guys calling her phone every day? Rachel was the one who got sweated—not the other way around. Joy had no problem catching them, but it was keeping them that was the problem. Maybe it was because Rachel was white, and blonde, and rich, and all of that. Joy hid it well, but was highly insecure, not only about her looks, and her family situation, but also because of the color of her skin. She feared that her dark skin, height, and skinny body would prevent her from ever getting the man that she really wanted.

But what she didn't realize is that everyone around her envied her—especially Rachel. They wished they had her rich brown skin shade, and tall, lanky physique. Rachel regularly visited tanning salons and took expensive growth pills that claimed to add up to four inches to your height. But instead it seemed as if she had gotten even shorter. Tracy had once sat out in the sun for four hours straight, trying to achieve the same skin tone as Joy, if even for just one day. She figured at a tan complexion, she was already halfway there.

Joy's house phone rang suddenly, and she jumped for it, hoping and praying that it was Mike. Ever since the day she met him in front of Tracy's job, she knew she had to have him. He called her the following week and they hooked up that same day for dinner at a Chinese restaurant in the city. That same night they were at a motel in Queens, nearly breaking the flimsy headboard.

"Hello?" she asked on the first ring, not bothering to check caller ID.

"Hey you," Rachel said wearily.

"Why didn't you just call me on my cellphone!" Joy snapped. She was highly annoyed at the sound of her friend's voice because it was not Mike's.

Rachel was silent for awhile. Ever since they returned from Los Angeles, Joy had been acting like a complete bitch. And she was using more too. "I just called to say hi, is that alright with you?"

"No, it's not. But anyway, what do you want?"

"Nada damn thing," Rachel said and hung up the phone in her friend's face.

"Whatever bitch," Joy said to no one but the dead phone.

Joy would be the first to admit that she had gotten caught up in a whirlwind. She and Rachel had become socialites on Long Island in a very short time. Rachel was always meeting new people and introducing Joy to them. It was only a matter of time before everyone who was anyone on the young social scene knew who they were.

The first time Joy had gotten lured into trying cocaine was about a year before, at a party thrown by Lara Cohen, the daughter of a real estate mogul who spent most of his time on the West Coast. She had parties at her house almost weekly, and only a select few were invited. It was a tight social circle that was kept that way with childish high school-ish tactics, gossip, and swift punishment for anyone who broke the rules.

Joy felt the pressure that day when one of the richest and most popular eligible bachelors in Port Jefferson, Timmy Wagner, offered her a plate with two lines carefully prepared for her to take in. She reluctantly grabbed the plate and dove headfirst into the lifestyle of the rich and shameless.

The following week Timmy had invited her to his parent's vacation house in the Hamptons. They had hooked up that weekend, and even though the sex was trash, she gave it up to him three times. His penis was so small that she was surprised he could truly be called a male of the species. After that weekend he never called her again, and when she saw him at parties, he completely ignored her. That was a huge blow to Joy's self-esteem and she became more and more mistrustful of this 'scene' that Rachel had gotten her into. But still, she was a participant, because she was too afraid to know what it would be like to not be a part of the 'it' crowd.

When Tracy had caught her using drugs in Los Angeles, Joy was devastated. At first she was annoyed, bothered by the fact that Tracy felt it was her business what she did behind closed doors. But as time went along, Joy was feeling more and more guilty. Tracy was right—Joy had no business doing coke just to 'belong' in a group of people. And Tracy had every right to call her out on it—they had been friends for as long as Joy could remember. Tracy always had Joy's back in school, when girls picked on her for being too cute or for stealing their boyfriends. Joy had been an athlete all throughout her high school career, and was even a member of the school's anti-drug committee. It was ironic that at 25, she had finally succumbed to peer pressure.

Joy got up and locked her bedroom door. She hated it when her mom came barging into her room. She opened her bottom drawer and pulled out the small stash she kept there along with her plate and blade. It wasn't as good as the cut Mike had given her, but it would do. She poured a little out on a plate and started chopping it up. She snorted up the two lines and then started thinking of the sensation Mike's hard thickness had given her the last time he was over. *Now that's a man*, she thought. She sprinkled a little more out on the plate and got to snorting again. Then she put the plate aside, leaned back on her soft pillows and spread her legs as wide as they would go, letting her fingers find their ultimate destination.

Chapter 20

It was New Year's Eve and Tracy was excited to be spending the holiday with Mike. She wasn't thrilled about the idea of going to his friend Chewy's house to celebrate, but as long as Mike was going to be there she figured she could relax. When they came in the house was already packed.

"Mooon," Bowen came up to his boy and slapped hands. "You was 'bout to miss the ball drop."

"Yea, I know man, what time is it?" Mike asked as he went for his cellphone.

"11:41," Bowen answered for him. "Chewy said everybody go ahead in the kitchen and grab a glass of champ."

Bowen's smile faded when Tracy and Mike turned around to head towards the kitchen. He had a feeling something was going to go down that night, but wasn't for sure, and even so there was nothing he could do about it at that point. He had tried to say something to Tracy. And when it came right down to it, his loyalty rested with his boys.

At 11:59 everyone was standing in front of the television watching the Times Square ball drop.

"10…9…8…7…" everybody screamed in unison. Most were already so drunk that they could barely stand as they counted down to 1.

"Happy New Year!" they shouted. Mike grabbed Tracy by her shirt and pulled her in for a kiss. Tracy was in heaven as she sucked and kissed on his plump lips. They tasted sweet like the Henny he had been sipping on all night.

Later on about half of the people at the party left to go to clubs, and the other half were in various parts of the house chilling. Mike and Tracy had resigned to a room in the back where there was a large futon. Mike got up and went to the kitchen again to grab them both another drink.

Mike's boy Rob came in with a freshly rolled blunt with Mike right behind him. Mike passed Tracy her new, bubbly glass of champagne.

"Yo y'all tryin' to hit that?" Rob asked as he held up the blunt.

"You want a toke?" Mike asked Tracy, who was already one drink away from being intoxicated. "Come on, give my girl the first hit. She don't really like smoking after people."

"Mike!" Tracy looked at him in surprise. "That's not nice to say."

"Fuck ever, these niggas don't care," he answered and lit the blunt for Tracy. She took a long drag from the blunt and laid her head back on the futon. The blunt crackled and popped a little, causing Tracy to look at it funny.

"Why is it popping like that when I pull from it?" she asked.

"That's that good shit right there," Mike nodded. She took another long drag and held out the blunt for Mike.

"Naw, pass it that way," he instructed and got up to go to the bathroom. "I'll be right back, don't worry. You cool?"

"Yea, I'm good," Tracy said as her eyelids got heavier. She looked around at the few other people in the room who were talking to each other casually.

The last thing Tracy remembered seeing before passing out was Bowen's face out in the hallway, looking at her sideways.

* * *

The pair of hands came out of nowhere, from behind. They

started choking Tracy mercilessly. Tracy opened her mouth to scream but nothing came out. The harder she tried to fight, the stronger their hold became.

She felt her eyes begin to bug out of her head as she scratched and pawed at the hands to get free. She looked up and saw a small mirror on the wall. She strained her eyes to see who was behind her, determined to end her life. At least she could know who killed her. All she could see was the hands and her own terrified reflection. As she felt her last few breaths escaping her body, she did something she hadn't done in years—pray. She asked God to please forgive her sins and to let this torture end now. She relaxed her hands as she felt the lifeforce leaving her body…

Tracy's eyes shot open and became fixated on the unfamiliar ceiling. She sat up and looked around, but had to lower her head because of the incredible aching feeling in her head. When her head finally stopped pounding, she looked around and saw that Mike was asleep in a chair on the other side of the room.

"Mike," Tracy called out. "Mike!"

Mike opened his eyes slowly and stretched before getting up and going over to Tracy on the futon.

"Damn baby, you was knocked out. That blunt had you on your ass," Mike said as he stroked Tracy's hair down into place. "I had to get my boy to let us have the room."

"What time is it?" Tracy asked as she searched around for her purse.

Mike pulled his cellphone out of his pocket. "8:31."

"In the morning? You let me sleep over here? I don't even know these people!" Tracy was starting to get upset. She found her coat on the floor near the futon, but didn't see her purse yet.

"It's cool Princess—I know these folks. Besides, you with

me. You know you ain't gotta worry 'bout nothin'," Mike assured her and then got up to use the bathroom.

"Where's my purse?" Tracy said to herself as she got down on her knees and looked under the futon. She moved some pillows and other things around and saw her small Louis Vuitton purse sitting there. "Thank God."

"Come on Princess," Mike rushed her.

As they were making their way outside, Tracy's cellphone started going off. She was shocked, because the only person that called her those days was Mike, and he was standing right there. She pulled the phone and her house keys out of the inside pocket of her coat. Mike scrunched up his face when he saw this—he had wanted those keys.

When she read the caller ID and saw that it was her mother, she put the phone on silent and kept walking.

As Tracy trudged up the stairs, she knew that she would be going right back to sleep. She was so tired. She pouted about the fact that Mike couldn't come up; she had been badly wanting to get some that previous night. As she walked down the hall, she slowed down when she saw something strange on her door.

The phrase "Snitch Bitch" was written in what looked like yellow chalk all over her front door.

"What the hell?" she said as she traced the chalk with her fingertips and tried to wipe it off. Even when she wiped at it, there was still a trace left on the red paint. Tracy looked frantically down both sides of the hall to make sure no one was watching her. When she saw that the coast was clear she fumbled with her keys and quickly let herself inside.

She couldn't think of anyone *she* had snitched on. She didn't even know anyone out there besides Mike *to* snitch on. After some thought she figured that whoever did it had made a mistake, and written on the wrong door. Or it was just a random vandal—there was other graffiti on the walls in her hall. She would have to call the apartment management on Monday to get it cleaned or repainted. But she knew that it was a shot in the dark that they would actually respond to this maintenance request.

Tracy threw her purse down on her couch and went right to the kitchen to get a drink of water. She had so wanted Mike to come in and hang out with her, but he told her that he had to go to his grandmother's house to spend time on New Year's Day.

She sat down on her bed and flicked on the television. She fell asleep again, watching an old episode of MacGyver.

When Tracy woke again, she was angry at herself for sleeping so late. She had wanted to do some grocery shopping for food while it was still light outside, but now it was going on 4pm.

She rushed to get dressed so that she could make it outside and back before it got dark. She grabbed her purse off the couch and hustled out of the apartment. But then she came back in to grab her switchblade out of the drawer and place it in her back pocket. Just in case that vandalism wasn't a mistake after all.

At the grocery store, Tracy didn't stop to look at prices or sales, she just grabbed what she wanted as quickly as possible, watching the time. The total came to $102.59.

Tracy opened her purse to get her debit card, but all she saw was a lipstick and mascara sitting at the bottom.

"What?" she said to herself as she rummaged through the two items as if her wallet possibly had become invisible and would magically appear. "Where the fuck is my wallet?"

She looked up at the cashier helplessly and tried to think of where her wallet could have gone. Then she remembered the New Year's Eve party.

"Oh, no," she said solemnly as her mind searched all the possibilities. There were at least 50 people at the party when she passed out—anyone could have taken her stuff. "Oh, noooo."

"I have to go look in the car," she mumbled, leaving the cashier and bagger with bags of unpaid food. As she was walking to the automatic doors, she fainted.

* * *

"Where have you been?" Joy screamed the instant that she saw him. Mike casually strolled into Joy's mother's house and started walking towards the stairs as if it were his own home.

"What took you so long to get here??" Joy asked.

Mike just kept walking up the stairs.

"Did you hear me?" Joy yelled again as she came behind him.

"Joy, leave me the hell alone, I'm here right?" he said, not really caring. If she started flipping too much he would just leave, and that would be the last time he saw this chick. "I came all the way the fuck out here to see your ass."

When Joy came to her bedroom door, she watched as Mike sat on the bed and pulled something out of his jacket pocket.

"What's that?" she asked, trying to hide her excitement.

"What you wanted," Mike said with a roll of his eyes as he threw the small baggie on top of her sheets. He looked at her and wondered why her skin was getting so blotchy—it was so smooth and even toned when he met her on the street months ago. That and her legs was what attracted him about her the most. She was also starting to get a little *too* skinny.

"What do you mean?" Joy tried to play it off. They both knew that this was what she had really been feening for all those weeks Mike had been MIA. Mike was smart—after he met Joy downtown, he had quickly put two and two together when they first spoke and she mindlessly started talking about how she lived in Long Island and was only in Manhattan to visit her friend

Tracy…

"Stop being stupid. Come here," Mike told Joy and held his hand out for her to come. "Lock that door first."

"My mom isn't here. She's out of town," Joy replied as she shut the door and obediently came over to Mike.

"Good. What, you wanna do it on her bed or something?" Mike's interest began to peak.

"No. No, I can't do that," Joy shook her head and sat down next to him.

"Why not? Come on," Mike grabbed her hand and yanked her up off of the bed.

"Mike, I said no!" Joy protested as she was nearly dragged out of the room.

"Where's her room?" he demanded that she tell him.

Joy snatched her hand away and started yelling. "I said no! I'm not going to do that in my mom's room!"

Mike looked at her thoughtfully for a few moments. "Alright. Well, I'm outta here then."

He went back into Joy's room and snatched the small pack off of her bed.

"What are you doing?" Joy's eyes grew wide. "You can't go anywhere. No, no, no. Okay Mike, okay!"

"Okay, okay, what?" Mike looked at her again.

"I'll do whatever you want!" Joy surrendered and crossed her arms in defeat.

"Good."

When they arrived at Joy's mother's bedroom, Mike raved at the decorations and even rifled through some of her mother's things. Joy opened her mouth to protest, but shut it again. She had already told him she'd let him do whatever he wanted. She would just clean up before her mother got home from Brazil.

"Mike. This may be a crazy question, but did you have

anything to do with my friend Kamira's boyfriend getting jumped?" Joy couldn't help but remember how she had told Mike everything about how her friend Kamira's boyfriend was hitting her, and how her friends had gotten into an altercation with him at a club.

Mike's eyes were glazed over as he put down a picture that was sitting on a desk nearby. "Didn't I tell you to stop being stupid? Why the hell would I need to do something to your friend's man? That don't even sound right. Long as he didn't hit *you*. I told you he probably got a lot of enemies right?"

That makes sense, Joy guessed in her mind. She was suddenly happy that Mike said "Long as he didn't hit you." That meant that Mike would fight someone over her. *He does love me*, Joy thought and smiled.

Mike stripped down to his boxers and sat on the comfy, expensive, white comforter that Joy's mother loved. Joy cringed when she thought of how her mother would trip if she saw this about to go down. Mike held the package up in front of him between two fingers as he reached into his boxers and pulled out his other, larger package for Joy.

"Now come here and give me what *I* want," he said with a smirk. Joy tried not to look at her baby picture on the wall above her mother's lamp as she fell to her knees.

Chapter 21

The plan was to talk to Tracy a few more times after stealing her wallet, and then disappear or make up an excuse to dump her. But strangely for Mike, he didn't want to let her go so soon. He was loving the sex too much, and actually enjoyed just being around Tracy. He figured he would let the whole theft die down over a few more days, maybe even weeks, and keep Tracy in his stable of women for a minute. All he had to do was keep doing his Oscar-deserving performance of how upset he was that she had lost just about all of her $4,000 savings out of her bank account, the nearly $1,000 in her checking, and $3,000 in charges on her platinum card. Tracy was a wreck.

She was lucky to have kept her house keys in her coat pocket that night, because being that they had her driver's license they would have been able to find and rob her house too. Though Mike kept dating Tracy, he was starting to get tired of hearing about her financial problems.

"The bank says they can't do anything about my savings," Tracy said from her spot on the floor. Her eyes were red and her skin was blotchy and uneven. She was sitting in front of the television sorting through bills in a pile. She was trying to figure out how she was going to pay them with absolutely no money in the bank and her last paycheck coming in a little under two weeks. She was so stressed out that her hair was beginning to fall out.

The week before, two days after New Years Eve, she had called into her job to tell them she needed two extra personal days. Her fear became a reality when one of the admins transferred her to the head admin, who Tracey hated, Sheryl

Cromby.

"Hey Tracy," Sheryl said in a fake, happy voice. She then immediately transferred Tracy over to the HR department. Tracy was no longer an employee of Elias Department Stores Incorporated and was asked not to come to the building anymore or she would be physically removed. She was considered too much of a risk and danger to her co-workers. They would mail her the contents of her desk that week. Tracy considered a plan to sneak into the building as a delivery person and punch Stacey in the neck, just once, and then go strangle Mary to death right in her office on top of the papers she always wanted re-typed so badly. It made Tracy giddy just thinking about it.

"I feel like such an idiot. What the hell was I thinking?" Tracy said and felt like she was going to cry again. She put her fingers in her scalp and held her head down.

Mike sat back on the couch behind her, tight-lipped. He began to feel that familiar twinge of guilt. It sucked that Tracy had lost her job around the same time Mike robbed her, but what was done was done. He wasn't supposed to have developed feelings for Tracy, but it happened. He was starting to feel as if he had picked a bad target.

"Princess, it's alright. You'll get back," Mike assured her. "Life is just like that sometimes."

* * *

On her way back home from work the following week, Tracy decided to go to the bodega to get a $2 turkey hoagie. It was either that or oodles of noodles that night. She had made a firm decision that she would only use $1,000 off of her credit cards to pay her rent and immediate necessities until she found another job. She really didn't want to get even more drowned in debt.

Out of everything that had gone wrong for Tracy in the past month, there was one thing that was bothering her more than anything. She couldn't understand why throughout this whole ordeal, and as a matter of fact throughout their entire relationship, Mike still hadn't offered to help her out with money. He was supposed to be her man, but when it came to money he was one of the stingiest brothers she'd ever met. Even Reggie's cheap ass had given her a five dollar bill to get some snacks from the store a couple of times. She figured it must have been because he was hustlin' rather than working a regular job. Maybe, as well connected he was on the streets, he didn't have as much money as she first thought he would. And at least he took her out to eat from time to time.

She had also been wondering lately how and why Mike didn't put her purse up after she passed out at the house, to protect her from being robbed. There were so many strangers there that even he didn't know. But then again, she figured that someone could have taken it while Mike was in the bathroom.

Tracy stepped inside of the bodega and let the smell of dry old fruit waft up her nose. The old dusty products on the shelf made it clear to her that this store wasn't just in the business of groceries. She walked to the back and ordered a hoagie.

"No more turkey," the young guy behind the counter told her.

"What? You ran out of turkey?" Tracy looked at him wearily. "How do you run out of turkey and you're in a deli?"

The man just looked at her blankly.

Tracy sighed and looked at the signs behind him. "Fine, let me get a roast beef then. How much more is that?"

"$1 more for roast beef," he answered.

Tracy thought about the $10 she had in her pocket to last her until the end of the week. "Let me get that then."

Tracy palmed the $10 bill and the hoagie in her hand and dazed off into space as she walked back up to the front to pay. Her eyes grew wider when she realized she was walking towards Bowen, Mike's friend who she had last seen at New Year's. He looked up from his Newport transaction and saw Tracy glaring at him hatefully.

"Yo, what's up Trace?" he said almost jovially.

Tracy had stopped in the aisle and was eyeing Bowen like a tiger that was about to pounce.

"Trace? You heard me? What's up? What's wrong?" he asked as he grabbed his Newports off the counter.

Tracy let her mind race and instantly remembered seeing Bowen looking at her strangely before she passed out. *He probably was the one who stole my stuff—mad because I didn't want to talk to him at the bar that time.* "Don't even fucking speak to me you bastard."

"Huh? What?" he asked incredulously.

"Don't 'what' me, you know," Tracy said, and looked him up and down.

"I know *what*?" Bowen squinted up his eyes at her.

"I'm not even talking about this," Tracy said adamantly. She stepped forward and waited for Bowen to step aside. "Excuse me."

Bowen backed up a few steps, but was still looking at Tracy as if she had insulted him.

"I said, *excuse* me," Tracy rolled her eyes and said to Bowen. It was becoming harder and harder to contain her anger. She wanted to let loose on Bowen so badly.

"And I moved," Bowen said, starting to become obnoxious. "What is your problem?"

"Give me some space! What, you wanna take my last $10 too?!" Tracy blurted out wildly. She couldn't hold it in any longer. "Here, take it!"

Tracy held the money out for Bowen with her eyes blazing and her nose flaring. It was a good thing she didn't have a gun, because she may have used it at that moment. As far as she could presume, this man standing before her was the reason why she was dead broke.

Tracy could feel the pressure building in her skull as Bowen continued with the stare down. She wished he would just leave her alone but he wouldn't budge. His beady eyes and roach face made her skin crawl. She wished she could do something to hurt him physically. She envisioned herself grabbing a pickle jar and bashing Bowen upside the head with it. But that would be a bad idea. Instead she decided that *she* should just hurry up and leave.

The grocery store clerk looked at Tracy as if she were crazy as she passed him the $10 and paid for her hoagie.

"What the hell are you looking at?" she screamed at the clerk and snatched her change off the counter. She turned and hustled out the door.

"Yo Trace, I don't know what the fuck you are talkin' about, but all I'm gonna say is you need to be careful of who you trust," Bowen said as he followed her outside. "On the strength sis."

Tracy just kept walking, but her ears were perked.

"People ain't always what they seem," Bowen said and then put a Newport on his lip. "That nigga Mike shady."

Tracy started walking faster and turned the corner. She blocked out what Bowen said and went somewhere else in her mind. *He's just trying to make Mike look bad so that he can have a shot at me*, Tracy thought.

Chapter 22

Rachel and Joy were shopping at the Massapequa mall, something they usually didn't do anymore. Massapequa mall used to be their favorite stomping grounds when they were in high school, but now they had graduated to upscale areas such as Fifth Avenue in Manhattan, Saks in Huntington Station, and the outlets for their clothing needs.

"Rach, don't you think we should call and check in on her?" Joy asked out of the blue.

"Who?" Rachel inquired, looking at her friend.

"You know who. Tracy," Joy confirmed Rachel's thoughts.

Rachel was quiet for a while. She had had Tracy on her mind just about every day since the throw down in California. She was feeling just as ashamed as Joy, but didn't want to let it be known. She was always the smooth one, the cool one, the one that left with her hands clean. Never before in her life did she feel responsible for her actions in the way she did with what happened between her and Tracy.

"I know, I've been thinking the same thing," Rachel finally admitted.

"You know how she gets, you know, when she's alone," Joy reminded her.

"Yea, I know." Rachel walked into *Gap*, tossed her newly straightened and dyed blonde hair over her shoulder and started sorting through their new fashions.

"But you know, she probably won't even want to talk to us though," Joy let the scenario of calling Tracy run through her mind a few times, but each time it ended badly. She bent down to adjust the buckle on her black, patent leather, Mary Jane style, high-heeled shoes and nearly lost her balance. "Uh, these things are killing me."

"I guess maybe I could get my mom to talk to her, or something. She has no reason to be mad at *her*," Rachel offered as she examined a shirt that was hanging on a brown wooden hanger. She cut her eyes and stole another look at Joy's face. Her friend was looking bad those days; sickly and rail thin.

"Good idea," Joy said and nodded her head too enthusiastically. "But what if she tells your mom about the… you know."

Rachel thought this over. "Seriously though Joy, my mom probably already knows I've dabbled. If she does say something about it I doubt mom would be surprised."

"But what about me!" Joy turned around and looked at Rachel with wide saucer eyes. "I don't want your mom knowing I've done that!"

Rachel shook her head and started chewing on the inside of her gums—a bad habit from childhood. "I need a cigarette."

"Seriously though Rach, never mind! I don't want my business out there to your mom."

Rachel sighed and continued to shake her head. She knew that Joy would trip if her mother called Tracy and her little habit, which had seemed to turn into a huge habit, was revealed. But at the same time, she felt that something needed to be done. She was really beginning to worry about Tracy—and Joy.

Chapter 23

It had been over a week since Tracy had heard from Mike, and she was beginning to think something bad had happened to him. He had told her that he had to go to Rochester to see family soon, but never gave her an exact date. If he *was* upstate he sure didn't call to let her know it.

She called his cellphone at least ten times a day, only to receive his voicemail automatically. When another few days went by she dialed his number and the dreaded lady answered.

"Doo doo doo… The number you have reached, 555-3164, in area code 914, has been disconnected."

Tracy checked all the nearby hospitals for a Mike Jenkins—none had him listed. She looked up Jenkins' in the Bronx only to find about 250 listings. After calling 30 numbers, she gave up and did a Google search, as if that would help in finding a street thug.

She was at her wits end one week in, and decided it was time to hit the block and search out her man. She had already gone to Prince's Towers, the building where Mike said he lived, and looked for a Jenkins on the list—but there was none. She considered knocking on random doors and asking, but decided it would just be easier to hit the places where he frequented. Tracy was getting very desperate.

The elevator was taking too long so she decided to go ahead down the stairs. On her way down the hall she heard a door open behind her.

"Hey *bitch*," a voice said from behind her. Tracy turned her head and met eyes with Elena, the woman who she had caught cheating on her husband. She had a healing black eye and it looked like someone had ripped a chunk of hair out of her head. Tracy turned and kept walking, this time quicker.

"You like your door mami?" Elena said with an evil smirk. Tracy stopped in her tracks, but after thinking about it, she just kept going.

"Bitch, if I find out it was you that told my husband on me, I'm going to kill your ass!" the woman threatened as Tracy let the door to the stairwell shut closed. "Black bitch!"

Tracy closed her eyes when she made it down to the bottom floor and breathed deeply. She hadn't said anything to the woman's husband, she didn't even know him like that. The way she was flaunting her boyfriend around, it could have been anyone that told him about her affair. She knew that threatening them about telling the husband would backfire in her face somehow, and now here she was. Tracy felt as if her whole world was falling apart. Everyone had it out for her.

Tracy's grey Hyundai crept down the street, virtually putt-putting from neglect, as she looked at all the stores she passed that looked familiar. She knew that Mike regularly hung out in this area, which was within a four block radius of her building. There had to be at least one or two people he knew out there on a Saturday night that could tell her if they had heard any negative news about Mike.

She turned the corner after the second time riding through, and decided to head up north. She was running out of options, and the only place she could think of at that moment was June's, the ghetto bar on Webster Avenue where Mike had met her before. He had said he did a lot of 'business' there, so it was probably her best bet.

Tracy was a complete wreck. Her eyes were swollen from crying so much—she missed her Mike so badly. She was crying again when she pulled her car into a spot around the corner from

June's and grabbed her bottle of Vodka off the passenger's side floor. Tracy guzzled the liquor like someone who didn't have a throat. Letting the Vodka take it's effect, she got up her nerve to get out of the car and walk across the street towards the bar, alone.

A group of three women were standing outside the bar, and looked Tracy up and down like the outsider she was.

"What's really 'hood?" one of them asked Tracy randomly and she kept walking inside as if she didn't hear the girl.

Her heart was pounding as she scanned the inside of the crowded bar, looking for anyone that was familiar. She sat down at the bar, in a rare empty seat, enduring stares from several patrons who were wondering, "who is this girl coming into the bar by herself?"

Tracy ordered a double shot of vodka and threw it back. She ordered a Coors Light and stealthily glanced down at the other end of the bar and thought she saw someone familiar. Before she had a chance to investigate further, she heard the door open behind her, and then the voice that she had been longing to hear for weeks.

"I told you I don't know her ass. Get the fuck off my back!" she heard Mike's voice booming over all of the other noise. Tracy's heart fluttered and she jerked her head around with the biggest smile across her face, ready to throw her arms around him.

But the smile quickly faded when she saw that Mike had walked in with some tall Puerto Rican girl that looked dangerously familiar. Mike had a close, clean cut and his green-hazel eyes were shimmering from the limited light in the bar as they usually did.

"You're fucking lying. You think I'm fucking stupid," the girl complained back. "You are such a stupid fuck."

"Bitch if you don't close your fucking mouth I'm going to toss you through that window!" Mike threatened as he turned back around to face her.

Tracy's heart dropped into her stomach as she watched the whole scene develop. Stevie Wonder could see what was going down here. Her body began to tremble with anger.

"C, I can't help it if every bum bitch that I pass wanna say somethin' to me," Mike told her.

"I can't believe you! You are so mean to me," Celia said shaking her head. Her long, dark-brown hair was in a high ponytail Janet Jackson style, and her face was made up. But when Tracy saw the scar badly hidden with foundation, she quickly recognized this girl as the chick from the baseball game that jumped her—Celia. *What the hell is Mike doing with her?*

"Princess, I ain't being mean. I'm just sayin', I don't want nonna those dicey faced bitches. It's all about you," he said sternly and gave her a kiss on the forehead.

Something in Tracy snapped when she heard Mike call Celia 'Princess', his special pet name for her. She stood up and started walking towards Mike just as he was turning back around.

"Mike, what is this?" Tracy said softly and felt a tear beginning in the corner of her eye. Her lip trembled.

Mike looked at Tracy with his eyes glazed over. Then he did the worst possible thing that anyone could do to Tracy—he acted like he didn't even know her.

"Ay yo, Troops, what's goin' on?" Mike called out to his friend that was standing nearby and slapped hands.

Tracy looked at his back and then back over to Celia, who was looking right back at Tracy with a smirk on her face that could launch a thousand wars. Celia strutted right past Tracy, being sure to switch her ass to the side as she walked, and grabbed Mike from behind.

The whole room began to move in slow motion for Tracy, and she lost herself. She didn't know what she was doing as she grabbed the bottle of Coors Light off the bar by the stem.

"I know, I just left from down there. I feel you," Mike was saying to Troops. The next thing he 'felt' however was a bottle cracking over the back of his head. He grabbed his head and became weak in the knees as he struggled to recover from the blow.

"You bitchhh!!" Celia screamed as she turned around, wet from the beer that was now all over her outfit. She made a charge for Tracy and swung at her face but missed. They struggled with each other, knocking over a nearby table and bumping into folks they didn't know. Chaos ensued in the bar.

People were fighting and cracking bottles over each other's heads. Then the inevitable happened when shots rang out. Everybody scattered and nearly trampled each other trying to get out of the bar's one exit.

Tracy managed to escape in the middle of the crowd of people running out, but someone suddenly grabbed her by the hair and snatched her back.

"Where the fuck do you think you're going?" Mike spat at her nastily. "You're dumber than I thought Tracy."

He pulled her to a nearby alley, threw her down, and began threatening her life.

"If you ever tell anyone anything about me, I swear, I will find you and your family and kill all of y'all. Don't underestimate me Tracy," Mike looked down at her and pointed. He was livid at the fact that someone had touched him, with a bottle at that.

"I know where you live at, your moms in Long Island, everything about your meaningless life, so don't cross me Tracy," he continued. Tracy just sat on the ground and cried her eyes out.

"I hate your ass!" she screamed.

"You didn't hate me that last time. When you were trying to scratch your name into my back," Mike laughed callously.

Tracy just cried as she thought about everything that had just happened. The thing with Celia at Yankees stadium. Mike had kept saying the plural 'hoes' when Tracy only told him that one person jumped her. She had wondered about that for a fleeting moment, but pushed it aside, just like everything else about Mike that had tugged at her Spirit. The warning from Bowen—he knew Mike was shady all the time, and even tried to tell her. But she had treated Bowen as if *he* were the bad guy.

"I don't know who was better though, you or that trick Joy. You've got some really stupid friends, you know?" Mike just had to add.

Tracy stopped crying and looked up at Mike.

"What did you just say?" she asked incredulously.

"I guess it don't matter at this point. Yeah, I had your simple ass friend Joy, the one with the long legs. Boy, that girl is eager to please," he looked up as if he were reminiscing. Tracy took that as an opportunity. She punched him in his balls with all of her might. Mike bent down in agony.

"Owwwww," he groaned and tried to let the pain subside before coming for Tracy again.

"You son of a bitch! You slept with my friend!?" Tracy screamed hysterically.

Tracy shakily got up and looked at Mike in disbelief. Just like that he had turned from the love of her life to her worst enemy. She watched him trying to recover from the pain for a few moments too long as she wondered where she had gone wrong. This was supposed to be the love of her life. She started shaking her head wildly, hoping that this was just another bad dream she would wake from.

"You slept with my friend?" Tracy asked again, this time in a soft, weak whisper. When Mike glanced up at her, she looked away before she could see his expression. He had slept with Joy? *That bitch!* she thought. *That sick, evil bitch. How?*

The tears were consuming her whole body as she turned around and tried to make her way to her car. When she turned the corner she saw police cars approaching in the distance, and quickly crossed the street to avoid them. She glanced back once more, in time to see Mike leaving the alley, walking funny and holding his balls. He disappeared down another small street to escape the police as well and never looked back.

All of Tracy's worst fears had come true.

By the time Tracy made it into her car, she was completely devastated. She didn't know why she didn't just stay there and let the police riddle her body with bullets, *Set It Off* style. It was official—she had nobody now; no family, no friends, and no man.

"Aaaaaaaaaaaaaaaaaahhh!" Tracy suddenly screamed at the top of her lungs through her tears and had a tantrum in the street beside her car. She turned around and punched down on the roof of her car so hard that it created an indentation and made her hand numb. She closed her eyes and thought of all those times she had given herself to Mike, told him her problems, and let him into her world.

"God, why me? Please, just kill me!" she cried out as she let her body slump forward onto the car, her head resting on the roof in defeat.

Chapter 24

Kamira was leaving her job in lower Manhattan and thought about heading back to the rental office to beg again before going back to Long Island. She had been praying that they would have mercy on her, and not have rented out the apartment she left, but that was a shot in the dark. That apartment had been rented out just a couple of weeks after she left. She wasn't even really supposed to be in the apartment at that price after her aunt died in the first place—they didn't know Kamira's aunt died; as long as they kept getting checks they didn't have anything to say. But as soon as the checks stopped, they looked into the situation and found out no one was living in the place anymore. So Kamira was assed out as far as a place to stay, and would have to keep commuting from her mother's apartment in West Islip to her job in the city. Her mother was livid when she learned about all that had went on.

As she was walking down the street towards the subway, she saw Karif's car screech up beside her. Karif jumped out and came around the car.

"Karif! Oh my God, I've been trying to get in touch—"

"Shut up bitch, and get in the car," he demanded as he grabbed her arm and threw her into the passenger side within seconds. As soon as she got into the car she regretted it, because Karif was steaming mad. She could see the impending violence in his eyes.

"You just thought you were so slick, huh? Setting me up and shit," Karif taunted her as he put the car in gear and pulled off.

"No baby, you gotta listen to me, it's all a misunderstanding!"

Kamira started pleading.

"Whatever, I'm gonna give your ass just what you deserve, you just wait," Karif said in a way that scared the living daylights out of Kamira.

* * *

"Gimme that rock Moon!" Mike's teammate Pit called out over and over again as he watched Mike show off his moves on the court. Mike went between his legs with the ball a few times before faking out his defender, shaking him easily, and charging for the basket. He swayed the ball from side to side to avoid it being blocked and slammed it in with authority.

"Damn! He snapped ya ankles homie. How you gonna come out here with them brand new Air Zooms on and get waxed on an easy fake out like that?" Chewy, who was one of Mike's teammates taunted Mike's defender Sammy, who had ended up on the ground. They all laughed at Sammy as he got up. He was never one that could take a joke though, and that's what made everybody fuck with him even more. "Nike should come and repossess their sneakers. You making them look bad."

"You go boy!" Celia called out from the bench and clapped hard and loud for her man. She licked her lips as she admired Mike's shirtless body glistening in the sunlight, dripping sweat from everywhere. He looked like he could have been the model for a statue of Adonis.

Mike winked at her as he grabbed his towel out of the back of his shorts. He wiped his face and took his time getting back in the game.

Some younger girls were also sitting on the bench.

"Damn he fine," one of them commented a little too loudly.

"What did you say bitch?" Celia whipped her head around

and looked back at the girls. They were all quiet.

Mike glanced over at the scene and rolled his eyes. He was starting to get tired of Celia. He had known her for a very long time, but ever since he decided to take her on as his main girl, she just got more and more possessively jealous as the days went along. The more frequently they had sex, the more she seemed to be losing her mind. She wanted it all the time, and he was becoming less and less interested. He was seriously trying to figure out the best way to drop her ass for good. She had the potential for being a serious stalker though. Not like Tracy though; when Mike was with Tracy she always let him have his space.

Damn, why am I thinking about her ass again, Mike thought. *I gotta stop that.*

But it was easier said than done. More and more, Mike was realizing that he had really caught feelings for Tracy in the short time they were together, and it wasn't just about the sex. She kept him on his toes, and he loved that. As hard as Celia acted on the outside, she was a weak chick on the inside and that turned Mike off. Mike thought back to the time Tracy had rolled off of the bed to hide her special book, which he had already known about from looking through her things, and chuckled to himself. She was so cute. He bit his bottom lip when he thought about how they had gotten down that night and actually considered giving her a call after the game.

"Yo, come on Moon!" his teammate Chewy broke him out of his daze. "What the hell you doin'?"

Mike grabbed the ball off the ground and made his opponent check it again. Then he took off and tried to do a repeat performance from before, but this time was fouled hard by Sammy, the same guy who he had left behind before.

"Yo, what the fuck is wrong with you?" Mike wanted to

know as he got up in Sammy's face.

"What you gonna do, call it foul?" Sammy challenged him.

"Come on ya'll, don't start that," Chewy said, laughing. He loved some drama though.

"Naw, but foul me like again and I'll send your ass to the cleaners on a clothesline the rest of this game bitch," Mike threatened as he glared down at Sammy condescendingly.

"Yo, Moon!" somebody called out from behind them. Mike turned around to look and his eyes grew wide when he saw it was Jimmy, his sister's boyfriend, carrying a large gun. Mike didn't even get a chance to react before he heard the ominous *click*.

Jimmy shot Mike twice in his bare chest without hesitation.

When the shots rang out, everybody on the court scattered, including all of Mike's 'boys'. The girls, all but Celia, were screeching as they ran from the scene. After that, all that could be heard was the basketball winding down from being dropped, and then rolling down the asphalt.

"Mike!!!" Celia screamed as she stood from the benches. She watched as Mike lay on the ground fighting for his life, trying to get up, but it was hopeless; the blood was pouring from his body. Jimmy stood over him with a blank, empty, indifferent look on his face. Despite his lack of expression, he was really enjoying the fact that he was finally getting his revenge. His heart beat faster as he watched Mike squirm and struggle on the concrete.

"Yo…JM…" Mike said right before he started coughing up blood. He could say no more.

"Yea, say my name bitch," Jimmy said with an evil smile.

Jimmy was happy that Mike wasn't dead yet. He pulled out a large hunter's knife and reached down to start carving something on Mike's lower torso. Jimmy chuckled to himself while Mike groaned in pain and tried to grab Jimmy's wrist to stop him, but he was too weak. When Celia saw this she ran down from the bleachers.

"What are you doing! You crazy bastard!!!" she cried as she tried to help Mike out, but Jimmy looked up at her with a crazy look that told her to stay away or she would be next. She backed up slowly and her beet-red eyes glazed over as she watched in horror and started to accept the fate of the love of her life.

By the time Jimmy had finished cutting the letter 'o' in Mike's flesh, Mike was dead.

That didn't stop Jimmy though. He finished slicing and then backed up a few feet to admire his work before walking off just as calmly as he came.

Celia came back to Mike's side and stopped in her tracks when she saw that Jimmy had etched the word 'hoe' in Mike's stomach. She fell to her knees at Mike's side and sobbed her heart out. His green eyes were still open and shocked.

"Babyyy," she whined as she stroked his face and stared into his eyes. She didn't even bother trying to wake him, because she could tell by how cold his face was getting that he was dead.

"Why God, why!" she cried pitifully, nearly choking on her spit. She howled so loud that her voice could be heard echoing in the distance.

Suddenly, she heard footsteps coming up behind her. She didn't get a chance to turn around.

Pop. Pop.

Jimmy shot Celia twice in the back of her head. He watched as she slumped forward on top of Mike's body. He heard her crying all the way back at his car, and decided that he couldn't afford to have someone that emotional about Mike's death sticking around.

Jimmy put his gun away again and looked around for any other witnesses before moving on.

Chapter 25

Tracy had no one.

She had been locked up for days, moving only to go to the bathroom, in her lonely studio apartment. She hadn't eaten in 48 hours. She was in a dangerous contemplation of life and death.

Out of all the things that had happened to her, the heaviest thing weighing on her mind was Mike and Joy's betrayal. She wondered how her good friend could have done her like that. How did Joy find out that Mike was her man, and why would she sleep with him knowing that? She had had so many visions of driving out to Joy's house with a loaded automatic weapon, and opening fire on her as soon as she answered the door.

But of course, she wasn't going to do that. She continued pulling strands of her hair out one by one instead. She examined each hair that she pulled, licked the length of it like a straw, and then laid it on her nightstand.

As she paused to rub at the bald spot that was forming at the front of her head, Tracy glanced over again at the newspaper she had saved for the past three days, still turned to the page. There was a picture of Mike there, and another dark-skinned man right next to him.

The headline read *Bloodbath in the Bronx*. Mike had been shot and slashed by a man named James Clark in broad daylight. Celia had caught it too. James was accused of not only murdering Mike and Celia but also of beating up Mike's sister Janet and leaving her to die in a boarded up house in Queens. Janet survived, and James was facing life in prison, possibly even the death penalty because of the cruel nature of the murders. The reports said that the whole incident was over a petty drug dispute. Tracy found out that Jenkins wasn't even Mike's real last name—his full name was really Michael Moon.

Tracy thought she heard a slight noise at her window and jerked her neck so fast that it made a 'cracking' sound. Her bloodshot eyes, worn out from crying for a week, became wide as she lay perfectly still and listened.

She trembled as she leaned up slowly and struggled to her feet. She tip-toed towards the window, which was now heavily covered with every dark sheet and blanket she had in the house. It made the atmosphere in her home very dark and depressing. She stopped and made a detour to retreive a long, wide butcher's knife from the kitchen. When she was standing in front of the sheets, butcher's knife held high in the air, *Psycho* style, she leaned in slowly and listened again. Then she heard the sound again.

"Whoever's out there, get the fuck away from my window! I'm not playing! I have a gun in here!" she threatened the imaginary person that was supposed to be sitting outside her third story window, 25 feet in the air.

She came closer and carefully pulled back an edge of the sheet to peer outside. A small sliver of sunlight caused her to blink, and when she opened and focused her vision, she saw two pigeons sitting on the thin ledge, flapping their wings around.

Tracy dropped the knife and let her head fall into her hands. For the hundredth time, she broke down in tears and her body was overtaken with grief. She sobbed and sobbed like a child that was lost. She finally lifted her drenched face and opened her eyes wearily. Her gaze fell on the gleaming knife that had just fallen to the floor.

She dropped to her knees and laid down on the hardwood as she picked up the knife to examine it. She wiped her face and then toyed with the sharp edge and the tip of it playfully. She giggled in delight, a giggle which grew to a chuckle, and then eventually into the raucous laugh of a mad woman. Her laughter filled the otherwise silent apartment like a soundtrack to Tracy's descent into insanity. Anyone watching this scene would surely leave and come back with a straight jacket in hand.

Mike was gone.

What did she have to live for.

She had no job.

Her mother hated her.

Her friends had abandoned her and betrayed her.

The love of her life had crushed her heart in the worst way.

And Tracy was losing her mind.

Chapter 26

A week later Tracy was sitting in the sunshine, on a nice quiet bench in Central Park. She couldn't think of a more serene place to relax and enjoy life. She never really got a chance to visit the attractions in the great city of New York, even though she had lived and worked in the midst of it for years. She smiled at a beautiful lady walking her perfectly groomed poodle. She was terribly afraid of animals, especially dogs, but she could appreciate this one. She let her head fall back and enjoyed the sunshine in her face. It was a very warm day in late March.

Tracy had gotten a message from Rachel that Karif had beat Kamira so badly that she needed a hospital visit. He took her to a motel room and took all of his frustrations out on her with a paddle, his foot, and his left fist. The sound of Kamira screaming and being kicked and beaten was so loud that a neighbor called the police. She was bedridden for a week, and her arm had been dislocated. Even in that condition, Kamira didn't want to press charges against Karif, but the cops didn't need her at that point. All they needed to see was Kamira's injuries to sentence Karif to a year behind bars for aggravated assault. With the evidence of Karif's visit to the police before the assault, it was decided that his attack was premeditated. With that on his record, Karif would never work on Wall Street again. Tracy had defended Kamira, even took a blow to the head for her, but did any of that matter? No. Tracy did not bother to return the phone call. She decided instead to shut off her cellphone service. She wasn't going to be able to make the bill that month anyway.

What Tracy didn't know was that Joy was the one who told

Mike about Karif. Mike had casually gotten Joy to talk about all of her friends, especially Tracy. He easily learned about Kamira, and the incident that occurred at the club that night. Joy had unwittingly ruined a friendship, caused Karif to lose the full use of his hand, and had caused Kamira to have a permanently dislocated limb. But then again, that last thing probably would have happened at some point anyway.

A lightbulb had turned on in Tracy's head the other day. She was not going to let the pressures of life get her down anymore. She was no longer going to let the people around her affect her life. She didn't need to contact her friends or family with all their drama. They were all due for some serious Karma. Especially Joy. Mike had already gotten his, and though she still loved him, she had learned to accept his death as just.

Rachel called a few days later, leaving another message on her home phone this time saying that Joy was at a clinic in Denver for her drug problem. Joy was doing about a gram a day and had started stealing from her mother. Someone had stolen $2,500 out of her bank account and used her credit card number to buy expensive electronics online. Her mother was so mistrustful of her daughter at that point that she actually accused Joy of using her own credit card online and then reporting the charges as fraudulent. But that wasn't what happened. Mike was the culprit, and had completely disappeared out of Joy's life as well.

"I didn't know it was that bad Tra… I really didn't," Rachel's choked up voice said on the message right before hanging up the phone. No "sorry Tracy," no apologies. Just updates on other people that couldn't give two flying flips about her. After that call, Tracy called her phone company and had her home service turned off too. She didn't have time to feel for Joy's trifling ass.

"How're you doing ma'am!" an officer on a horse called out to Tracy. He had the biggest, warmest smile on his face.

"I'm doing great! How are you?" Tracy shouted back.

She watched as he trotted along. She almost felt sorry for the horse in that heat. She wondered when was the last time the horse had some water.

Chapter 27

Mrs. Samuels dialed Tracy's number for the tenth time that week. The first six times the phone just kept ringing, and then the message system would pick up. Mrs. Samuels didn't like talking to machines. The next three times the message center notified her that the voicemail box was full. This time it said that that phone number was disconnected. Now she was starting to get a little concerned.

Amazingly, Mrs. Samuels didn't even know her daughter's cellphone number. She couldn't remember Tracy ever even giving it to her.

"What is this girl up to," Mrs. Samuels said, sucking her teeth. Tracy was always doing something to cause her to worry. Her daughter loved for people to be thinking about her all the time.

She had now officially not heard from Tracy in a month.

The phone rang and Mrs. Samuels picked up on the first ring.

"Hello?"

It was her boyfriend Robert. This was the first time she wasn't happy to hear his voice. She was hoping for Tracy's.

"Hi sweetheart," Robert said in a syrupy-sweet voice that gave Mrs. Samuels a toothache. "How are you doing?"

"Hi, I'm alright I guess. I just still haven't heard from my daughter."

"She still hasn't called huh?"

"No, and I'm starting to get a little concerned. It's been close to a month I think. She usually comes to check on me at least two Saturdays out of the month."

"I thought you said you were happy not to see her this month?"

Mrs. Samuels was quiet and actually thought about whether she had said that or not about her daughter to a virtual stranger.

"I don't think I said that," she denied. "Listen, I've got to go."

"But I wanted to take you out tonight? So that we can talk about AC."

"Uh… I don't know. Maybe another time. Later this week," she said and hung up.

"Mom," Jenny, Tracy's sister came out of the back room and called to her mother. She was dressed in what looked like a brand new outfit; a pair of khaki shorts, stylish white blouse, and name brand designer sunglasses. Yet Jenny hadn't made even one contribution to the household since she came back six months before.

Mrs. Samuels looked up at her eldest daughter and raised her eyebrows as if to tell her to go ahead.

"I need some money, I've got this thing at the shore," Jenny continued.

"Jenny," Mrs. Samuels sighed and rolled her eyes. "How much do you need?"

"Like $250."

"$250! What the hell for?"

Jenny rolled her eyes this time with a lot of attitude. "Ma, please. If you don't have it, just say so. I can try to get it from Grandma on my way past the city."

Mrs. Samuels examined her daughter for several minutes. 30 years old and she was still living at home, asking for money. Copious amounts of money. She gave up and went to look for her purse.

"Tracy never asks me for money," she commented as she

handed Jenny the contents of her wallet. Jenny stood there and counted it.

"This is just $185?" Jenny said ungratefully.

"That's all I have. Take it or leave it," Mrs. Samuels snapped back. *The nerve of this girl*, she thought.

"It's not like it's *your* money anyway," Jenny said instead of thank you. "It's Dad's."

Mrs. Samuels opened her mouth in shock at what her daughter had just let slip from her lips, but before she could find the words to say, Jenny was out the door. Mrs. Samuels chased after her and snatched open the door to say the first thing that came to her mind.

"Get a job!"

She closed the door and couldn't help but let a tear fall as she thought of how Jenny was treating her. She thought about how Tracy had refused to take money from her in the past—and instead tried to give her some, even in her hard times between jobs. Mrs. Samuels wasn't exactly rich, after all. She was living off of insurance money and savings. All Tracy wanted to know was that her mother was healthy, and Mrs. Samuels had pushed her away. The guilt shot up her spine and racked her brain, causing the tears to start flowing. Suddenly she felt that something was seriously wrong.

"I need my Tracy," she said suddenly and went back to call Tracy's home number again, in vain.

Chapter 28

Tracy went over to her bed and fixed the sheets so that they were perfectly straight. Once the bed was made, she sprayed some Febreze on the top, and on the pillows and took in a long whiff of the fresh scent.

"That is so nice," she said with a smile.

She looked around the rest of her apartment and saw that for the first time in ages, it was clean! She grabbed the Swiffer she had just purchased out of the corner and started setting it up.

As she pushed the Swiffer across her hardwood floor, she thought about a dream she had had the night before.

Rachel was wearing a brand new pink Versace blouse and pants, Kamira looked like she had lost a little weight—she had on a white top and jeans, and Joy looked like a supermodel as usual in a pair of skinny jeans and a long black sweater. Her shoes looked as if she had definitely paid over $500 for them. They all looked like they were doing very well. Very happy.

"Are they treating you right there Tracy?" Kamira asked as she sat down next to Tracy.

"Who?" Tracy had asked.

They all were quiet for a long time, and then Joy spoke up. "Tracy I want to apologize. I'm really sorry for everything. It wasn't my fault."

Despite her conscious anger at Joy, Tracy wasn't angry in her dream. She was just happy to see her friends again all in one place.

"I've been practicing on those Blow Pops," Rachel said with a smirk and a wink.

Tracy smiled as she thought of the dream. When she was finished cleaning she went into the kitchen to check on her meal.

It was daytime, going on three o'clock in the afternoon, and the sun was shining beautifully into Tracy's wide open windows. She decided to eat an early dinner tonight, and enjoy the sun.

Tracy wasn't much of a cook, but that day she had outdone herself. Macaroni and cheese. Chicken. Green and Cornbread. All her favorites.

She had purchased a bottle of Patron at the liquor store, and a bottle of rare, aged Merlot, her favorite kind of wine. The Merlot had cost her $145. It was the most expensive bottle of liquor she had ever purchased.

She sat down at the table with her food and turned on her new flat screen television. She sat and watched an old episode of the *Sopranos* as she ate. Then she was excited when she saw that they were running old repeats of *Martin.*

She laughed and relaxed for several hours, watching television and getting progressively drunk from the wine. Now it was time for the Patron.

She took three shots in a row of the Patron, which hardly burned her throat.

"Ooooo!" she shrieked out in delight after the last one went down oh so smooth. She laughed and went across the room to retrieve the remote control for her brand new stereo system. It memorized her favorite songs on each CD and played them randomly at a push of the button. She had never had anything high tech like that.

She had put in a mix of Billie Holiday, Etta James, Nat King Cole, Marvin Gaye and the Temptations—all of the old favorites.

She swayed and danced with the Patron bottle in hand as the sounds of the Temptations started flowing through the speakers. She was entranced by their voices, especially the bass.

She remembered how her dad used to try to teach her the familiar steps the Temptations used in their early routines. She wasn't much of a line dancer, but she had gotten a few of the steps down. She tried to recreate them right there in her living room/bedroom/dining room/kitchen. She cracked up when she realized that she couldn't remember them for shit.

Finally, she grew weary. And she was quickly becoming plastered, even with that large meal in her stomach. For the first time in a long time she didn't want to get too drunk, so she went back over to her cherry cabinet and placed the bottle of Patron in the middle. She closed the door and touched the fine wood with appreciation. It was so sophisticated. Tracy smiled at it.

She shut off the TV and left the stereo playing, just not too loud. The last thing she needed was that crazy bitch Elena down the hall knocking on her door. If she did, Tracy just might commit her first murder. As much as she hated Elena, she knew that her kids needed a mother. Tracy suddenly moved her lips and prayed that Elena would be a good mother to her kids.

She decided it was time to take her bath.

She stripped down and remembered the first day she had met Mike, and had masturbated in the tub thinking about his face. She tried her best to push the thought to the back of her mind. It did not work.

She drew her bath and rummaged through the bag of bath bubbles that she had just purchased from the mall. She decided on the black raspberry vanilla scented flavor; it had always been her favorite.

Tracy was coming down from her high as she settled into the hot bath. She listened to Marvin Gaye sing about sexual healing and couldn't help but remember the time she and Mike had made love to that song in the back of his Acura. She saw him smirking at her devilishly as he made her body twitch and tingle.

"Uh, I can't do this anymore," she said, shaking Mike from her thoughts permanently. She dunked herself under the water and forced herself to stay there. When she finally came up, she gasped for air, and then reached up to grab an object from the shower caddy.

Her pocket knife.

She had carried this thing around with her for years for protection from people hurting her. How ironic that now she would use it to hurt her*self*. She had sharpened the knife to perfection.

There was no hesitation. After the cuts were made, quick, deep, and painful, Tracy moaned with grief as the lifeforce began leaving her body. *That should be deep enough*. She could already feel it. She had purposefully filled the tub halfway full so that it wouldn't overflow. As she relaxed, she thought about everything that she was leaving behind and realized that she wasn't really, since nobody really cared anyway. The life insurance policy from her job wasn't lapsing until that following month, so her mother would get that. Her car would probably be donated to a children's charity; at least that's where she would have wanted it to go. Her apartment? They would have that rented out before her blood was cleaned out of the tub. She breathed in the last long breaths of the black raspberry vanilla bath bubbles that she had added to her water and couldn't resist the urge to think of Mike in her last moments of living. It didn't matter anymore anyway. She was going to a *new* place, a *new* life.

No one could touch her there, no one could hurt her there, and no one could leave her there, because she had already been left. Sure, her mother had been there with her through some hard times but here it was over a month since they had spoken or seen each other in the flesh, and her mother didn't even bother to come visit to see what was going on. In fact, her mother hadn't been to her daughter's apartment since she moved in. Sure Rachel had tried to contact her, as well as Joy through Rachel, but they had their own agendas, their own social lives and their own problems to solve. Fuck them, it didn't matter anymore. Kamira was mistaken, but she probably would never learn to value her friends over her men. That was a dead end friendship. They were all probably going to forget about Tracy soon enough and go on with their lives. And it was only right that they did. Tracy didn't feel worthy of their attention anymore.

After a while, the room began to spin around her and she felt herself slipping out of consciousness. Then everything went black.

Unfortunately Tracy had only grown to be a pebble before her foundation was rocked. Now she was just blowing in the wind.

.
.
.
.
.
.
.
.
.
.
.
.
.
.
.
.
.

.

.

.

"Tracy! Tracy!!" Mrs. Samuels knocked and yelled intermittently. "Open this door girl!"

Tracy could faintly hear the voice calling her from beyond, and imagined it was someone calling her to the afterlife.

"I'm not playing with you girl. I saw your car outside, so I know you're in here! Open this door!" Tracy's mother screamed from outside the red painted door that still said 'Snitch Bitch.' Mrs. Samuels listened in closely for any signs of movement from inside her daughter's apartment. When she didn't hear anything again, her heart started beating rapidly and she was thinking the worst.

That's it, Mrs. Samuels thought as she put the basket of flowers she had been holding down on the ground and strapped her large bag across her body, pushing the purse part to the back. She closed her eyes and took a deep breath, then said a silent prayer to God before taking action. She summoned her strength and remembered the techniques she had learned in her Karate and self-defense class. She was thankful that she had worn her gym sneakers.

"Mmmmm," she hummed and then grunted as she suddenly jumped up and kicked Tracy's door with all of her might, Bruce Lee style. She hit it in the exact right spot because the door flew open immediately.

"Tracy!" she said as she hurried into the apartment, looking around and noticing how clean it was. Tracy had always been a messy pack rat as a child; this was unusual. "Tracy!"

When Tracy's mom finally made it to the bathroom and saw that the door was slightly ajar with the light on and the fan buzzing, she instantly became frightened. She called out her daughter's name once more. "Tracy?"

Fighting her fear, she eased the door open and her eyes grew wide when they beheld the sight of her daughter laying in a pool of blood, her hands crossed, and her head resting back as if she were in a coffin already.

"Oh my God!" she said, barely whispering as she rushed up to the tub. "Oh my God!"

She grabbed Tracy by her shoulders and shook her violently. "Tracy!!! Tracy, baby, wake up!"

She trembled as she tried to find the source of the bleeding and lifted Tracy's hands up, revealing the deep cuts on her wrists. Her flesh was still warm.

"Oh my GOD!" Mrs. Samuels shrieked again.

When Tracy's hands flopped back down in the water lifelessly and splashed blood all over Mrs. Samuel's face, then came the shrill screams.

"Aaaaaaaaaaaaaaa!!!" was the sound that could be heard two floors downstairs.

Mrs. Samuels ran out of the bathroom with her hands flying in the air. She wasn't thinking straight. She just kept screaming over and over for someone to call the police, even though she had a cellphone right in her own bag.

Epilogue

Something, rather, someone had told Mrs. Samuels to get off of her lazy behind that day and come see her daughter, finally. She hadn't been to the Bronx to visit Tracy in years, and that was a shame. She had a dream the night before where Tracy, Tracy's father, and Robert all flashed across her mind. Robert was looking at Tracy's father's back, and Tracy's father was just staring at his daughter, who was sitting in mid-air, looking down at the ground. Then Tracy's father looked at Mrs. Samuels, and the dream was over. After fighting her reluctance to get in her car to drive to the Bronx all morning, Tracy's mother finally found herself in her Forerunner heading for the Cross Island Parkway.

The doctors told Mrs. Samuels that if she had been just an hour later, Tracy would have died in the tub. She had already lost close to four pints of blood and was in the fourth stage of hypovolemic shock. Unfortunately, Tracy fell into a coma due to the loss of blood and was in critical condition, under close watch by the hospital attendees and her mother. They were still optimistic about her chances of coming out of the coma soon.

Mrs. Samuels was a wreck. She couldn't believe she had come this close to losing her daughter. And it was all due to her own selfishness. She would have never had a chance to apologize to her daughter, which she now did profusely. That first night at the hospital, she got up the nerve to make a call that would signal the end of her false pride.

"Sandra Moretti of West Islip please," she asked the operator. She remembered how flippantly she had thrown Sandra's business card to the side when she had visited. Now she was searching her out—how ironic.

The operator connected her through and Mrs. Samuels closed her eyes tightly as she listened to the phone ringing on the other end.

"Hello?" she heard a groggy voice ask.

"Sandra? Is that you?" Mrs. Samuels said weakly.

"Yes? Who's this?"

"It's Terri Samuels. I apologize for calling you so early in the morning," Mrs. Samuels paused as she prepared to swallow her pride. This was greater than her now—it was about Tracy. "It's Tracy."

When the news hit the Island, Rachel and her mother rushed to the hospital in record time. Anyone who wasn't family was not allowed in that wing of the hospital, but Mrs. Samuels managed to sneak them in for a moment. When they saw the condition Tracy was in, and looked at her damaged wrists, they were devastated. Rachel cried her eyes out in a corner of the room and fell to the floor in grief. Mrs. Moretti had feared for a long time that something like this was going to happen. The nurse came in and rushed them out, but before they left, Mrs. Moretti gave Mrs. Samuels the name of the psychotherapist she had been referred to by her friend. They hugged goodbye, and it was very genuine. As soon as Tracy left the hospital, it was decided, she was headed to a mental facility in Long Island as an inpatient, whether she wanted to go or NOT.

Kamira was too ashamed to go to the hospital when she got the call from Rachel. She and Joy were dealing with their own demons. Everyone, from Reggie, to Joy, to Stacey from Tracy's job, sent flowers, to the point where Tracy's room was completely adorned with arrangements of lilies, roses, and tulips. Tracy's sister Jenny was MIA; no one knew where she was, not even her boyfriend.

Mrs. Samuels sat at the side of Tracy's bed and tried to stroke her daughter's hair down into place. Her face still felt as clammy and cold as it did the day she found her lying lifeless in her tub. Her skin tone had become pale, about two shades lighter than before, and her eyelids were very dark. Tracy looked like an old woman lying there, and it hurt Mrs. Samuels to look. But she did—because it wasn't about her anymore, it was about her daughter and what she needed. Mrs. Samuels had spent every day for the past week at Tracy's side, waiting for her to wake.

"Oh Tracy. You're the child. I should have been more of a parent," Mrs. Samuels commented with a tear in her eye, and then opened up her bible to read Tracy her daily affirmation:

"In thee, O LORD, do I put my trust; let me never be put to confusion. Deliver me in thy righteousness, and cause me to escape; incline thine ear unto me, and save me. Be thou my strong habitation, where unto I may continually resort. Thou hast given commandment to save me; for thou art my rock and my fortress. Deliver me, O my God, out of the hand of the wicked, out of the hand of the unrighteous and cruel man. For thou art my hope, O LORD GOD; thou art my trust from my youth. By thee have I been held up from the womb; thou art he who took me out of my mother; my praise shall be continually of thee. Psalms 71, 1-6."

"A little at a time," Tracy's mom said with a smile after she finished speaking. She closed her bible slowly. Reading the scripture eased her mind. "I know you can hear me baby, I just know it."

Mrs. Samuels then got up and gathered her things to go get some lunch from the cafeteria. She would be staying with Tracy all day again. Then she said the words that Tracy had longed to hear from her mother for most of her life.

"I love you baby," her mother said as she held the door open before leaving, and smiled. "I truly do. I love you!"

After she left, a feeling of euphoria overtook Tracy's mother, and she suddenly felt that everything was going to be alright with her daughter.

Back in the room, there was silence other than the sound of the machines working. After a few minutes, Tracy's eyes started moving rapidly beneath her lids, as if she were having a really good, exciting dream. Her heart rate increased. Then as quickly as her eyes started moving, they stopped, and a look of satisfaction and calm fell on her face. A few seconds later the heart monitor flatlined and a loud, steady, beeping noise filled the room. By the time the nurses and doctors arrived and tried to bring her back to life, Tracy was gone.

Tracy had lived her entire life in fear, of people, of places, and of betrayal. But it turned out that Tracy Samuels' biggest threat was her own mental deficiency. Fortunately, her mother's last minute love had given her a second chance at finally getting some peace within.

What was painfully ironic was that all of Tracy's paranoia did nothing to protect her from herself in the end.

Message from the author

(Do not read this page until you have completed the book.)

I realize that the ending to this book is morbid and kind of sad, but I had to keep it real. I do not advocate what Tracy did at the end—it is just a reality of life. The premise of my books and my company is 'This is Real Life. It Ain't No Fairytale.' In real life a person as weak and unstable as Tracy, without support from *someone*, whether it be a friend or family member, would most likely make the same mistake. In my personal opinion, the act that Tracy performed in the end is a trick of the enemy; a quick, easy way for the devil to pull people who are weak of Spirit into his clutches.

I guess the moral of this book is to get people with mental instability help before they hurt themselves and others. Be a REAL friend, not a phony one, value your family and loved ones, and think about other people sometimes; not just yourself. Also, to people who feel the whole world is against you, stop feeling sorry for yourself and open up to getting help for your problems.

You can't walk two blocks in a major metropolitan city—New York, Philadelphia, Chicago, San Francisco, DC and others—without seeing someone who is mentally ill just roaming around. And they didn't become that way by accident. Something, or someone, happened in their life to make them that way, just like with Tracy. Cliché, but we need to get help for ourselves, and those close to us, before it's too late. And if we're honest, we have all been in tough life situations where our lives seem almost hopeless, myself included. Ultimately, it's that support around us that gets us through. But what happens if you don't have any support or help? Tragedy.

God Bless - J.Gail

Give the gift of this exciting book
to your Family and Friends...

Check out *all* of Jazoli Publishing's
exciting line-up of books!

Get it at
jazolipublishing.com !

Get it at
karmabook.com !

Get them at **thugbooks.com**!

about the author

J.Gail has been writing creatively on and off for the past decade. She currently has four novels, *Thugs are for Fun*, *Thugs Ain't No Fun At All*, *Karma's a Bitch* and now *Stop Looking at Me!* She is currently working on her fifth book, *Cap'n Save a Bro*, the story of a young woman who tries to save all of the bad men in her life, but really they are just corrupting her soul. The author can be emailed at jgail2911@yahoo.com.

Thank you God!

acknowledgements

This book dedicated to the only *true* female friend I've ever had. E.B. - I still love you girl -J.Gail

Want to order through the mail?

Stop Looking at Me! by J.Gail
Price: $14.00
Shipping & Handling: $1.75 each book
($1 S&H for each add'l book ordered)

All books will be shipped via USPS Media Mail, which takes anywhere from 3-10 business days. If you want your book quicker, send $4.50 S&H so that your book will ship via USPS Priority Mail.

Call 888-715-9599
Fax 888-645-1615
if you have any questions that can't be answered on our website: http://www.JazoliPublishing.com.

Truth Hurts Publications is an imprint of Jazoli Publishing.

Make your check or money order payable to *Jazoli Publishing* and return with this form to:

Jazoli Publishing
P.O. Box 1316
Code B-OF144-1
Brookhaven, PA 19015

www.JazoliPublishing.com
This is Real Life.
It Ain't No Fairytale.

(feel free to rip out this page and send with your order)

Stop Looking at Me!

by J.Gail

* * *

Book Club Discussion Questions

1) What do you think caused Tracy to become so paranoid? Have you ever known someone like Tracy?

2) Discuss the meaning of Tracy's dreams.

3) Were Tracy's friends good for her? Discuss each one, and how she affected Tracy's life.

4) Did Tracy's mother contribute to her madness? Was she justified in wanting to stay away? Do you believe the women in Tracy's family made her this way?

5) What made Kamira into the type of woman she is; accepting abuse and choosing men over her friends?

6) Discuss Joy and her desire to be a part of the 'in crowd,' her own insecurities, and where she went wrong.

7) Do you think Mike was in love with Tracy despite what he did to her?

8) Did the absence of Tracy's father cause her to turn out how she did?

9) If someone in your family had a mental illness, would you get them help? If so, how would you go about it?

Subscribe to the Newsletter - Give Your Feedback

Provide your own personal feedback on the story.

Share your *own* paranoid story!

Go to:

www.jazolipublishing.com

Have you ever thought of writing and publishing your own book?

Well then stop just talking about...

and BE about it!

Take action towards your dream.

One Stop Books can help you turn your rough manuscript into a professionally laid out paperbound or hardcover book for a reasonable price, and in just one stop.

Services offered:

- Professional editing services
- Book Layout and Typesetting
- Cover Designs that Grab Attention!
- Design and Printing of Marketing Materials
- Copyright Registration
- Website Production
- ISBN Numbers & Bar Codes
- Turn Handwritten Book into a Microsoft Word file
- Dictation
- Marketing and Consulting Help, and more!

We will create a unique, eye-catching cover for you, layout your book, and have it printed by one of our reliable book printing firms. You will also have a basic webpage created for your book.

* *Package deals available* *

Get finished books for as low as $5.50 per copy!*

(* based on 150 Microsoft Word pages, 12 pt, double spaced, 1 inch margins, minimum 1000 book order)

Contact Us @ One Stop Books 888-275-2098

or email onestopbooks@yahoo.com www.1stopbook.com